Col

By Colin Llewelyn Chapman

Cold Call

All Characters in this publication are fictitious and any resemblance to real persons, living or dead, is purely coincidental.

Enquiries should be addressed to
Percy Publishing
Woodford Green,
Essex. IG8 0TF
England.
www.percy-publishing.com

1st Published July 2014
1st Edition

ISBN : 978-0-9929298-0-0

Percy Publishing is a Clifford Marker Associates Ltd Company

Colin Llewelyn Chapman

Colin lives in Southend-On-Sea with his wife Michele, three children aged from 12 to 18, and 2 step-children. His writing comes from the Dark Side of his mind.

This book is dedicated to:

I would like to thank my wife Michele for her continued support and encouragement. She has shown an unwavering belief in me since the first 'I think I could do that' moment.
She is my rock... x5x

Joseph V Sultana, Clifford and Ruth... All deserve my gratitude and respect for their wisdom and guidance.

My Mum... Who has walked every inch of this fantastic journey, right by my side.

Lastly I would like to make a special mention in memory of my late Uncle Gordon. He taught me to live life to its fullest and most importantly, to chase my dreams. He was an inspiration to so many.
Gordon David Chapman (14/01/1950 – 12/5/2014) xx

CHAPTER 1

34 PELDON RISE

Adam Pickering strode along the balcony of the tenement block with his usual sense of urgency. Like every day of his life he was ten minutes behind pace, late for work as usual. Adam worked in a bustling seafront bar in Southend's main tourist hotspot collecting glasses, wiping tables, and other menial tasks. He longed for the favour and limelight that was bestowed on the bar staff, rather than the disparaging comments and 'Pot Man' insults he suffered almost daily. At 22 Adam had seen plenty of the brawls and bust ups that Southend's drunken revellers indulged in every Friday and Saturday night. The bloodshed bruises and broken bones were commonplace, and even at his tender age he thought he had seen it all.

As he stepped out of his flat the stench of stale urine and discarded beer cans greeted his nostrils. Below him in the street, amongst the litter, broken benches and dog excrement, three hooded white lads shouted at each other as they kicked their ball against the rusty garage door that bore the tags of every youth in the district that could lay their hands on a paint can or permanent marker. The tinny twang of a mobile phone speaker filled the echoing passages with its inaudible drone of rap music, distorted and scratchy. Glancing back over his shoulder he caught sight of his neighbour's door ajar. He paused. A cursory glance at his watch told him that he was well behind time. The door ajar, the watch ticking, he gave a deep sigh and turned towards his neighbour Katya's flat.

"For fuck sake!" he raged silently to himself. "Like I need this - silly bitch always leaving that fucking door open!" he couldn't just leave it ajar; some of the estate urchins made easy money as sneak thieves and he didn't want her to be their next victim.

"Katya!" he bellowed with one hand on the door, one foot in the hall and one eye fixed on his wrist. Time was speeding away from him: another late showing at work and he really would have more spare time than he wanted.

"Katya, you've left your bloody door open again... Katya?" Silence met his frustrated calls. He rounded the door into the warmth of Katya's first floor flat, anxious to complete his neighbourly deed so that he could get to work. Adam's helpfulness was more selfish than it would first appear, trying to get into Katya's good books and ultimately he hoped, her knickers. Adam held a torch for his sweet foreign neighbour despite her elusive and introvert nature. The entrance to her flat smelt of cigarettes and perfume, but was bitterly uninviting. The dated carpet was threadbare and the wallpaper was peeling at the edges, but there was something alluring about the place - Katya. She always looked better than this flat, this estate.

Passing the empty kitchen, Adam moved through to the lounge, where the TV filled the small room with the dulcet tones of some wannabe teenager singing on yet another 'get famous overnight' talent show. Nothing! No sign of his pretty Polish neighbour. Adam was struck by how sparse her flat was; compared to this his parents' place looked positively palatial. He exited back into the hallway and turned sharp right to her bedroom door, a room he longed to be invited into. Tonight he would enter Katya's bedroom for the first time, hoping, dreaming that she might be asleep. Perhaps she would be half naked, and then he could finally leer over her lithe young body. He stood hesitating for a moment; it didn't feel right entering her room without consent, but something inside him drove him on. "Katya?" One last call out to her, before he went in. Then more softly, as if not wanting to disturb her, he uttered her name again, imagining her sprawled naked across the bed. He could feel himself getting excited as he slowly pushed the door open.

Instead, what met his gaze in Katya's bedroom caused him to reel sharply backwards, banging his elbow on the door jamb. He all but fell back into the hall, his hand clasped to his mouth, stifling a cry of horror. Retching from the very depths of his gut, he vomited uncontrollably, the contents of his hastily consumed dinner bursting through his clenched fingers onto his coat and splashing across the hall floor. He crashed through the flat to the open door and hit the waist-high balustrade. "Help!" He screamed with a mix of terror and desperation. The fish and chips he had scoffed earlier that evening surged once more from his gullet, billowing over the balcony and cascading onto the squalid pavement below. Initially only one of the boys looked up, clearly aggrieved that he had nearly been spewed on. "Watch it, you fucking tosser!" he snarled. To start with, the lad thought it was just another rowdy piss head having a domestic, or getting ready to moan about the persistent noise they made. The long-suffering residents were always moaning about one thing or another, but the gang usually just ignored them!

Adam was now screaming at them to call the police, and suddenly the lad realised something was badly wrong: this was not just some normal occurrence on the Estate. The boys knew Adam well, and the terrible distress in his voice was clearly genuine. They couldn't possibly have imagined what horror he had seen. What could be so vile it would cause their neighbour to be screaming blue murder? Fumbling for his mobile, the hoody Adam had narrowly missed with his vomit hastily struck three nines on the keypad of his mobile and engaged the operator at the Emergency Centre.

"Which service do you require?"

"Police, innit," replied the lad with some trepidation.

"Hold on while I connect you!"

There was a pause while the operator connected him to the Police Control Centre.

On the first floor balcony Adam was looking increasingly unsteady. "There's been a murder! She's been fucking murdered!" he screamed.

The hoodie was now talking into his phone "There's some guy here and he's bangin' on 'bout a murder and shit, the bleedin' muppet! Reckons there's blood everywhere an' that. Ya better get dem cozzers down 'ere!"

"Can you give me your address please, Sir, and we'll send a car straight away." The operator was used to handling emergency calls and filtering the usual panicked waffle, prank calls and needless domestics that deluged their office every day without fail.

"I think it's Flat 34 or 36. I'm not sure, innit," the hoodie replied. "Peldon Rise, first floor. You know," he added, "near the council offices."

Meanwhile, Adam had started to sway backwards and forwards as his head began to spin. He was struggling to regulate his breathing, his heart thudding in his ears louder than a nightclub bass. His vision blurring he slumped forwards, stooping down to his haunches. Then his body went limp as he passed out, falling forward onto the damp asphalt walkway. The hoodie saw Adam dip slowly behind the concrete barrier and feared the worst. Having no desire to rub shoulders with the Old Bill, the rest of his gang had already fled the scene, leaving him to face the music all alone. The operator listened intently as he reported that Adam had collapsed, and then kept him talking while the Police made their way to the scene.

***

Peldon Flats was a regular haunt for Southend's Emergency Services. If it wasn't the communal bin store ablaze, it was one of the countless junkies comatose in a pool of their own vomit and urine, or the

Flanagan family beating seven bells out of each other or any other mug that dared look in their direction. As soon as the sirens began to close in on the tenement block, the hoodie thought better of it and was on his toes, into the warren of rat runs and alleyways within the estate. Next moment, with siren blaring, a Police car sped into view and screeched to a halt. Two officers leapt out, leaving the doors open behind them, and raced up to the balcony where Adam had passed out.

"Here we go, another pissed up fucking idiot! Probably had a scrap with his skank of a wife," remarked the young rookie copper, Paul Semple.

His older, far more experienced colleague shook her head in disapproval, aware that he was still novice enough to be excited at the prospect of a Murder Scene.

"The report was of a murder," she reminded him acidly, "so just be careful - and watch what you touch!"

WPC Vicky Ward moved like an agile cat as she made her way up the stairs. She kept herself fit, and even though she was in her mid-thirties had the body of a younger woman. In her eighteen years' service Vicky had mentored countless young PC s like Semple, full of vim and vigour, diligently exercising all the authority and knowledge they had gleaned from their brief but intense training regime. Still in their formative years, they had vowed to change the world, to make a difference. Then the stark reality of life on the beat slowly crept into their lives: instead of the excitement depicted in the crime dramas and movies of their youth they would find themselves confronted by endless paperwork, politics and red tape.

PC Semple knelt beside Adam and shook him gently, slowly bringing him back to consciousness. "Hey Sir, are you OK? What's happened?"

Adam looked up at him through bleary eyes. "She's in the bedroom – she's been murdered!" he moaned.

Vicky leant down towards him. "Come on fella! Take a deep breath, breathe slowly." She spoke with compassion and patience. "Who has been murdered?"

Adam pointed to the open door and shook his head vigorously. He was fighting hard to speak but found himself devoid of words. His emotions were in tatters; all he could muster was "Katya... Katya!" Then he collapsed once again, distraught and inconsolable.

"Get him an ambulance!" Vicky told Semple. "I'll take a look in the flat, and you stay with him until the ambulance arrives. He's in shock."

She took a deep breath and then made her way into the flat. On the left hand side of the hallway the small bathroom was empty; to the right the kitchen was equally bare - nothing untoward in it, just fast food remnants and surfaces laden with unwashed crockery. Further along to the left was the lounge, a barren room which contained very few comforts. The ageing two-seater cloth sofa was stained and frayed. A TV was on inside a dated black cabinet with shards of laminate fractured from its edges. On the nest of tables in front of the sofa lay a clutch of old magazines, some in Polish and others tattered and dog-eared like those in a doctor's waiting room. A solitary cigarette stained with vivid pink lipstick fresh from Katya's plump lips had been stubbed out in the bottle brown glass ashtray. With nothing particular in there to attract her attention, WPC Ward moved on to the bedroom and pushed open the door.

The sight of Katya's mutilated body smashed across her consciousness with the impact of a crashing freight train.

CHAPTER 2

ALTER EGO

A full three and a half hours earlier Robin Bradford sat in his car, his mediocre existence stretching before him. His work phone nestled neatly in its cradle on the dash of the tired Ford Focus; his pens, CDs and other effects were arranged in different compartments, all neat, tidy and regular. Perusing the contacts list of his personal phone, he found his girlfriend's mobile number. Just for a second he halted, his conscience pricked. Thoughts of his girlfriend Lizzie finding out about his illicit indulgences flashed through his mind. Then in a flurry of taps the call proceeded.

***

Lizzie stepped briefly from her equally shabby Vauxhall Corsa and greeted her friend and confidante, Maria. They exchanged the usual hugs and air kisses, full of tattle and gossip - the idle prattle of their mundane lives. Maria begged Lizzie to go with her that evening to a new Yoga class that was opening in nearby Billericay. Lizzie dutifully agreed: after all, there was nothing waiting for her at home. Back in the Corsa her phone buzzed excitedly on the dash as Robin tried to get through to her. Then it fell silent again.

***

Robin greeted this unanswered call with a smile; it's so much easier to lie with a text, so much less hassle. A carefully woven fabric of untruths was constructed and the message was duly sent. That would stave off her interest in his whereabouts until at least tea time. He knew he had to try and stop her from contacting him for a while. How could he possibly enjoy a stroll on the dark side if she was going to be harassing him every ten minutes?

'Got 2 more appointments yet love. Shud be home bout 6ish. Call u when i get out of last 1. Phone off 4 a while now xx'

This was not out of character for him, and Lizzie knew he wasn't to be disturbed when he was 'trying to close a deal' as he put it.

He replaced his personal phone on the dash in a second cradle next to his work phone and sat nav, and began leafing through the back pages of his local paper. 'Cherrie's Exotic Massage', 'Tiffany's Massage', 'Crystals of Leigh', 'Ebony and Ivory': they all sounded so alluring, so exotic. These beautifully crafted names and descriptions soon had Robin hot under the collar. His finger came to rest on one that drew his attention. 'Bubbles, Uniformed Girls. Visit Us – Visit You'.

Smiling to himself, he pushed his hand deep beneath the seat, his fingers searching for the cool hard plastic of his 'very' personal phone. He was very careful to dial 141, followed by the number for 'Bubbles'. Tracing his hand up his thigh and across his crotch, he let out a slight moan. "Is that Bubbles?"

"Yes my love," a sexy female voice replied.

"Who do you have working today?" he asked as he stroked himself ever so gently.

"We have Anja, an Eastern European blonde, twenty-two, a shapely thirty eight DD bust. Or Tamara, an English brunette, who is nineteen and very slim, with legs that go on forever."

"Tell me more about Anja," he pressed.

"She likes to please. What sort of service would you be looking for?"

"Just a little on the rough side."

"She does like to be treated rough, but she expects more money. It'll be eighty pounds for half an hour."

"Fine, that's fine!" He breathed heavily down the phone unable to contain his excitement.

"The address, please?"

"Thirty-four Peldon Rise, just off Winchester. Do you know it?"

"No, but I'll find it."

"Four-thirty ok for you? But don't be too rough on her, Tiger!" She was cheeky, flirty and playing up to her punter.

"Thank you, I won't." Robin hung up his phone, switched it off and put it back under the driver's seat, his naughty little secret safely stowed away. Robin's penchant for indulging in illicit sex in Southend's

seedy underbelly of backstreet parlours and brothels had surfaced once more.
His job took him all over South East Essex. Maldon, Wickford, Basildon, Canvey, and Southend and the surrounding areas all featured in his daily routine of meetings and sales spiel. He boasted to his clients that his business sold lucrative slots in plush European timeshares. He advertised his wares in the very same local rag which contained his massage parlour beauties. His business had served him well until the recession hit, crippling people's spare cash, and his outfit was nowhere near as fruitful now as it had been. Both he and Lizzie had enjoyed a lavish lifestyle for the last few years, providing them with countless holiday opportunities, flash cars, a nice big house and only the finest dining.
He began to visit lap dancing clubs while entertaining male clients. During one of these saucy 'work' nights a rather naughty young dancer had tempted him into a small private booth. As soon as the drapes had swished shut behind them, she made it clear that more than a dance was on offer - if he had the cash. He happily agreed for her to perform oral sex on him for £20. His first encounter was decidedly nervous and somewhat brief. A mixture of over excitement and seeing the fresh-faced, topless dancer's mouth writhing around his penis sent him over the edge in a flash. Back home, it seemed like Lizzie was always either too tired or too stressed to do anything. If she did, it was always on her terms, with no variation and she had a total dislike to sucking his cock, much to his disappointment. Over the ensuing weeks and after a couple more trips

inside the booth, one of the dancing girls let slip that she worked in a parlour during the day to bolster her income. She discreetly suggested Robin paid her a visit; that way she could give him a more relaxing and unhurried servicing. He knew exactly what she meant and was soon knocking at the dingy flat door.

He loved his devilish assignations; quickly learning he could have what he wanted if he paid for it. He was addicted to the buzz and the thrill of 'strictly business' sex, craving more and more. Soon his salacious appetite was spiralling out of control.

He had always been smart at extracting money from the unlikeliest of sources. Despite all his promises, he never delivered 'opulent dream flats' to his clientele, but he did fleece them of their money to fund his lavish lifestyle of call girls. Suffice to say, his small print tied his clients up in knots and left them with little chance of reimbursement should they pursue him. If they did track him down and corner him, the money was long gone.

At 5'8" tall, Robin Bradford's plump physique was testament to his fine dining. In his youth he had been strong and muscular, but so much time spent travelling around the country in his car soon put paid to that. Lethargy crept in, and his once muscular frame quickly succumbed to flab. Robin's mop of jet black hair showed signs of greying, but his face was always clean-shaven: smooth and silky, just like his sales patter. Sadly, his morals where not as clean and fresh as his sales talk. In that respect he had more in common with a sewer rat!

Robin keyed 'Peldon Rise' into his satellite navigation

system and his cheery electronic host led him on his way.

***

Katya was a very attractive and clever Polish girl. She was down on her luck, isolated and lonely. Her days were filled with a mixture of emptiness and crap daytime TV. The only visitor she ever had was Adam, the weird neighbour who seemed obsessed with her every move, albeit in a kind and seemingly harmless way. Despite a lack of company, Katya didn't want to encourage his visits. He always made her feel a little uneasy and she felt it best to shy away from his dinner invites and constant offers of help with the 'man jobs'. To date, he hadn't even got past the threshold of her flat and she wanted to keep it that way. At around four o'clock that afternoon she was huddled under a throw on her grubby sofa, listening intently to the television and trying to piece together the babbling English conversation, when her mobile rang. It was Katya's madam advising her of her latest client's imminent arrival.

"You have a gentleman due at four-thirty, Love. He likes things a bit rough. You know the boundaries, so stick with what you're comfortable with, Darling, ok?"

Sadly, Katya no longer recognised where the 'boundaries' started or finished. This former strict Catholic girl had left her ethics behind when she arrived at London's Victoria three years earlier. At home in Poland she had worked long hours across two jobs, just to save enough money for the coach trip to England. Katya had left her beloved family and rural life back in her native Polish village after finding an online company claiming to be an elite au pair agency offering 'stunning opportunities' with 'a large client base of rich families'. The stark reality was a million miles from the vision they had painted. She found no cash-rich jobs awaiting her; no posh flats, just poverty, hardship and then... prostitution. She was met at the bus station by a scruffy old East-End chancer, whose sole ambition went no further than living off immoral earnings and sex on tap. The whole website was nothing more than a façade to lure in pretty young women, and then enslave them in a live of misery and depravity.

Disorientated in a large foreign city, she could do nothing but let herself be taken in by him, despite her immediate misgivings. As soon as she got to his flat the nightmare started; he kept her locked up in a cramped room, only visiting her periodically to drug her. Soon a string of his 'friends' took turns fucking her semi-conscious carcass, till she was left with no option but to submit to their demands, or face the brutal beatings. Once she had been humbled and became compliant, the drugging stopped. Ironically, for this small mercy, Katya was grateful, and eventually she lost track of time. Days melted into weeks, weeks into months and soon a whole year had elapsed... every day the same: sleep, fuck, eat! In time she was given the freedom of the flat and small unkempt garden, but was never allowed outside the boundary walls. Every minute of every day was filled with desperation to escape this living hell.

One morning she was woken early by sounds of arguing from the lobby downstairs. She eased from her room, tip-toed to the banisters and cautiously peered over. Her captor was lying in the narrow hallway clutching his hand to his head, blood seeping through his fingers and onto the carpet. Without a second thought Katya was down the stairs and aiming for the door, but even as she fled, her dressing-gown was grabbed by a huge ape of a man she didn't recognise. Dragging her to the floor, he put a hand over her mouth, stifling her cries. Then, motioning silence, he gently eased his hand away and a middle-aged female entered the hallway and gestured for her to get up. Within seconds, the two intruders had hurried her out of the building and bundled her into a car parked outside. During what turned out to be a short journey east along the A127 the pair explained what was happening. They told her they were heading for a coastal town she'd never heard of called Southend-on-Sea. The old guy had crossed them once too often and she was being taken in lieu of payments owed. They then tabled a proposition the broken girl knew she couldn't refuse ... a flat, a wage and some protection. In return she sold herself willingly, but to a better class of punter. To these people she was no more than a commodity they were happy to exploit, just as her previous captor had before them. They needed her to do business with a smile, though, and some ground rules were set.

And so it was that Katya moved to Peldon Flats.

***

Robin Bradford leant forward and listened for his sat nav's commands.

Turn right at the next junction. He dutifully obeyed.

At the roundabout take the third exit; continue for two hundred metres. He was close now.

Take the next right. You have reached your destination.

Robin eased his car into a space opposite Peldon Rise and surveyed the building. The estate was like any other up and down the country. The darkness of the winter's evening began to creep over the town, and one by one the street lights fused together creating safe passage to Peldon's entranceway. Checking his watch, he began the ritual of hiding his sat nav and phones in the glove compartment safely out of sight. After all, people round these parts had no scruples. He removed the cash from his pocket, placing it inside his sock, and then with a series of beeps and flashes he locked his car and was away across the courtyard. As he neared No.34 he stopped momentarily in front of a small frosty bathroom window, adjusting his tie in the reflection and smoothing down his eyebrows, as if he were about to attend a sales appointment. He cleared his throat and reached for the buzzer. Cathedral bells chimed behind the door.

***

Katya rose from the grubby sofa and went to greet her client, shutting the door to her personal space as she made her way to the front door. Before she reached out to open the door she straightened her short pleated skirt and released one more button on her tight white blouse so that her already ample breasts spilled out gracefully over her red lace bra. A quick pucker of her pink lips and 'Anja' was ready too.

Pulling the door back tightly on its chain, Anja spied through its gap into the eerie half-light of Peldon's balcony.

"Hi, Anja?" enquired Robin.

"Tak, Tak... yes. Please come in!" Anja's English was getting better, but she still had a heavy accent. Robin perused Anja's body from top to bottom. Her blonde hair was closely cropped, and her immaculate make-up topped off with tarty, shocking pink lipstick. She held herself well: had fate been kinder, she could easily have graced the pages of the countless magazines she endlessly pawed over. Her blouse parted gently at her bosom to reveal an ample cleavage, so Robin could see clearly what he would soon be enjoying. Her midriff was exposed, showing off a slim, sleek waist adorned with an angel shaped belly piercing. Her skirt hung just over the hips and barely covered her buttocks, leading neatly down to fishnet hold ups. Anja had chosen well: these were Robin's favourite garments. To finish, she wore the shiniest black patent high-heeled shoes, which gleamed back at Robin as his gazed at her feet.

"You come through, please!" Beckoning him inside, Anja turned to reveal her shapely buttocks teasing out from below her skirt, her red lace knickers just visible and barely covering her. Robin was clearly elated at the sight of Anja's arse as she guided him to her boudoir. He resisted the urge to slap her bum as she sauntered sexily ahead of him; his time to slap and grope was fast approaching.

Anja's bedroom was something of a contrast to the rest of the flat. Although they were one and the same,

Katya's alter ego Anja commanded the bedroom. It was, after all, her office and needed to befit its purpose. To this end Katya despised sleeping in her bed. The only half-decent room in the house just served to remind her of her own failure. Instead, she chose to sleep on the lounge sofa, and no client was ever allowed to enter that room - her personal space. Sadly, Katya envied Anja: she was confident, wanted, and sometimes even loved. One of Anja's well-off regulars had begged her to give up her degrading job and take up residence with him, but she declined. At least this way she was only a part time whore, not at his beck and call all hours of the day and night. Katya was so very different from Anja. Katya was demure, shy and quiet; she liked the arts and had studied the historical buildings and monuments that were scattered far and wide through Poland's old cities. Like a well-schooled actor, Katya played her role as Anja brilliantly. If there was an Oscar going for playing a brass, Katya would definitely be in the running.

Robin brushed up close behind Anja as she slid her hand across the door handle, the warmth of his breath breezing past her neck and partly exposed shoulder like a zephyr, sending a chill running through her. She quickly opened the door and made for the bed. Robin removed his watch and placed it on the tacky purple leather stool at the bedside. The décor was cheap and garish, awash with pinks and purples; everything was low-ticket factory shop, but clean nonetheless. The freshly laundered sheets lay invitingly open, and the bedside lamps suffused the room with a soft amber backlight. Fluffy pink and mauve heart-shaped pillows snuggled together at the head of the bed, creating the illusion of a loving romantic assignation. The truth was that Katya had carefully put all this together with the help of charity shops and car boot sales. Here and there around the room various "work" clothes hung from the picture rail: slinky, sexy and some outright slutty. Anja's outfits were not the usual comfortable blouses, jumpers and skirts that most would associate with a day at the office. Hers were provocative, indecent and tarty, designed to set the hearts and pulses of her rampant clientele racing. Anything Katya could do to speed up the inevitable climax and get it over with, the better.

Robin was pleased with her attire. She reminded him of his pubescent fondling with Sarah Pearson in Fifth Grade of Secondary School - young, but far from innocent. He removed his clothes in a flurry, stripping down to his boxers and socks. Anja began to unbutton her blouse.

"Wait, leave it on... please." Robin stopped her. "How old are you Anja?"

"I am twent two."

"No, surely you're younger! You look much younger." Robin was steering Anja in a direction he wanted her to play. "Sixteen, I think Sixteen. Maybe even younger. You could pass for fifteen, no sweat!" Robin's arousal was now evident from the swelling in his baggy underwear. Anja remained silent. He reached up the back of her stockinged thighs and caressed her firm arse, before steering her to sit on the edge of the bed.

Anja was more than familiar with what this meant and dutifully obliged by removing Robin's penis from his boxer shorts and firmly stroking it with her warm clammy hands. Leaning slowly forward, she reached for her dressing table where the tools of her trade lay waiting, as if on a surgeon's trolley. Oil, tissues, K.Y, condoms, wipes, an assortment of phallic shaped toys, and lastly an air freshener to rid the room of sex's musky odour. She ripped the condom packet open with her teeth and, still using her teeth, slid a condom onto his shaft with all the skill and guile only a sex worker could command. Once the condom was on, she removed his penis from her mouth and eased a wipe from its packet. Not liking the taste of spermicide, Anja used it to stroke the full length of Robin's glory. She tossed the wipe into the basket by the bedside table - the obligatory wicker bin, pre lined with a carrier bag for ease of removal and then focused on the task in hand. Leaning into his crotch, Anja's warm pink lips greeted Robin's throbbing cock, and as she drew her head back and forth she left a trail of candy pink saliva along the length of his latex-clad member. Robin placed both hands on her head, applying an increasingly firm and steady pressure. Gritting his teeth, he tightened his grip more and more until Anja winced.

"That'll teach you to fuck about in my class." His authoritarian voice was bitter and aggressive. "You naughty, dirty little slut! You'll learn the fucking hard way who's the boss!"

She tried to pull away but Robin was in control, and he wasn't done yet. He lifted one hand from her head and cupped her breasts through her top. Then he reached round the back of her head with the other hand and pulled at the hair on the nape of her neck. His large palm all but encircled her slender throat. Gripping, pulling, groping, he now used Anja's head to satisfy his salacious greed. Grunting loudly, he drove hard into her mouth, forcing himself deep into the back of her throat. Anja tried to protest, but couldn't speak, her hands trying to stop Bradford's thighs from slamming into her chest as he rammed harder and faster. As she struggled to push him away, she unintentionally scratched his leg with her long painted nails.

"Nasty little bitch! You slut, fucking slut!" Robin released his unwilling victim from his cock. "Bend over the bed, you dirty slag! Fucking DO it - now!" he snarled.

The fear building inside her, she turned her back to him as instructed and bent over the bed, praying for the ordeal to be over. He pulled her skirt up over the small of her back and snatched at her lacy underwear, dragging her briefs urgently down to her ankles. He stood for a second admiring her arse, before raising his hand and slapping her fleshy buttocks hard. Anja squealed in pain, which only excited him more. His penis was rock hard as he slapped her again.

"Swinya, grube swinya!" Her native tongue took over as she felt the burning pain course through her body. Angry crimson welts surfaced instantly on Katya's tender flesh, but her protests merely served to spur Robin on and he pulled at her blonde hair with renewed vigour. She leaned back and guided his cock towards her vagina. Her hand was shaking, and she was struggling to get him inside her because of his rampant stabbing. Anja was dry from fear: she wanted this over, wanted him to cum because that usually did the trick; once they had cum they always calmed down. With the K.Y. well out of reach, Katya elected to spit on her fingers and rub the saliva onto her vagina in front of him, hoping this would spur him into fucking her - she couldn't take much more of the slapping - and In one sharp jerk, he was deep inside her. He pulled harder at her hair now, virtually tearing it out by the roots, his other hand clawing at her buttocks and hips. His fingernails dug into her flesh, breaking the surface of her smooth, soft skin, and a faint smudge of blood filled the underside of his nails. He pumped harder and faster, each time more dramatic and forceful than the last.

"Fucking whore! Cheap, fucking little whore!" Robin could feel himself about to cum. "You filthy bitch... BITCH!" Groaning loudly and jubilantly, he came in her with a final powerful thrust. He was done.

Now she knew she was home and dry, her legs buckled under her and she collapsed onto the bed. She turned to see him removing the soiled condom, which he dumped unceremoniously on her purple, heart-shaped rug. An act of defiance and humiliation, designed to teach Anja who was the master. Humbly she got off the bed, removed it from the mat and placed it in the bedside bin. Reaching for the wipes, she pulled some for herself and offered the packet to Robin. He snatched the packet from her and set about removing all traces of their sordid coupling. Unfortunately for Katya, she couldn't rid herself of the encounter so easily: her body bore clear and open testament to his vile rage, the scratches still weeping blood from his coarse nails.

Bradford removed the money from his shoe and slung it across her bed as she dressed. "Whore's wages!" he snarled.

"Thank you." Despite his disgusting manner, Katya was still grateful for the money; she had bills to pay like everyone else. Once Robin had finished teasing his tie back into place, he swept his jacket from the stool and stepped into the hallway. She followed him to the door, one hand on her sore arse, caressing the swollen hand prints. After he'd left she re-applied the security chain, bent forward and let her head rest on the cold door. Then she sighed out loud, relieved it was over.

Katya returned to her lounge and began leafing through a magazine, trying meanwhile to calm her nerves with a cigarette: she never could understand why these men liked to hurt Anja so much.

***

Robin placed the keys in the ignition of his clapped out car and the engine rumbled into life. A cursory glance at his wrist told him that in his haste to leave Anja's flat he'd forgotten to put his watch back on. "Oh you fucking tosser!" he moaned to himself. Relocking his car, he again found himself heading for the steps of Peldon Rise. Once more the musical chimes echoed incongruously through the shabby hallway. Katya looked up nervously, taken aback by the doorbell so soon after her last client's departure. In some trepidation, as she wasn't expecting anyone else, she stubbed out her cigarette in the glass ashtray and left the lounge.

"My watch!"

Katya was shocked by Robin's reappearance.

"I left my fucking watch in your room!"

Foolishly, Katya opened the door. "I get watch for you, but you not nice man. I tell you that you have hurt me!"

"You got paid, didn't you? I paid through the nose for my extras, so get over it. Now piss off and get my fucking watch!" he demanded.

"You are not nice man!"

Robin brushed her aside and went to the bedroom to retrieve his timepiece. Katya followed.

"You don't pay enough for hurt me like that!" she moaned.

Bradford grabbed Katya's jaw and pushed her head up against the toilet door. "If you don't shut your mouth... I'll shut it for you. Got it!" he snarled into her face.

Flailing her arms she broke free from his grasp and pushing against his chest with all the strength she could muster, she told him to leave. "Get out my flat, get out!" she yelled.

"No fuck arse tom tells me when to go!" He drove his palm hard into the underside of Katya's chin, knocking her flying. She fell backwards, unable even to scream, striking her left temple on the door frame and with her pretty blue eyes shut, her head hit the floor. Katya had no idea that Robin came at her again, kicking her hard in the ribs: she was already unconscious. Still raging at her motionless body, his mood worsened. "Actually, you skanky, fucking slag, I don't reckon I had value for money, so I think I'll take this back while I'm at it!" And lifting the notes from the side table, he pocketed her wages and then rifled through her drawers.

Not until he was satisfied there was no more money in the bedroom did Robin Bradford take his leave of Peldon Flats for a second time.

CHAPTER 3

COPPER AND BRASS

WPC Vicky Ward had a wealth of experience to draw on, as well as her training and her own sharp wits. She ushered young Semple to the open doorway of 34 Peldon Rise with strict instructions. “Don’t move, don’t touch anything, and don’t let anybody in!” She reached down for her radio and spoke to her Duty Sergeant. After having briefed him on the scene, she cautiously re-entered the flat, nerves jangling, senses heightened. Sergeant James McEwan, or Sergeant Macca as he was affectionately known by his colleagues, sent out instructions to his foot soldiers left, right and centre. Macca hurriedly carried the news upstairs to C.I.D, as he very much wanted to be involved. A sad but rare glimmer of excitement in an otherwise uneventful shift, and Macca wanted in! He had only ever seen a few suspicious deaths in his years as a policeman. None was ever pleasant and he knew that details, albeit minute, near enough always held the key. Time as they say, was of the essence.

***

Detective Inspector Vincent Ambrose sat daydreaming at his desk, thinking about the weekend's Police Charity Golf Tournament, which Southend had the honour of hosting this year. Vincent was a giant of a man, standing 6ft 2" tall, with an impressive 56" chest. In his twenties he had held the Home Counties Police Boxing Belt for six consecutive years, and despite being forty seven now, Vincent still trained every day. He was very proud of himself, always preening and titivating. He had divorced five years ago and was enjoying his newfound freedom. There was a wealth of opportunity for a fit, healthy, well groomed man and he exploited it. His confidence, stature and charm had women queuing to gain his attention, while his rugged features, bent nose and crumpled ear lobes just seemed to add to his lovable rogue label. Thanks to a well-paid job and some shrewd property investments, he was sitting pretty financially too. Vincent had no desire to change his job, as it fuelled his need to be respected and also opened many doors. He had never crossed the line, but often sailed close to the wind with his outside business interests.

When Macca bounded into his office, Vincent was pushing papers around his desk trying to look enthusiastic while tapping his teeth with a pen.

"Vol au vents or crolines, Macca?"

"What?" Macca was caught off guard by Vincent's random question.

"Sunday week, the golf comp! What do you think?" Vincent smiled.

"Who cares about vol au vents or golf, Vince! Will there be lager and strippers?" joked Macca.

"Not sure if there'll be strippers, it's a respectable event - unless of course your missus is going!" Both enjoyed a good bit of banter, it made for an easier life. "But there will be plenty of lager!"

"Vince mate, listen! One of my arms and legs has just called in a suspicious death on the Dodge City Estate. Much as I'd like to keep it to myself, I know I can't because it's well over my pay grade! I guess you boys will want to poke your flat noses in - take all the glory while we do all the running as usual!"

"Why thank you, Macca me old mate! How very kind of you. If you want to help, perhaps your flat footers can do some of the more interesting tasks for me. Like door to door, hours of trawling through CCTV, witness statements, and of course fingertip searches on your hands and knees and rummaging through the waste bins!"

"So kind, Vince, so kind! Can I also polish your fat bloody ego?"

"Nothing fat about me, Macca!" he quipped, patting his enviably trim stomach.

"I've put four officers down there already and called through to S.O.C.O. Probably get that poncy pillock who wears a syrup again. Do you think he knows how bad it really looks?" Macca glanced at Vincent, who now looked deep in thought. "WPC Ward was first on the scene, Vince; she's keeping it secure for you lot."

"Thanks for that, Mate. I'll try and keep you in the

loop as much as possible. Oh, and have you contacted Him Upstairs yet?"

"No, that's one job you can do. I have no wish to deal with that cantankerous bastard."

"Perhaps I'll email him, or send him a text on his Blackberry!" They laughed raucously at their own joke, as they both knew the "Man Upstairs" was far from being a tech head. Vincent grabbed his keys and phone off the desk and made his way out into the open plan office space, which was littered with desks and busy looking bodies.

"Listen up! We have an unconfirmed report of a suspicious death on the Dodge. I need the meeting room next door as an Incident Room. Nicky, start getting me any CCTV footage; Brian, you get me an autopsy slot sorted. I want this processed and wrapped up in three days. I've got the Charity Golf to sort out still. Come on, let's get cracking!"

His request was met by a wave of activity, chairs grinding on floors, desk drawers clattering and doors banging shut. Vincent took the stairs down to the basement car park and marched towards his vehicle. He didn't feel the need for sirens and lights: he knew the victim wouldn't be going anywhere until he had given her the once over. He slipped quietly across town, his mind already racing.

***

Peldon Flats was now overrun by police officers, their cars parked all over the place, and half the Estate's residents were being held back behind a cordon. This was the biggest news to hit the police radio network in months. As Vincent made his way across the courtyard and under the blue and white tape, his metal-kegged brogues clinked against the paving, letting all around him know that he was coming. When PC Semple saw him approaching the doorway of the victim's flat, Vicky Ward's instructions echoed through his mind. He stepped bravely into Vincent Ambrose's path and delivered his lines with confidence and authority. "Stop right there, Sir, this is a restricted area! Nobody goes in here without clear instructions from my superiors." Not wishing to cause this ambitious young copper any embarrassment, Vincent flashed his warrant card and politely asked him to step to one side. A wry smile graced his face: he had always liked the obedient rookie types, and took a mental note to remember the young constable's name - could be future CID.

Reaching inside his smart designer suit, he pulled out a pair of crumpled blue overshoes. Putting them on over his brogues he looked down in distaste. They didn't make him look quite as cool and sharp as he wanted. WPC Ward glanced over and saw Vincent enter, his huge frame filling the open doorway. She was more than pleased to see him, but wished it could have been under better circumstances. Ever the charmer, he put his arm round her shoulders, asking if she was ok. Vicky was beginning to show signs of stress. "A bit shook up, Vince. I wasn't expecting such a brutal end to a quiet shift! The body's in the bedroom. Looks like she's a youngish tom, possibly Eastern European judging by the magazines and stuff in the lounge. Not managed to get a name yet - the flat's registered to a letting agency."

"Ok Vicky, go get yourself a brew in the Incident Wagon, then come back up and see me when you've had a breather." Vincent was worried about her; she looked a little peaky.

"Thanks, Vince." Vicky was still reeling from seeing the effects of the victim's grizzly demise, and his compassion was very welcome. "Do you want one brought back up?" she asked with a smile.

His cheeky spirit was unfazed by the butchery within. "Not unless you've got a livener to spice it up with!"

"See what I can do!" Collecting PC Semple on her way out, she left for the mobile unit stationed in the courtyard below.

As he made for the bedroom, Vincent cast his eye briefly over Katya's meagre possessions discarded around the flat. Tit bits had already begun filtering through to him, and even from Vicky's brief summary, he knew it had been a brutal assault. This made it easier for Vincent. Unlike poor WPC Ward, he knew it would be a ghastly scene: he had been forewarned.

***

Adam was sitting in the Incident Unit with the obligatory 'hot, sweet tea' cupped in his hands when WPC Ward entered the wagon. After removing her hat and coat she signalled to the constable next to Adam by forming the letter 'T' with her mitts. "How ya bearing up?"

"I'm not doing too well," he replied, still clearly in deep, deep shock.

***

Back in the flat, Vincent Ambrose had just caught sight of the carnage in Katya's bedroom. Her body lay sprawled across her once prized rug, Robin Bradford's earlier act of defiance now totally erased by the copious quantities of blood pooling around her. Her blonde hair was stuck almost gel-like to her scalp with the blood that had oozed from a large gash on her temple, and her nose and lips had also bled profusely. Her white blouse, torn open along with her brassiere, was stained scarlet by the blood from a deep cut across her exposed breasts. Her left arm lay upwards between the bed and her dressing table, the contents of which were now spread across the floor. Heavy bruising, alongside numerous scratches, was already visible on her forearms, and her right arm - clearly broken - lay under her lifeless body. Katya's silky smooth stomach had been ripped open, her intestines spilling across the laminate floor like the remains of a road-kill fox. This attack had been wild and frenzied, merciless and crazed. Katya's skirt and briefs were still protecting her dignity - a small mercy for such an undignified end. Her left leg, which was bent at the knee, was tucked neatly under the bed; her right lay straight and unmarked, except for tears to her fishnets. Within the congealed blood which lay to the right of the corpse were two shoe prints, one crystal clear, the other distorted and around twice its normal length. On the wall was a scuffed and bloody hand print and numerous splats and splashes, like something created by a mad artist. Katya's slayer had shown no mercy. The room was a forensic dream with clues at every turn: blood, fibres, hair, it was all there. The answer was surely here in the room. The bin beside her bed held keys to her day's visitors.

Vincent stroked his chin pensively. Clearly a knife had been used to disembowel Katya. So where was it? He decided that for now it was best to retire from this sickening scene and let the specialists take the place apart stitch by stitch. Unbeknown to Vincent Ambrose, the murder weapon was right there in front of him, less than a metre from where he stood. But it would be several hours yet before it was discovered by the S.O.C.O. The mind of a killer is never the easiest thing to fathom, but when this particular monster struck, he or she was clearly and seriously unhinged.

CHAPTER 4

FLAT FEET AND THEORIES

As Vincent left No 34 and ventured out into the hallway his eyes scanned the crowd below, wondering whether the killer was there, ringside, satisfying some kind of obsession or morbid fascination for the drama he had caused. PC Semple was leaving the Incident Wagon, tea in hand, about to head back up to his sentry point as Vincent Ambrose approached. Vincent's usual deliberate and calculated composure faded briefly. "Sick bastard!" he groaned. "What kind of sick bastard could do that to a woman?"

"I've not seen her yet, Sir." PC Semple sounded relieved that he had sat this one out.

"My advice would be to avoid it if you can, Lad. It won't ever leave you otherwise."

Having Adam to contend with, Vicky Ward had been gratefully distracted from her earlier discovery, but now Vincent stepped inside the mobile unit and ushered her to the back, out of Adam's earshot.

"That has to be the worst thing I've ever seen Vincent! How could anyone do something so terrible?"

"What about this lad here - Adam? What's he given you so far?"

"Nothing. He can barely speak, just keeps mumbling crap!"

"Ok Vicky, keep a close eye on him, I want him in an interview suite with Nicky Meers and me within the hour."

"You don't suspect him, surely?"

"At the moment he's all we have, Vicky. Maybe he did it, or maybe he holds a clue to whoever did. Don't lose sight of that!"

"No way! He's too distraught."

"Wouldn't you be, if you'd just slashed someone to death? Jesus!"

"But surely he would have bolted long before we got here, and there isn't a speck of blood on him! I'm sure you're wrong!"

"That's why I'm the detective, WPC Ward. So kindly let me get on with my job and stop bloody surmising!"

Vincent eased through the trailer and confronted Adam. He spoke formally and with no emotion. "Mr Adam Pickering, I must ask you to accompany my officers to the station and answer some questions."

Adam froze. "You're arresting me!" he exclaimed.

"No, not at present. We need to ask you some questions relating to our enquiries, and for a DNA swab. Hopefully, we can then start building up a picture of what's happened here today."

"Are you fucking serious? 'Build up a picture'? What the hell's wrong with you people! Start looking for the fucking killer!" Adam shouted.

Vincent interrupted him. "Now you listen up, Sunshine! I will tell YOU what's happening, not the other way round! WPC Ward, arrange a van to collect him and get Macca to book him in."

"Vincent?" she protested.

"WPC Ward!"

She knew it was pointless to question Vincent's judgement, he could be very single minded at times. He pulled his phone from his pocket and called his office.

"Nicky, it's Vincent! How are things moving?"

"Hi, Vincent! Well, Brian's arranged for a meat wagon to collect the body - they should be with you any time now. The post mortem's booked for nine-thirty tonight. Oh, and Brian's sorted the Incident Room too."

"What progress have you made with CCTV?"

Nicky had been trying to get the operators at Southend's Council Office to browse Peldon, Victoria and the local streets from their Security Centre. So far she hadn't had much luck, but she was in no rush to get the information anyway. She wasn't the detective solving the case. She knew now, though, that she'd be getting a right royal dressing down from Vincent if she didn't get moving with it. He seemed very impatient and agitated on this one.

"I'm still waiting for footage to be emailed over from Council HQ for the two hours leading up to the 999 report," blagged Nicky.

"Push them then, Nic! We need those images. And call Simon Warby to get his backside over from

Chelmsford. He's shit hot at enhancement and video editing."

"Ok boss, on it right away!"

When Nicky hung up, she immediately logged off the social network account which had been dominating her time whilst everyone else was pandering to Vincent's demands.

***

As the Police van pulled out of Peldon Rise car park with Adam Pickering tucked neatly in the back, Forensics' head honcho William Mumford sauntered in, bespectacled and studious. Pushing his glasses back up his nose he asked for Vincent Ambrose or the Crime Scene S.O. Thorough and professional, he was a man who came across as seriously lacking anything resembling emotion. His ill-fitting wig indicated his only apparent weakness. Refusing to succumb to his receding locks, vanity had overridden any chance of him balding gracefully. Mumford was very unpopular with most of Southend's Police hierarchy, having an arrogance about him that didn't sit well with the likes of Vincent Ambrose. He was one of England's most accomplished forensic scientists, but his interpersonal skills left a lot to be desired. Tact wasn't William Mumford's strong point; finding needles in haystacks was, though. Much as Ambrose detested him, he was sure he would draw a wealth of hidden information from Katya's flat.

***

WPC Vicky Ward stood close to Vincent and engaged him in a hushed conversation, while he tried to draw as much as he could out of her in the hope that something might strike a chord.

Her radio chirped into life with Macca's familiar voice bleating from her pocket.

"Vicky, can you tell Vincent we managed to track down the 999 caller! The number's registered to our old friend James Flanagan, 4 Peldon Rise. I think the caller was possibly his son, Benjamin."

"He is standing right next to me, Sarge. But yes, I will tell him."

"Ooh, lucky you, Vicky! You want to watch yourself with him!" Macca laughed over the radio, implying subtle flirtations and veiled innuendos simmering between Vicky and Vincent - that was Vincent's way. Vicky's cheeks reddened and Vincent mustered a knowing grin. Though they had both been in the same station since Vincent's divorce, they had never got closer than flirting.

"Who did you have with you, Vicky ... when you first went up?" Vincent asked.

"The new lad from Colchester, PC Semple."

"Take him with you and go round to the Flanagan's' flat. See want you can find out. See if it was his lad that rang through to Control earlier, but don't go in too heavy - you know what the Flanagans are like!"

***

Vicky Ward knew the Flanagan family of old. Although James was a pain in the arse, always fighting, getting hammered and causing mayhem in the bars, he was 'old school'. He wouldn't think twice about putting Semple on his backside, but Vicky was sure he wouldn't hit a woman. Or at least, she hoped!

PC Semple was relieved of his guard duty and soon he and WPC Ward were on their way to the Flanagan's' flat. James Flanagan had come to Essex from Ireland's West Coast in the late sixties, seeking gainful employment. Not long after, he had met Monica, a young singer working the many clubs around the Essex towns. Both smitten, they set up home together. Monica had given James three sons, each as fierce as their father, and their reputation spoke volumes on the Peldon Estate. Most locals feared the Flanagans, and only the pissed or plain stupid crossed swords with James and his brood. Benjamin, the youngest, wasn't as tough as his older brothers, but living on their reputation he got by. His dad would secretly taunt him, joking that he wasn't from Flanagan stock at all. "Probably the postie's!" he would say. Nobody wanted to provoke the fearsome wrath of the Flanagan family, so Benjamin went about his business unhindered.

Monica Flanagan kept an immaculate house, despite their impoverished life. "Cleanliness is next to godliness!" she would say as she relentlessly mopped, polished and cleaned. Ward and Semple knocked at the ground floor flat and waited patiently as the bolts, chains and locks banged into life. Keeping people out, or keeping them in: you could never be sure with James Flanagan. Vicky had already warned PC Semple to keep quiet, and he was starting to feel like a ventriloquist's dummy. All he needed was a stick up his arse, he thought.

Monica Flanagan opened the door to her modest cas-

tle and beckoned the officers inside. Nothing if not polite, Monica had little to fear from the police. James Flanagan called out from the lounge, “Who’s dat at the door Mona?”
“It’s the police James, looking for young Benny.”
“What’s the little shite done now?” He bellowed.
“Nothing bad, Mr Flanagan. We believe he may have reported a serious incident earlier,” WPC Ward stated. James Flanagan came bounding out of the lounge. “My son’s no fuckin’ grass, Missy. You’ll have gotten it wrong!”
“This is a little bit different to the normal squabbles, Mr Flanagan. There’s been what we believe to be a murder in the block above you. Benjamin merely reported the incident on behalf of a distressed resident. We need to evaluate what, if anything, he saw.”
Flanagan began to relax and retreated a step or two, his raised, wagging finger returning to his side. Monica asked if the PCs would like tea or coffee while James tried to dig his son from his pit of a bedroom.
“Come out son! Ya gotta talk to da officers.”
Benjamin was understandably apprehensive; after all he had legged it earlier on in the evening and wasn’t keen to rekindle his conversation with the Police. Eventually with a little gentle encouragement from his dad, he was led into the lounge by his ear lobe.
“Now bloody well speak up, son!” James wasn’t one to dispense the namby-pamby parenting skills preached on T.V.
“I ain’t done nuffink!”
“We just need to ask you a couple of questions, Benjamin. Don’t stress yourself, you aren’t in any

trouble." Vicky's manner was soothing to the troubled youngster and he settled himself at the family dining table ready to be grilled.

"Earlier on this evening you made a call to the Emergency Services. Correct?"

"Yeah, but I didn't see nuffin. That Adam told me to!"

"Okay, okay! Just take things easy! Why did Adam ask you to call for him?"

"He was going mental, bruv! Shouting and chucking up. I just called you lot, like he said."

"When did you first become aware of Adam's presence on the first floor balcony?" Her pen poised to scramble more notes down in her little black flip pad.

"Few seconds before he started shouting. I 'eard 'is flat door bang, and looked up."

"Is that all?"

Ben nodded; he was keen to rid himself of these coppers.

"If we need to ask Benjamin any further questions, Mr and Mrs Flanagan, would that be ok?"

"He's told you all he knows. Why would you want to be talking to him again?" James Flanagan growled, while Monica put her arm round her son's shoulder giving him the comfort and love only a mother can. James saw them over the threshold, pausing for a second to ensure they had cleared off into the night.

***

They now headed back up the flight of stairs towards Number 38, home of Adam Pickering and his mother. PC Semple was close at Vicky's heels like a lap dog, posing questions to her at an unanswerable rate, trying to make sense of the evening's events. All this enthusiasm was not helping the WPC's concentration: she needed a clear head and Semple's constant chatter was driving her batty, sooner rather than later he pushed her to the brink. "For Christ's sake, Semple! Will you just shut up for two pissing minutes?"

***

William Mumford was fast approaching retirement and time hadn't been kind. His forehead constantly wore a frown, with deep scar-like lines running from side to side, giving him a permanently pensive expression. What little hair he had left was grey and thinning around the sides, a stark contrast to his poorly made black wig. He always wore the same old two-sizes-too-big tweed shooting jacket, with leather patched elbows and a crumpled handkerchief spilling out of the breast pocket. It clashed wildly with his plum corduroy trousers, tan sandals and grey socks. His ties were typically of an indeterminate sand colour, and an equally drab fawn cardigan hung off his emaciated frame. He was ushered into the Mobile Unit and introduced to Vincent Ambrose. Both had met before and each had reservations about the other, for different reasons. Now, though, they needed to forge a working relationship - and quickly, if they were to catch the killer.

Mumford shook Vincent's hand firmly and realised straight away that they had more in common than either had imagined. Albeit from different lodges, both men were prominent Masons. It was the first time he had tested Vincent with the famously encrypted gesture, and Vincent's subtle reply fell like deafness on all except Mumford himself. Maybe this revelation about their mutual passion and kinship might smooth the path for future assignments.

"Best get you up to the flat, William: I need you to give me some insight into tonight's events. At the moment we're staring at a blank canvas and scratching our butts."

"Let's see what we can do for you then." Clutching an aluminium case in each hand, with a white disposable suit tucked under his armpit, Mumford stepped to one side and allowed Vincent to lead on. Vincent duly escorted his new-found Masonic Brother to the entrance of Katya's flat and told him that to his knowledge only three people had been inside - Adam Pickering, WPC Ward and himself.

Mumford carefully set down his two cases in the hallway and slid the catches aside. Lifting the lid on the first, he revealed a vast array of pots and brushes arranged in neat compartments. In the second was an expensive and highly complicated camera, with numerous lenses nestled in a bed of foam and engineered into small black pyramids. Below the camera was a compact tripod, which he immediately retrieved and set about erecting.

"You need a two day course just to set this bloody thing up!" he quipped.

"Rather you than me!" replied Vincent, non-plussed by the sight of the complex contraption. William Mumford began a pictorial log of 34 - the balcony, the doorway and hallway - occasionally pausing to fill his micro sized Dictaphone with relevant verbal notes.

"No obvious blood traces to the door area, although we do have fresh vomit along the passage. Pattern suggests the person who was sick was travelling outward at some speed." Reaching again into his case, he produced an ultra violet lamp which emitted an eerie magenta light.

"I understand that the lad who discovered her vomited in here and outside, William," Vincent advised.

"Switch the lights off please, Vincent!" The room was filled with a magenta haze.

"Hmmm, small traces of blood towards the far end of the hallway consistent with a strike or blow. Height of splatter would indicate upper body or head injury."

Vincent was always fascinated by forensic examinations. They had this magical ability to conjure hidden clues. Clues he urgently needed.

"D'you mind if we view the lounge, kitchen and bathroom first? Don't want to cloud my judgement by seeing the body yet."

On entering the kitchen Mumford repositioned his tripod and began capturing the scene again.

"Kitchen drawer open, otherwise generally nothing of interest."

Earlier on Vincent had missed the utensil drawer, which he now saw was partly pulled out from its housing. Inside the drawer all the different compartments merged together, forks, spoons and knives randomly scattered. There was no way of knowing if anything was missing, it was a total mess.

"Possible source for our weapon do you think, William?"

"Not sure, but I'll dust the whole place for prints soon. I certainly wouldn't rule it out."

Moving to the lounge William Mumford was visibly excited by the cigarette, until Vincent remarked that the victim seemed to have been wearing the same pink lipstick. Moving swiftly through to the bedroom Mumford beamed broadly, unsettling Vincent.

"My, my, our killer was careless! We should be wrapping this up quite quickly, Vincent. Usually with a spur of the moment attack like this the killer is unprepared and clumsy. Likelihood is a disgruntled client, or maybe even a pimp she was holding back on. They lose their cool and strike out without care or caution."

"Fact or speculation, William? Can you tell from what's here?"

"Speculation at this stage, old fellow, but I'll have a damn good go at unearthing the killer. My gut reaction would be an overzealous punter."

William gathered his case and effects from the hallway and reset them down on the bed next to Katya's stricken and lifeless body. First he photographed the room in its entirety, taking in the whole room in interlocking frames. He then turned his attention to taking pictures of Katya, leaning in close to her body and snapping away at each and every wound. Eyes falling to her stomach, he began to dictate into his Dictaphone once more.

"Deep lacerations to the stomach, approximately sixteen inches in length, exposing the intestines."

Scratching his cheek he panned back to her head wound.

"This is strange, Vincent. Look at the blood on her left temple! Do you see?"

"What am I looking at?" Vincent mused.

"The blood around the cuts to her arms and chest are still sticky and congealed, whereas the blood on her temple is dry! I would say at least an hour or so earlier than the other injuries," he surmised.

"So she was subjected to an attack that lasted over an hour. Tortured?" Vincent struggled to come to terms with some people's sadistic behaviour.

"Maybe. Post mortem will be more conclusive. Bruising has formed, suggesting she was still alive at the time. It also looks like that wound has been cleaned."

Vincent instinctively looked for the bedside bin. Peering in, he discovered several blood stained tissues, an abundance of cleansing wipes and, more importantly, half a dozen or so condoms.

"She was certainly a busy girl; there must be a good few clients' DNA in here, William!" Vincent was feeling more confident by the minute. "Can we get these back to your lab post haste? I really need to get these condoms processed and start tracing the users."

"I still have a lot to do here, Vincent. I need to record these prints and go through the place with a fine tooth comb."

"Ok! Listen, I'm going back to the station. If you find anything important, contact the guys in the wagon downstairs, or give me a ring if it's really juicy."

"I should be wrapped up inside the hour. Have her back on the slab about nine-ish! Will you be gracing me with your presence?"

"Damn right, I wouldn't miss it for the world!" Vincent made his way back towards his car.

***

Meanwhile, Constables Ward and Semple were visiting Mrs Pickering, Adam's mum. A gritty old East End girl, Maggie Pickering was the salt of the earth, still wearing clothes that were fashionable twenty years ago. Maggie had always worked tirelessly for her brood, forsaking any of her own comforts to see them well fed and clothed. All in all she had seven offspring, five girls and two boys. Like Benjamin Flanagan, Adam was the youngest and one of only three still left at home. The apron strings positively knotted, and his pay and prospects being so poor, he wisely chose to stay put. He joked to his mates that he was waiting for a rich 'Milf' to take him under her wing - or duvet! The reality was a complete contrast to Adam's boast. Despite being well placed to find a Milf, especially amongst the divorcees that frequented his workplace, the women all found him a little creepy and always brushed him off quite swiftly.

"Mrs Margaret Pickering?" enquired WPC Ward.

"Yes, Love! What's wrong? We don't normally get you lot up 'ere knocking unless some fink's up."

"Can you confirm the whereabouts of your son Adam from around four-thirty to six-thirty this evening?"

"Well now, he'd have been leaving for work about five thirty. I was making a cup of rosy for my ole man during the advert in that soap. What's it called now - Hollyoaks? I don't really like it but there's not much else on till Corrie and East Enders." Vicky cut in abruptly. "Sorry, Mrs Pickering - the time?"

"Oh yeah - sorry love! I'm fairly sure Adam left while I was in the kitchen. I called 'im back coz the silly bugger left 'is keys on the sideboard in the hall. He'd leave

his bleeding 'ead if it weren't screwed on tight."
"You're sure?" WPC Ward pressing again.
"Yes, Love, definitely!"
Ward turned to PC Semple who was on his radio in the hallway.
"Semple, check the incident report time with H.Q. please."
"I just did, Ma'am. They confirmed it as five-thirty pm."
Vicky lifted her radio and called through to Sergeant McEwen. "Macca, Mrs Pickering has confirmed Adam's movements. Anything further for us here?"
"Not at the mo, Vicky. Head back to the unit with PC Semple and await further instructions."

***

Back in No.34 William Mumford continued scrutinising Katya and her dishevelled bedroom. In the distance he could hear faint murmurings of music coming from elsewhere inside the flat, and he followed the noise till it led him to the lounge coffee table. The music emanated from under a pile of dog-eared magazines next to the ashtray. As William brushed them aside to reveal a dark blue mobile phone, he read 'Work' flashing on the screen. 'Ah-ha,' he thought, 'We have contact!' He pressed the answer key with his latex clad hands, and nestled the mobile to his ear.
"Hi Anja, I have another client for you."
"Hello! Could I ask who's calling?"
"Who are you? Where's Anja?" a startled female voice enquired.
"I am William Mumford from Essex Police Forensic

Department. We need to speak with you urgently, Anja has unfortunately..." The caller hung up.
William immediately scrolled through Anja's call list. The last few calls were WORK: in fact her only callers were work! Six calls in all, about an hour apart. Anja had been popular today. He gave over the contact details to a grateful Ambrose and then proceeded with his more usual task of fingerprinting Katya's room.

***

WPC Vicky Ward had exhausted all her enquiries at Peldon Rise, so she settled into the support van with PC Semple for some toast and a warming mug of tea. Having time on her hands to reflect on the evening's events didn't help her mood: when she thought of Katya's disembowelled body she shuddered and felt nauseous.

***

The customary black van with 'Private Ambulance' emblazoned on all four sides backed up to the stairs in readiness to receive Katya's corpse. Flanked by two police officers to keep back the growing crowd, the two suited occupants left the vehicle and put on their white disposable overalls. As they entered the flat William Mumford was packing his last pieces of equipment neatly back into his case,
"Please be extremely careful with my girl, Gentlemen, I have yet to give her a proper examination!"
"Right you are, Guv!"
They placed a large black holdall on the floor next to the body and unzipped it, Katya totally unaware of the

indignity surrounding her penultimate journey. Being carted out in an oversize bin bag seemed so callous and degrading: fortunately those who had this dubious honour were blissfully hardened to its terrible pathos.

***

They moved carefully out of the flat and down the staircase to the waiting van, amidst the buzzing of voices from the vultures circling the cordon. There is nothing the baying public likes more than feasting on someone else's misfortune. Like rubber-neckers at a crash scene, they all enjoyed a ringside seat as her cold, lifeless body met the chill of the van floor. The camera flashes from mobile phones heralded her retreat to the mortuary table as Katya left Peldon Rise to make her way through Southend's dimly lit streets. Despite her vocation, she was a daughter and a sister. Her family would soon be devastated by the news of her terrible death and worse still by the knowledge of where she had ended her days, destitute and alone.

CHAPTER 5

HOME AND DRY

Robin Bradford arrived home to his rented two bedroom terrace house, flushed from his encounter with Anja. The miniscule, yet overgrown front garden languished neglected, and the peeling paint and cracked window pane only served to remind him of his failure. His humble residence was aeons away from his former abode, a grandiose four bed town house in Thorpe Bay's most desirably affluent road. When his business collapsed he lost everything - cars, houses, and nearly his girlfriend. Lizzie had been his rock throughout the whole embarrassment of bankruptcy. Now he needed her more than ever as she held all the cards financially. On paper she controlled the new business. Even the clapped out cars were registered in her name to prevent the insolvency buzzards from stripping his dignity further. Maybe this slight on his masculinity had contributed to his sexual deviance - as a yearning to prove his mettle and regain dominance.

Understandably, with all that he had done behind Lizzie's back, he felt a pang of guilt as he entered the hall. As with all drugs, the high had been followed by a tremendous low. He made his now familiar routine checks in the hall mirror, aware of Lizzie in the kitchen preparing his dinner.

"Hi, Love!" she called out as she heard him come through the hall door. "Alright? How's your day been?"

"Not too bad. Usual crap," Robin answered.

"Oh, and by the way, I'm off out shortly with Maria. There's a new yoga class starting in Billericay, so we're popping along. Probably cop a glass of wine on the way home as well."

Robin was pleased with this revelation. He needed a long soak in the bath - not just to cleanse his body, but to try and purge his soul of the illicit sex he had enjoyed earlier.

"What's for dinner love? Smells lovely!"

"Spaghetti Bolognese, Babe. It'll be ready in about five minutes!"

Robin embraced Lizzie and tenderly kissed her neck as she prepared to serve his meal, all traces of his sick, animalistic urges now gone. She backed away from him and scowled.

"What? What's wrong?"

Robin had quickly become accustomed to Anja's fragrant aroma, but Lizzie's nose was alert to the sweet floral perfume and registered it instantly. Eyes darkened, brows furrowed, she fixed her gaze on his face.

"Where the fuck have you been? You smell like a whore's handbag!"

Robin was used to surviving on his quick wit and ability to back out of corners. He was blessed with the gift of the gab, and his escape route was primed and ready for use.

"Calm down, you scatty mare! Do you still not trust me, Lizzie?" Buying himself valuable thinking time was his only objective.

"You reek of cheap pissing perfume! Where have you been?"

"Well I would! When I came out of my last appointment in Westcliff, I bumped into Mickey and Alice Finn. He shook my hand, she hugged me. You know he buys all that knocked off shit from 'Billy Fingers' who drinks in The Ship? He got her some Coco; apparently it was spelt with a bloody 'K'. God, it made my eyes smart!" Laughing as he spoke, his story was altogether plausible. Using Alice was a very clever tack. He knew Lizzie had fallen out with her over an argument involving her best friend Maria. They hadn't spoken for six months, so she wouldn't approach her over his claim. Lizzie paused briefly before retracting her unwarranted tirade. He hugged her again and forgave her like the decent man he purported to be. As she sought solace in their loving embrace Robin sighed inwardly over her shoulder.

'That was close, damn close!' he thought. 'Need to be much more careful in future.'

***

Lizzie Fenwick went upstairs with her tail firmly between her legs, mind racing. She wanted to believe him, but she wasn't convinced. He had spun too many yarns in the past, so she resolved to be more watchful of her slimy tongued man. Trying to compartmentalise her thoughts, Lizzie got ready for her yoga class with Maria. She was only five foot two inches tall and a very sporty size eight. Her flat chest gave her an almost boyish appearance, and the constant Keep Fit and yoga had given her a well-toned physique, which she was immensely proud of. Her face was sharp with feline features, making her look permanently waspy. Her long auburn hair was usually pulled tightly back into a pony tail, making it more manageable for her various activities.

Robin would joke that her 'Croydon Facelift' saved him the expense of cosmetic surgery, but if they entertained or partied, she would wear her hair down and straight. With a slinky dress clinging to her svelte figure, she would look stunning, and was the envy of her female friends. Yoga required somewhat less inspiring attire: allowing the body to flex and move unhindered was the foremost concern. Tonight Lizzie selected her favourite loose-fitting orange tracksuit bottoms and her green sweat top. Waltzing into the lounge and parading in front of Robin, she was a veritable cacophony of colour. "How do I look?"

That bear-trap question woman always ask, leaving their men to ponder on a suitable response! Not one to mince his words, Robin delivered the killer reply. "You look like a packet of fucking fruit tic- tacs!"

Not surprisingly Lizzie's retort was equally damning. "Perhaps you should get that fat arse of yours off the sofa now and then, and make an effort to exercise like I do," she retorted. "Then maybe I would have some interest in sleeping with you!" She paused and then added, "You ignorant wanker!"

Inside herself, she was deflated by his spiteful assessment. Meanwhile, Robin sought consolation in thoughts of his romp with Anja only an hour or so earlier.

When Lizzie asked him for his car keys the tell-tale panic swamped him again, "Why do you want mine? Take your own bloody car!" Quickly remembering the phone hidden under the seat, he tried in vain to encourage her into her own car.

"You've got sat nav, and we don't know the way. Is it too much to ask!"

"Mine hasn't got much petrol - better take yours!"

"No Robin, you tight bastard! I'm taking your car and that's the end of it! Now give me the keys! I'm late as it is."

Robin's heart sank as he scrambled to his feet. Dashing to the car, he muttered something about needing papers from his briefcase. As soon as he opened the door he saw his copy of the local rag on the passenger seat, neatly folded on the Personal section. 'Bubbles', circled about ten times in black ink, stood out like a sore thumb, and pencilled at the top of the page was '34 Peldon Rise, S-O-S' was scribed. He grabbed the paper, along with his mobile, and secreted it inside his briefcase safe from view.

Lizzie packed her gym bag with a change of clothes, water, make-up and a thousand other things. You'd have thought she was off for week. A carefree swing saw it neatly over her shoulder and she made her way towards the dirty Ford Focus.

"Don't bother to wait up!" she barked as she snatched his keys and left.

Robin could not have cared less: he'd had his fill already today and was looking forward to a chilled night without a browbeating from Lizzie.

***

Soaking in his deep Radox laden bath, Robin stroked his manhood, closed his eyes and let his mind wander, turning himself on with memories of saucy Anja. She needed to be taught a lesson: she was rude and disrespectful, but she wouldn't make that mistake again - he'd shown her who was in charge. She'd learned some respect the hard way! He was happy in the knowledge that he was firmly established as master.

CHAPTER 6

JIGSAW PIECES

William Mumford stood in his laboratory coat watching the two burly undertakers wheel in Katya's body on the bright, stainless steel trolley. His thoughts drifted briefly to his own daughter, who was about the same age as Katya; he couldn't bear to think that such a fate might befall his own little angel. What a tragic waste of life! Despite Katya's poor career choice, she had still left loved ones behind. Just a young girl trying to survive in the world, caught out by Fate's cruel twists and turns. Mumford's pretty assistant Lucy bounded cheerfully in like a breath of fresh air, completely unfazed by the grisly task ahead. Her brow was sticky with sweat and she was out of breath.

"Sorry, William! Got here as quick as I could." She apologised. "Just about to order dessert when you called, so you've probably done me a favour! All those calories!"

"Calories? Since when do you need to watch your weight!" Munford smiled.
"Moment on the lips, and all that." She chuckled.
William thought his eager technician more than pleasing to the eye. 'Curves in all the right places' he would tell his friends, tracing an hourglass with his hands. She stood about five-four in her heels and had streaked blonde hair, neatly bobbed. Her face was warm, inviting and always wore a smile. William often joked that he should buy her a more appropriately glamorous tailored white coat, rather than the plain ones they had. Lucy was keen to expand her already growing wealth of knowledge in forensics. He would have liked more, but Lucy was settled with her new man; besides, he was much older than her.
The Brothers Grim carefully placed Katya on the polished stainless steel table and bid William and Lucy good night. The two pathologists then set about reaping the clues Katya's body had generously saved for them. William asked Lucy to set up the video recorder and link it to his pc, so that he could review it later. Lucy carefully combed through Katya's hair in the hope of finding additional hairs, and then they both made a brief scan of her clothing for fibres or follicles. Caught just inside her blouse were four of five hairs which were tight and curly, possibly public. Lucy photographed these in situ before carefully bagging them.
"Lacerations to the chest, arms and thighs. Closer inspection of the cut to her right arm would indicate a defensive wound, possibly from raising the arm in front of her face or chest to prevent further attack". William was very thorough, spending several minutes exam-

ining each injury. "As previously discovered on scene, left temple head wound has dried more than the others, pointing to either a prolonged assault or secondary attack. Location and severity of this wound would almost certainly have rendered her unconscious."

Lucy studied the numerous cuts to Katya's arm and motioned for William to look again.

"What have you found?"

His eager aide looked nervously at the camera, not wishing to make a mistake that could be endlessly replayed to her. "The wounds on her arm: more specifically this one here. It looks to have a clear serrated edge or pattern to it."

"Let me see! Yes, yes - you're right, well done! It's consistent with a kitchen knife. Get a close-up, please Lucy.

"Examining the fingers on the right hand: index finger is broken, and there are small abrasions to her knuckles; signs of blood and tissue under the finger nails. Lucy, would you scrape and pot up for me."

Lucy was pleased with her participation, and so was William. For her to find something while working for him was proof she was close to her goal - ultimately to lead examinations herself.

"Numerous grip marks around the body; prominent markings to neck and upper arm consistent with restraint." William made grabbing gestures for the benefit of the video recording. "Moving to the stomach: major lacerations to the abdominal area, crossing downwards from right to left. It would seem that our assailant is left-handed. Judging by the injuries, our girl was prostrate at the time of the attack to this region."

Lucy had tagged various fibres and hairs passed over by William, and was now busy staring into Katya's open gut. "William!" again apprehensively, "I can see a metallic object inside the lower part of her stomach. Here - look! Just below the last rib."
"Oh my god!" she exclaimed, "That's a bloody knife... How sick is that!" Losing her cool momentarily Lucy covered her mouth and averted her eyes
"Well, at least now we have the murder weapon young lady!" Mumford teased the blade from Katya's Vagina . "Exhibit 1, I think! Listen, there's not much more to do here - you go and chase up our samples. Also check the bagged items from Peldon Rise that are in Bay 14 - reference them against the items we have found here."
William looked at Lucy, "Once you've done that you can go home for the night, I will wrap up here."
She was relieved, but would have liked to finish the post mortem.
"And just for future reference..." William held his dramatic pause to create maximum effect. "You have done fantastic work tonight. You should be very pleased with yourself."
"Thank you!"
"No - thank you, Lucy!" She will definitely make the grade, he thought.
Lucy left the chill of the mortuary room and retired to the warmth of their office. As she went in, the phone rang on her desk.
"Forensics! Lucy speaking."
"Lucy, hi! It's Vincent Ambrose from Southend Nick. What did you guys get from the autopsy? Anything interesting?"

"Well, we're still processing quite a few fibres etcetera. William's asked me to concentrate on DNA analysis from hairs, condoms and so on. Oh, and we're confident we've identified the murder weapon."
"That's great news! What was it? Where was it? - I didn't see it!"
"It was a kitchen knife."
"Damn!" Vincent fell silent for a moment as he gathered his thoughts. "Tell William I need those reports, pictures and DNA details as a matter of urgency!"
"I will." Lucy looked at her watch: one-fifteen am - no goodnight cuddles for her tonight.

***

Back at the station, Nicky was busy with the monotony of viewing the countless hours of CCTV footage. There were eight cameras within a four hundred metre radius of Peldon Rise. The nearest and most significant of these covered the main artery that linked Victoria Avenue to Peldon Rise Flats. Although there were numerous other ways in by car, let alone on foot, this would be the route of choice for most drivers. Nicky froze and saved the image of every car that entered during that period, all forty two of them. When her colleague from Chelmsford arrived he would wave his magic wand over the images and produce licence plates. Nicky would then scour the DVLA and PNC (Police National Computer) for driver details, in the faint hope of springing a known offender. If only it could have been that simple.

***

Nicky's judgement was right, Robin Bradford had travelled this very road; his journey was on there for all to see. However, he had inadvertently drawn a cloak over his passage to Peldon Flats. When checks were made on all the vehicle IDs, the shabby black Focus would show up as being registered to one Elizabeth Fenwick, 162 Hadleigh Crescent, Leigh-on-Sea. At this stage no one would link Robin Bradford with Lizzie's car, and the under-pressure officers would just put it on a long list with all the others to 'look into' later on.

***

Brian had been searching through Madame Bubbles' phone records and was busy tracking details of all the callers. Robin Bradford's call was listed, but again it was masked. If they did manage to decipher the withheld number, all they would be greeted with was a 'pay as you go' sim bought from a back street off-licence. As one metaphorical avenue opened for Nicky and Brian, the previous would close. A series of blind alleys and stone walls met their every move.

Vincent Ambrose called both of them into his office for a progress update; he was at best disheartened by the feedback. "There must be something we've missed somewhere! Get back on to William Mumford, Nicky - I need detailed reports. Brian, you put together a small press conference for me for ten am tomorrow - and I mean small! We need to limit the damage the Gutter Press will do to us if this blows up. Let's just hope this is a one off, or we'll be grilled big time."

Brian left the office and began preparations for Vincent's request. They would try to stifle the Media's voice before Southend became a news freak show. Just as Nicky re-entered the Incident Room at three-twelve am, the fax machine began spewing pages into its eagerly waiting tray. Sifting through the lengthy document, she picked out the bones: six sets of DNA were present in Katya's flat, excluding her own. Nicky would have a mountain of work laid at her feet when Vincent clapped his eyes on this little lot.

"Vincent, forensic analysis is in. There were six different people in the victim's flat that day. Well, that they can establish, anyway. The knife is confirmed as the murder weapon, and cause of death is cited as severe blood loss resulting in major organ failure. They also believe the knife was from Katya's own kitchen drawer."

"Where was the murder weapon? I never saw one at the scene."

"Vincent, it was inside her vagina."

"Jesus, what sick bastard would do that to some young girl!" He paused. "Look at the time! You'd best get home and catch a couple of hours' shut eye. You and Brian are going to be run ragged in the morning. I want this evil sod in custody by the end of tomorrow."

"Guv, it's morning already!"

"I'd best get some sleep myself then." With that he got up, opened his filing cabinet and removed a red tartan travel rug. Plonking himself heavily back in his chair, he lowered the back rest, dumped his feet on his paperwork, threw the rug over his legs and smiled back at a grinning Nicky.

"Switch the light off on the way out!"

Nicky shook her head and laughed. "'Night, John-Boy!"

"'Night, Mary Ellen!"

CHAPTER 7

COLD LIGHT OF DAY

At six thirty am Robin Bradford roused from his deep slumber to find himself alone. Initially drifting back to sleep, he woke again at around seven and realised that Lizzie wasn't beside him. That was nothing untoward, as she often moved to the spare room when his bed-hogging and snoring became too overwhelming. Eventually he made his way downstairs to the kitchen to scoff his poached egg on toast, orange juice and coffee. He was surprised to see Lizzie already seated at the breakfast bar in her housecoat sipping coffee. She normally had to be prized from her bed with a crowbar, but this morning she already had the percolator on and was staring out into the garden. She didn't even acknowledge his presence, so he decided to try some of the old Bradford charm in the hope of raising a smile.

"You alright, hun? Not like you to be down so early! Is

everything ok?" In the back of his mind he was hoping she wasn't still smarting from the perfume incident.

"Just had a rough night, that's all. You kept me awake with your grunting." Still sipping her drink, she returned her gaze to the window.

"You look like shit."

"Thanks! That makes me feel so much better! Perhaps if I didn't have to sleep with a walrus, I might get a decent night's sleep."

Robin was far from convinced; she seemed distant and anxious.

In the background the news was airing on Local Radio. News just in of the suspected murder of an Essex prostitute. Police are currently refusing to comment, but have called a press conference for ten o'clock this morning. We expect to be bringing you an update in the one o'clock bulletin... This afternoon Shoebury W.I will be holding a charity...' Robin Bradford went white, clasping his hand over his mouth to stifle his shock. Luckily Lizzie was still daydreaming and didn't clock his obvious anxiety.

***

Simultaneously, Vincent Ambrose snored so loudly that he woke himself up with a jolt. As his vision cleared and he regained his senses, he realised he was not alone in the office. Makossi the Columbian cleaner was busy vacuuming and wiping.

"Hello, Mr Vincent! You wake up now?"

"Yes Makossi, I am waking up. Must be the whine of that vacuum cleaner, Love!" Vincent moaned.

"You whining and grunting too, Mr Vincent!"

Vincent slowly lifted himself out of the chair and stretched, shirt tails hanging out and trousers hanging round his backside. He reached into a drawer, pulled out his emergency wash bag and spare shirt, and then headed for the Gents'. As the hot soapy water ran down his body, Vincent's mind wandered through yesterday's fiasco. He so badly wanted to find the missing links and sort this case out. He hated the Press and was not looking forward to the usual Spanish Inquisition grilling later on.

When he eventually got to the Incident Room, Nicky and Brian were already sorting this and chasing that, and Nicky was on Vincent straight away.

"I've cross referenced the DNA profiles and have names for four out of the six. The other two are not known to us. William's office has matched three different hair samples to three of the DNAs. The most interesting sample is one of the two 'unknowns'," mimicking inverted commas with her fingers. "The body sweep at the mortuary gave up five pubic hairs, probably matching her last client. Basically, they're saying in their report that she washed between clients, judging by samples from the shower. That sample stands out because his hair was on the corpse, inside her blouse, so he was almost certainly her last punter. Also, particles of his skin were found under her nails. He's our man!" Out of breath, Nicky halted as if waiting for praise or applause.

"Sounds very promising, Nick. But take stock! Don't be blinkered by this one detail. Please, both of you, keep open minds and clear heads."

"Sorry, Guv! Just excited, that's all. Three of the four

that we have DNA matches for are being chased up by Sergeant Macca's foot soldiers. The fourth sample, Kalvin Johnson, was in custody at Basildon Nick after an altercation with his estranged wife. They took him in at..." flicking through a pile of notes she had on her desk... "three-fifteen pm and released him after nine-thirty, so he's definitely out of the frame."

"How long till the other three matched guys are being brought in for interview?" Vincent asked.

"Macca's got officers out now. They'll all be getting a rude awakening this morning! Hopefully, we'll have them all in by the time your fifteen minutes of fame is over." She grinned.

"Thanks for reminding me!"

Brian pitched in, not wishing to be outdone by Nicky's efficiency.

"Well now, her full name is Katya Peta Lesniak. She was born in Keblow, just outside Lublin in Poland on 27th November 1987, and came to England in early 2007. It would seem she's been working as a prostitute since she got here. No indication of a boyfriend, but then she was probably getting plenty of action at work!"

Brian's humour irritated Vincent. For one thing he was already too much under the microscope from upstairs, and for another, he had little time for Brian anyway. The guy was not a team player at all. Everything he did was all too obviously for his own selfish reasons.

***

Back in Leigh-on-Sea, Robin Bradford had finished his breakfast and was sorting through his day's work load.

He had numerous appointments to attend, as well as calls to make. Trying to get 'Joe Public' to let him through the door wasn't as difficult as getting him to part with any cash. Robin used his paltry dining room as an office and would spend half his week in there, head jammed into the computer, phone welded to his ear. Lizzie was heading off to work, so he would soon have the place to himself: just another day at the office, he thought! Switching on his PC, he began highlighting potential clients from a list of cold call leads he'd got from a marketing consultant.

Lizzie worked three days a week at a caravan park on Canvey Island. Although cleaning static caravans wasn't the most exciting of jobs, it paid the bills and gave her some independence. She couldn't stand being cooped up with Robin every day. The park had a high turnover of guests in the summer time, but winter tended to be much slower. This gave the park owner the ideal chance to spruce up the caravans ready for the seasonal deluge of visitors. Lizzie would scrub and clean each unit from front to back, check for breakages and report faults. The only thing she found annoying was trying to find each van's keys amongst the huge heap of identical ones. She would stand on the trailer steps for ages some days as she searched through a bundle of tags as big as a wasps' nest.

***

Back at the station Vincent Ambrose was making last minute adjustments to his pre-prepared speech in readiness for the press onslaught. Nicky was still delving through the huge report from William's efficient assistant.

"The cigarette in Katya's ashtray only had her D.N.A. on it so that's a dead end. They've also found numerous fibres on her rug and body, which are possibly the assailant's - light grey fibres which have been identified as being from 'King Speed Sports'. They're a local company with quite a niche market, predominantly high-end sportswear shops. Problem is they use the same fabric in various products, from socks to tracksuits."

Vincent entered the press conference amidst a bombardment of flashes and questions.

"Essex Police have issued the following statement..." Vincent Ambrose began his carefully prepared spiel.

***

Whilst Ambrose was confronting the Media, his team worked endlessly behind the station's gloomy exterior to process and eliminate all the information they could find. Mumford and Hockley retraced their every step, checking and double checking. Meanwhile, Macca's boys dragged the three irate suspects from their houses, kicking and screaming as their horrified wives and children looked on. Innocent or not, their activities within the walls of Peldon flats would have ramifications for days, weeks and in some cases years to come.

There remained two as yet untraceable visitors to 34 Peldon Rise. Neither Mumford nor Ambrose could identify the two owners of the DNA samples. Despite the mass of resources at their disposal, both were baffled - and indeed, stumped.

***

William Mumford and Lucy Hockley met at a cafe a mile or so from Peldon Rise and discussed her future over a latte. William's workload could have done with being lighter, but he always thought it important to distance himself from the lab when reviewing his assistants' progress.

"Lucy, I think you know how much I value your help, and how pleased I am with your professionalism." She looked down at the floor, clearly embarrassed by his accolade.

"Well, I think it's time we elevated your status within our ranks. Do you believe you are ready to fulfil a bigger, more challenging role?"

She grinned wildly. "William, I am... speechless. I don't know what to say!"

"Perhaps you could save your joy till after I've told you the news." Mumford suddenly turned serious.

"How remiss of me! Sorry!"

She had worked tirelessly to achieve her ambition. Now they were both savouring the moment, each knowing what was to come! The only jarring note was the ludicrous frothy moustache appended to William's top lip as he quaffed his almond syrup skinny latte.

"The next time we have a field based assignment, I want you to lead." Mumford paused to judge Lucy's reaction. "In layman's terms, the next 'stiff' that turns up in Southend will be yours to evaluate."

That honour was destined to come her way sooner than either of them had anticipated. In less than a week our killer's thirst for blood would once again be satisfied.

CHAPTER 8

PAYING LIP SERVICE

Robin Bradford had been struggling all week with the lack of sexual activity at home and was becoming frustrated. The encounter with Anja had faded from his memory, and now he needed a new high: something saucy to get his blood pumping again. He swept the papers, case and other effects to the side of the boot and lifted a black carpet-clad board. The well housing his spare wheel was where Robin kept his 'trophies': ladies underwear, bras, a couple of high-heeled shoes and even a variety of studded collars - all the bric-a-brac accrued on his travels. Some collected coins or baseball cards, but Robin Bradford had a penchant for ladies' lingerie or similarly provocative attire. If he got the chance during his numerous visits to brothels and massage parlours, he liked to purloin the odd garment here and there while the girls weren't looking; preferably items still fresh with the musky aroma of his dalliance. The thrill for Robin was taking something he wasn't allowed: the forbidden fruit, as it were.

Below his bag of souvenirs was a second bag: this was his emergency kit. If lack of money was a problem, he would draw on this bag for his kicks. Stealing away to a quiet country lane or derelict industrial estate, Robin would leaf through the seedy magazines and pleasure himself; hence the hand cream and wipes that also nestled in the bag. Amongst the grubby, dog-eared books was a contact magazine. This was what Robin sought right now, with its wealth of housewives, mums and divorcees advertising their services to all and sundry. The magazine's editorial staff made claims of 'free contacts for like-minded people': the grim reality was that all these women were common whores, no different from the street corner brasses, or parlour tarts. They just chose a less vocal advertising platform to promote their wares and hopefully hijack a more discerning and well-mannered clientele.

One such advert was for two girls who worked together from the same flat. Robin knew it was a front for a Parlour, but wasn't bothered; he also knew that at some point they would ask for payment, compensation for their extra time and trouble. He didn't mind, though, he was happy to dig deep for his favourite hobby.

'Tamsin and Marina, two lonely and bored mums looking to play during the day.

Both guaranteed to please. Naughty or nice, you decide!

Based near Southend on Sea.

Call 0700 2789287. Go on, show us you've got the balls!'

He duly rang the number and was greeted by a girl calling herself Tamsin. As always, it would be an alias; she was probably a Sharon or a Tracy, or something similarly unglamorous. She eased into the financial aspect after he had already agreed a visiting time. He knew it was coming, so he was unfazed. Seventy quid wasn't excessive, he thought - not much different to a night out, or a round of golf plus a pint.

"Who will I be seeing?"

"We're both here today, so it's your choice."

"Fine! What do you both look like?"

"Marina's about five-ten. Very curvy and busty with dark hair, brown eyes. I'm a petite five-two, with blonde hair and a very athletic figure."

"Ok! And is Marina going to be free when I visit you? No disrespect intended, but I do prefer the fuller-figured woman."

"No offence taken, Darling! And yes, she's on till two-thirty. Working mum and all that."

"Then I think I'll settle for Marina. Is she the naughty one, or the nice one!" Tamsin had made him feel comfortable, so he was happy to show his humorous side.

***

About an hour later Robin reached his destination, a busy car park a stone's throw from the Sea Front. Riffling through his pockets, he counted his change as he stood in front of the parking meter. "Bollocks!" He didn't have enough coins to meet the two hour charge, but then glancing around the parking lot he decided to chance his luck. He beat a path through the hordes of shoppers, tourists, loafers and vagrants that congregated around the town centre, eventually arriving at the Tango Top-Up Sun Bed Salon. This was the facade behind which Tamsin and Marina's knocking shop plied its trade. On the face of it the place was a reputable tanning salon, doing a roaring trade among Southend's innumerable wannabe WAGS. Young women seeking that healthy orange glow to impress the local bar-brawling men, fixated on having trophy wives and glamorous girlfriends to show off down the Seafront. The crafty tanning shop owner let out the upstairs room to the two harlots for a nice handful of cash, which they palmed his way once a week. No invoices, no questions, and a discount on services if and when he needed relief. As instructed, Robin approached the receptionist and asked where the Therapies Room could be found. She obligingly led him through the shop and into a back room which housed a long staircase, leading up and out of view.

"Up there, Sir. Ring the bell at the top."

"Thank you, Darling!" he replied, smiling. His charms were wasted on her, though. She knew exactly who he was and what he was: a punter.

The staircase turned halfway up to reveal a large, royal blue door. Covered in an array of different locks, it was obviously designed to prevent the Old Bill, disgruntled clients and irate wives from getting at the working girls. Robin pressed the buzzer on the small intercom and waited somewhat impatiently for a reply. As he stood shuffling from foot to foot, wringing his hands in anticipation, he felt a twinge of fear. Stories of mugged punters and blackmail victims started to play out in his mind.

What if I get inside and some big beefcake robs me?
What if the police raid the place while I'm ankles deep in a tom?
What if they try and blackmail me?
But the ever present 'what if's' were quickly beaten back down by a much more pressing matter: Robin's rampant desire to satisfy the lustful urges seething in his loins.
The silver, pepper-pot fronted intercom speaker crackled into life and brought Robin's mind back into line instantly.
"Hello! Who is it, please?"
Despite having already passed the first line of defence, namely the drone working the 'Front of House', Robin was subjected to several encrypted verbal trials from the intercom. While it was gabbling away at him, asking him all sorts of trivial questions, he started to become distracted by an idea that the voice coming from the silver box of buttons seemed vaguely familiar. No matter how hard he thought, he couldn't place it; the sexy overtones disguised her natural voice.
At last the door opened. Robin surveyed his potential purchase, beginning at her black high-heeled shoes and sheer hold-ups. Moving on up, he paused briefly at her lacy red knickers, a matching brassiere barely restraining her ample breasts. When he reached her dark tousled hair, his mouth fell open.
"Fuck me! ...You?"
It would have been hard to say at that point who was the more alarmed, Robin or his lacy lady.
"Fancy meeting you here! How very awkward - for both of us!"

The female in question was Maria, Lizzie's best friend. Robin had broken the deadlocked silence first to establish his strength and dominance within this excruciating situation. He was hoping to capitalise on Maria's obvious embarrassment.

"Robin! What are you doing here? How could you? Lizzie would be devastated if she knew!"

"Why am I here? I would have thought that was fairly bloody obvious, wouldn't you? And as for lecturing me on my moral conduct, I think the phrase pot and kettle springs to mind! I'm sure Lizzie would be equally devastated to find out her best friend is a brass!"

"How dare you! I do this because I have no choice. Who are you to judge me!"

"Well now Marina! It would seem we have reached a bit of an impasse, wouldn't you say?"

"If I knew what that meant maybe I could comment, smart arse!" Maria was now flushed with embarrassment, conscious that she was standing before her best friend's fella in just a skimpy, matching red lingerie ensemble.

"It's a funny thing, Maria - or Marina, which do you prefer?" He smiled. "Me and my lovely lady - you know, your best friend - we've been trying for years to work out how you manage to do so well. Lizzie would often say it was damn near impossible for a single mum caught in the State's measly benefit system to be so financially stable. Now, here's the killer! I always thought you survived on hand-outs from your kiddy's dad, whereas Lizzie - your bosom buddy - she assumed you'd reverted to type and starting knocking out the old white powder again, like your ex!"

"Promise me you won't say anything to her, Robin!" She begged.
"Like I said - impasse, or stalemate! We both have naughty little secrets we wish to keep from Miss Fenwick. Well, the ball is fairly and squarely in your court, Maria."
Maria was finding the way Robin seemed to have taken control of the situation very unsettling. His cold self-assurance was making her squirm, and not only that, but he was still surveying her body with a lustful look in his eyes.
"Cards on the table, Maria. I've always fantasised about giving you a good shagging. I never in my wildest dreams thought I would get the chance, so I'm guessing today's my lucky day."
"Fuck off!" Maria's voice started to rise and her tone grew more determined as she tried to hide her body from his lecherous gaze. "You are joking, right? Surely you don't think I'd go through with it now? No fucking chance, mister!"
As the argument continued, Tamsin came out from one of the other doors, clutching a towel to her naked body, and told them to keep the noise down.
"I'm trying to work in here, thank you! And you're putting my punter off his stroke. Quite literally! What the hell is going on Marina?" Despite the fact both names featured in the advertisement, it was blatantly obvious that Tamsin was the key face behind the duo's shenanigans. She kept order in the house, took bookings and balanced the finances.
"This wanker is my best mate's boyfriend, for Christ's sake! I can't do a trick for him: it would be wrong on so many different levels."

Maria's head had been bowed throughout the whole conversation. Robin had caught her red-handed: he was positive he had the advantage and was determined to exploit it. Tamsin had fewer scruples and more business sense than Maria, which was evident in her starchy reply.

"Trust me, Maria, you've done far worse things and we most definitely can't afford to upset the landlord by having a slanging match on his staircase where his staff or clients can hear. We have it easy up here! I strongly suggest you shut your mouth, open your legs and think of your future. I have a queue of fresh girls waiting to fill your boots, and I'm not cutting you any more slack, Darling! Either way, sort it out now - and quietly!" Tamsin turned her back on the pair and shut the door, but not before Robin got a bird's eye view of her naked buttocks slipping away behind it.

"Well, Marina, what say you?" Robin was smirking from ear to ear. He already knew the answer: Maria's face said it all.

"It doesn't look like I have much of a choice really, does it!"

She looked dejected and beaten as she made her decision to bed Robin. She knew Tamsin was right: she would have to swallow her pride - amongst other things, no doubt.

"You never know, you might even enjoy it!" Robin was revelling in his new found power, and relished the thought of holding this secret over poor, disheartened Maria's head. The apprehension he'd felt on arriving at their gaff had long since gone. "I think I can safely say this'll be the best seventy quid I've spent since Lizzie's

engagement ring. You never know - I might even give you a tip!"
"Don't push it, you wanker!" Maria resigned herself to just getting it over and done with.
"Now love, you toddle off and show me the way while I follow on and enjoy the view. I'm quite keen to get your knickers off."
"Gross bastard!" she snapped back at him. As she walked the short distance to her room, she knew his eyes would be burning a hole in her arse.
"I hope you can give a convincing performance, young lady. I want my money's worth, you know. Customer satisfaction and all that!"
Maria sat on the side of the bed and reluctantly encouraged Robin to remove his clothing. He enjoyed stripping in front of her, convinced she would be agonising over every moment. Whilst he took off his boxer shorts Maria unclipped her bra, and Robin's watchful eye scrutinised every inch of her, adamant he wouldn't miss one second of her discomfort. As soon as her breasts were free, so were Robin's hands, fondling and groping her as she tried to move away. No tender embrace or intimate touches, just selfish, clumsy advances: he was enough to turn a nymphomaniac frigid. Begrudgingly Maria asked him to lie down beside her, keen to get her unwelcome guest serviced and shipped out the door as quick as possible. Robin tried in vain to plant kisses on her lips, breaching the unwritten rule, but she wasn't entertaining his advances, at least not in that way.
"Come on Maria, play the game! It's not like it would be the first time we've kissed."

"Greeting your friend's man with a customary peck is totally different to this and you bloody know it!"

"Oh well, let's try a different tack then!"

Sliding his hand across Maria's stomach, Robin's fingers met the lace of her tiny red thong. He teased the thin material to one side and ran his hand over her fluffy mound, gently prizing her lips apart. She grimaced as she reached down and grabbed his erect penis, guiding it towards her vagina as he grunted, squeezed and moaned, subdued by the erotic encounter. His entry was clumsy and degrading, and Maria closed her eyes tightly, praying for the ordeal to be over. Her teeth were gritted tight as she bucked beneath his touch, unable to fight her impulse to withdraw, desperate to escape his foul breath and lustful advances. Despite Robin's groans, Maria had an eerie quiet in her head; her senses seemed to be on overdrive, tuned in to his every move, as if punishing herself further. She tried to seek tranquillity in her thoughts by imagining herself at the waterside, peaceful and calm, water lapping at her feet: anything just to distract her from his oafish groping and groaning. But even that was soon shattered by Robin's strident voice berating her, taunting her. He was nothing more than a vile bully, venting his life's frustrations on a weakened and vulnerable woman.

"We should do this more often. Say once a week, when Lizzie's working down the camp site cleaning caravans. You can be giving my helmet a good clean with your tongue!"

Maria lay motionless and silent as he pounded away at her unwilling body, his overweight torso bearing down heavily on her, making it almost impossible for

her to breathe properly; his rancid breath clawing at her nostrils as she bucked her head left to right trying to avoid his mouth, still trying to get to her lips.
"Jesus, this is so good, Maria! You have no idea how much I've wanted to do this to you! I have often fantasised about finger fucking you and screwing you, just like this. Are you enjoying it? Is it good? Well, Babe?" He was growing impatient at her lack of response to his endless questions and demands.
"Yes," Maria lied through her teeth. She would have said anything at that moment, just to hurry him along.
"Say my name, Babe! Go on - tell me how good I am!"
Maria was desperate not to succumb to his request but knew that if she did, it might help her plight by appeasing his grotesque demands.
Robin was close to cuming now, but still hell-bent on shredding Maria's dignity. He pulled out from inside her and stood beside the bed, thrusting his hard cock towards her face.
"Suck it!" he raged insistently. Maria protested.
"I fucking said suck it, you cheap whore!"
Maria unwillingly obliged, cursing as she leant in to take him in her mouth. "You bastard!"
Robin was unstoppable now, pulling her head back and forth by her hair. Maria was choking as he rammed harder and faster, but then he suddenly pulled his cock out of her mouth and stood there looking at her. "Turn around. Get on your hands and knees!"
She turned and did as he said, with Robin standing behind her. He slapped her hard on the arse. Maria squealed. "You like that you cheap whore?" He slapped her again, and then again. Suddenly she felt both his

hands on her arse, pulling her apart. "I've always fantasied about fucking your arse. Maria!"

"No!" Maria shouted. "No, I don't do that! No!"

"You do today, Lover." Robin held her hips as he forced his cock into her. He could feel the resistance as he pushed harder, but the tension dissipated and he was in. She cried out as Robin pumped into her, the anguished cries only making him harder. "Take this, you bitch! Take it all!"

Maria dug her head into the sheets as Robin fucked her. She could feel him about to cum and then he pulled out of her.

"Come here bitch, and take this!"

As he reached climax he snatched the condom off his cock, casting it aside. Grinning wildly, almost demonically, he erupted over her face and breasts. "That's a good girl; you know you've always wanted me deep down, haven't you! I can see it in your eyes, the way you look at me." Having fulfilled his loathsome desires, he was lording it over her now, twisting the metaphorical knife wherever he could.

Maria felt utterly degraded and humiliated. She rolled away from Robin, sobbing, but he wasn't having that, so he faced her back towards him.

"Now clean me up!"

She leaned over the bed to get a tissue. "Not like that, you stupid slag! With your fucking tongue!"

He grabbed her by the hair and pulled her to his crotch, forcing his now limp dick towards her face. She cleaned him up without uttering a single word. Once he had dressed again he waved the money in front of Maria's face, tempting her, cajoling her. As she leant forward, trying to cover her naked body and recoup some dignity, her hand strayed within grasping distance of the cash. Robin withdrew it, just enough to humble her.

"Just one more thing, my sexy little whore!"

"Don't talk to me like that! I don't choose to do this: I do it for my kid, to give him a better life."

"Ok, calm down! Just playing with you. I want your knickers as a keepsake... a little reminder of this momentous occasion."

"You really are one sick bastard!"

"Is that a yes, then!"

"Just take them and piss off!" Maria snatched the money from his hand and searched her bedside drawer for more underwear, something to make her feel less vulnerable. Swiftly pulling on her knickers, she stood up and grabbed her dressing gown from the corner of the wardrobe, humanity restored once more.

Picking up the knickers from the floor, Robin raised them to his face and eased them over his nose, inhaling deeply.

"Mmm, that's nice! They still smell of your sweet, moist honey pot. I shall cherish these, Marina, you horny little tart!" His teasing provoked Maria's temper for the last time, and she pushed him towards the door.

"Just fucking well go, Robin! I swear if you ever breathe a single word of this to Lizzie or anyone else, I will slit your fucking throat! Do you hear me?"

"Ooh, feisty! I like that in a girl: it shows you care."

"Care! I care alright - just not for you, you sick fucker! Get out!" She shoved him out of the door and into the hallway, slamming the door behind him.

"I've got to get myself another job!" she thought. "I can't put up with the Robin Bradfords of this world any longer!" Maria was petrified of Robin and the damage he could do to her reputation, she also had a nasty feeling that this would not be the last she heard of their encounter. She got dressed and went into the small kitchen for a cigarette; a nicotine fix was what she needed to settle her nerves.

***

Robin Bradford paused in the hallway at the bottom of the stairs and drew his mobile from his pocket. A second or so later, Maria's phoned chimed as the text came through.

She saw it was Robin. 'Till the next time! This is just the start, my sexy little Marina! Xx ;)'

"Fuck! Fuck! Fuck!" She knew she would never get rid of him now.

Robin slipped his phone back in his pocket, smirking at his good fortune as he left the tanning shop and headed back to his car. As he approached his vehicle he could see a traffic warden taking pictures of the small clear, sealed envelope on his windscreen. Rather than remonstrate with the surly looking warden he pulled it from under the wiper laughing.

"Something funny, Sir?"

"If only you knew, if only you knew! There's nothing even you could do that would ruin my day, Mate!"

CHAPTER 9

'STRICTLY' BUSINESS

The following Thursday, over a week later, Robin Bradford sat transfixed in his small dining room office. He cooed with delight as a series of erotic images scrolled enticingly across his computer screen. Lizzie was busy beavering away on Canvey earning her modest wages sprucing up caravans, so the coast was clear for more shenanigans. Robin was supposed to be using this quiet time to extract money from his 'cabbage green' timeshare fools. Instead, his thoughts had strayed from work and ventured into the murky world of call girls and massage parlours. Lizzie was a distant memory as he focused his mind on appointments of an altogether different kind. Seeking somewhat more adventurous encounters, Robin searched the internet for houses of ill repute. He wanted to act out his growing desire for sadistic sex. He needed a willing and submissive slave to dominate and inflict pain and humiliation on.

Mistress Helena, his on-screen, latex clad beauty was to be his chosen dalliance. Her gothic charms, studs and chains sucked him in instantly, and as he perused her gallery he began to imagine the vile things he could do to her while she begged him to be lenient. Helena stood over six feet tall in her stiletto heels; she was shackled at the ankles and tethered to a 'D' ring fixed low to the wall, her smooth pale legs covered in his favourite 'fish net' stockings. She wore latex panties with zips front and back and little suspenders attached to her stockings. Her stomach was bare, revealing a waif- like abdomen with muscles just protruding, and her top was awash with studs and chains. Conical breast cups tipped off with tassels jutted out aggressively. Her arms were high and wide, clasped in metal shackles above her head. A startlingly pallid complexion was emphasised by the dark make up which surrounded her eyes, with virtually black lipstick giving her face an almost death-like look. Completing the 'theme noir' was Helena's jet black hair, which was wild and frizzy like an eighties rock star. Her sorrowful and submissive air, with her whole persona epitomising a weary, downtrodden slave, gave an extra high to Robin's beastly ego. There was even a trickle of theatrical blood strategically dribbling from her dark lipstick. Unlike other girls he came across, Helena seemed as if she would genuinely relish all those beatings, whippings and sadomasochistic rituals, the money merely a bonus. He retreated to his car to make contact with her on his very personal phone.

"Is that Helena, Mistress Helena?" He enquired when the sultry voice greeted him.

"Yes, it is! Do you vish me to serve you?"
"I certainly do. I see from your website that anything goes."
"Yes Master, I surrender to all your darkest desires. Vill you please come and teach me the error of my vays!"
"Oh, I'll teach you alright! How much?"
"Services start from one hundred pounds, depending on how naughty I have been and how strict your corrective measures are!" she teased.
"Well, I have a budget of two hundred in mind. Will that suffice?"
"Oh yes! But I would need to be punished a great deal for that. Come und see me very soon please, Sir!"
"Would four-thirty be good for you?" he asked excitedly.
"Oh, yes!" she purred. "You come left at the top of York Road, behind the garages. It is the basement flat on Flitch Crescent... Number Thirteen A"
Robin went straight upstairs, showered and changed, killing time before his sexual extravaganza. Donning his grey hooded tracksuit top, he grabbed his keys and left for the 'Dungeon'. He liked to wear sports gear, not because he was active, quite the contrary. He wore it because his portly frame felt more comfortable inside the loose, baggy fabric.
His charming sat nav hostess was soon leading the way. York Road is one of the most infamous roads in Southend. The working girls took up residence many years ago, its proximity to the lucrative Sea Front bars and Amusements providing them with a mass of potential clients. Nowadays they were few and far between, but our Helena was there, waiting patiently for

Robin. He cruised casually along, watching all the nubile teenage girls going in and out of the Arcades. The Kiss-Me-Quick hats of summer now a distant memory, winter brought only local girls, bored or cold, and using the Amusements like a youth club. At the height of the season Robin would roam the area, ogling and 'goosing' every young female he could get close to.

Leaving the seafront via Burdett Road, he eased up towards York Road and into Flitch Crescent, then parked his car and headed for the basement flat.

Bashing the large brass lion's head door-knocker onto the 'off white' paint of Number Thirteen A, Robin waited patiently for his mistress to allow him in. Soon the roles would be reversed: she would wait on him, be at his mercy. At last she opened the door and beckoned him inside with her stud- encrusted PVC gauntlet.

"Come through, please! Zis is ze first visit to me, Mr Bradford, yes!"

"Yes, it is. Hopefully the first of many, I hasten to add." Robin smiled at her lasciviously.

"Vell, ve must establish some ground rules. Vunce these are in place, virtually anything is acceptable to me."

"Ground rules?"

"Yes! 'Although I vill submit to your vishes fully, zere are certain procedures zat must be in place for my vell-being and protection," she explained.

"I see!" Looking somewhat puzzled, Robin allowed Mistress Helena to continue.

"Ve must establish a safe vord. Ven I say zis vord, you must stop vhatever you are doing immediately. Zis means I am uncomfortable vith the act, or am suffering severe pain."

"Okay! And you say anything goes?"

"Within reason, Mr Bradford, but I vill not accept cuts or bruises to my face. Zis is agreed, yes?"

"Yes, yes!" Robin started to wonder how far he could push this lowly slave.

"Also, no excrement. I vill not indulge zis in any vay! Anal is good either way, but not shit."

Even Robin could not begin to imagine what sick people would involve defecating in their role play but, resolved to go along with the adage 'it takes all sorts', he pressed Helena for the 'safe' word.

"Ve have two. The first von is a varning for you to back off, or be a little less forceful: zis is 'ocean'. Ze second vord is important von - zis means desist immediately from your actions."

Puzzled by this odd request, he asked, "Ocean! Why ocean?"

"I vill explain zese vords in a moment."

"Why not 'stop', or 'help'?"

"Let me finish, and you vill understand zis logic."

"You're the boss!" Ironically, she was. Despite her submissive manner, she called all the shots - for now.

"Ze second vord is 'forest'. Zese vords are chosen because zey represent tranquillity and calm. Vords you vould normally associate viz stopping are our most common play vords - like 'no', 'stop', 'help' and 'get off me."

Robin began to understand Helena's train of thought. She would regularly indulge in rape and torture, so her 'safe' words needed to be far removed from the normal protestations!

"Have you a scenario in mind, Mr Bradford?"

"Well, I quite like the idea of forcing myself on you while you try to stop me - and my name is Mr Smith." She led him to the 'Play Room' and paused at the door. "Ven ve enter zis room, ve begin. I vill be your villing servant, but not villing to let you fuck me. You vill have to try very hard." She winked suggestively and entered the dungeon.

The room was quite dark, with numerous industrial looking contraptions nestled around it. Clamps, shackles and chains hung like ornaments, and mirrors reflected back and forth, as if talking to each other. A large leather swing took centre stage, hanging from the ceiling on huge iron chains. Initially Robin was sceptical of all this cumbersome paraphernalia. It was like something out of a corny horror movie.

Helena called him to the far side of the room where a bench lay outstretched. "Vould you like to secure me to ze bench, Master?" Suspecting this man was a Dungeon Virgin, she egged him on gently.

"Yes, yes! Lie down on your stomach... Bad Girl!" If only she had known, she wouldn't have enticed this monster from his hiding place.

Robin took hold of her hand and placed it in a clamp to her right side, then did the same with her left. He then proceeded to shackle her ankles. More than accustomed to this ritual, Helena began to remonstrate loudly. All part of the game! Pleased with his enslaved hostage, Robin slowly stripped in the corner of the room, taking time to fold each item of clothing. Once naked, he stood in front of Helena and lifted her head by the hair; then placing his erect penis inches from her face he began to masturbate.

"Please, don't! Please! I promise I vill not to do it again, Master!"

"Your type always does. You're mine, and I'm going to teach you some manners, you little whore!" He pushed his cock to her lips and began his tirade of abuse.

"Fucking suck it!" Helena bucked her head wildly - screaming out to be left alone, set free. Robin inched forward and held her hair tighter, prizing her lips open with his rigid phallus.

"Fucking suck it, you bitch!"

Despite her verbal outburst, Helena enjoyed being forced, and Robin enjoyed forcing. He leaned across her back as she eagerly devoured his cock and struck out at her buttocks with the flogging tool. She screamed in agony and he struck again, each time harder and with more intent: he was just warming up. She would wail and moan with each blow and sink her teeth into his penis, making him wince. He would then thrash her harder in an unbroken cycle of pain and violence, with him screaming obscenities at her and Helena apologising and begging for mercy.

He replaced the 'cat' on the wall and returned with a studded paddle.

"This'll teach you! Who's the fucking boss? Who?"

"You, Mr Smith, you! Please, no more!"

He clawed at her thighs and started to force her legs apart.

"Condom! Use a condom!" Helena's protests were now more genuine.

"I don't fucking want to! I'm going to force my way inside you and spill my seed deep up your dirty snatch!"

"No! Condom!" she bellowed, but Robin was already at her moist entrance.

"No!" she screamed. "Ocean! Ocean!"

"Fuck your stupid word! Shit! ... I'm in your fucking 'forest' now!" and he rammed away at her vagina, slapping her buttocks with his paddle harder and harder.

She was begging now. "Zat is not part of ze deal! Stop, please! Forest!"

Helena realised she was trapped and helpless. Not so much fun now she wasn't in control, he thought.

"Please, I'm begging you! Please, not zis!" To Helena unprotected sex was a cardinal sin: risking disease or death was unthinkable.

Robin ejaculated far inside her womb, then his euphoric high began to subside and he slumped over her back.

"Get out of me, you bastard! Get off." Robin now had a very irate brass on his hands, and wasn't quite sure what to do.

"Listen! I'll give you three hundred quid, if you just shut the fuck up and pretend this never happened."

"Let me go! Let me go, you fucking bastard!"

Robin stood silently in the corner of the room and dressed while his victim lay thrashing and yelling. He was in a terrible quandary: he knew if he let her go she would flip completely and probably attack him or call the police. He couldn't let her go, but he couldn't leave her there either.

"If you calm down I'll let you out, so shut up and stop struggling." He tried to reason with her.

"Ven you let me out I promise" - speaking softly, almost remorsefully at first, then with genuine venom and menace - "I vill tear your bollocks right out viz my bare hands!"

Robin had no doubt she meant it, and that he was facing a huge dilemma. "Time! I need time," he moaned to himself as he gagged Helena with one of the straps. All her fight was gone, and she lay still now, hoping her captor would be merciful. He knew that if he wasn't very clever, this could bring his whole world crashing down around him. Money was the only thing Robin could think of that would save his arse.

"You lie there nice and peaceful and I'll be back soon, I promise." Leaving straight away, he took a further £200 from the machine at a nearby petrol station, and went back to thirteen-A. As he was approaching the basement steps an elderly neighbour called to him over the fence of the adjoining flat.

"Excuse me! Is everything alright? Only my wife and I could hear a woman shouting, and she sounded distressed."

"Yes, everything's fine. You go back in out of the cold! My girlfriend's just fallen over and hurt herself, but it's nothing serious. Just got some aspirin from the garage." Clearly unconvinced, the old man withdrew from Robin's view and shut his window. Still peering through his net curtain he watched as Robin descended the steps. Back inside, Robin placed four hundred pounds on the floor in front of Helena and fanned it out for her to see. "You take this for your trouble and I promise I'll go - just leave. Ok?" She stared at the money for a minute, and then nodded in agreement. As he released the gag she gasped loudly and gave a great sigh. Robin stooped to the floor and unclasped her ankles, her blood smearing his fingertips. The sharp edges had cut deep into the flesh of her wrists when she struggled to free herself, desperate to escape.

"You are going to behave yourself now, aren't you?" Now she was free, he wasn't convinced Helena would still submit to his requests and accept the extra cash.
"Yes! Yes! Let me go!"
Robin sensed that his captive's spirit was returning. Unsure of himself, he lifted a phallic shaped wooden truncheon from the bevy of torture instruments adorning the wall and looped the chord over his wrist. Raising it menacingly to her cheek, he pressed it to her flesh. "Last fucking chance!" he screamed, and Helena lowered her head and muttered her submission. He unclasped her left arm from its anchor, leaving a chain around eighteen inches long swinging from the shackle. As he knelt to unfasten the right hand side Helena whipped the chain furiously across his shoulders and right arm, knocking him to the floor. Her onslaught was valiant, but poorly timed. She had rocked him, but still being secured via her right wrist left her vulnerable. Quickly retaliating, and still smarting from her attack, Robin regained control with a series of brutal blows, beating her mercilessly with the wooden cock.
"You shouldn't have done that, you stupid bitch!" and with a bone-shattering crunch he rendered her unconscious. Leaving her trussed up, he vowed to return later on or in the morning, once he had given himself time to compose his thoughts, plot his course of action and decide her fate.
Robin's hooded top had been blessed with copious amounts of Helena's blood, this time not the theatrical sort used for effect on her website. He folded it inside out and headed for the neighbouring petrol sta-

tion, in his haste failing to observe the old man still spying through his curtains. With a cursory glance around him, he dumped the soiled top in a large galvanised wheelie bin and shut down its lime green lid. Once back in his car, he slipped Helena's keys into the door pocket and made for the sanctum of home.

Meanwhile, the old man at 15 Flitch Crescent was jotting down his dealings with Robin in a small red diary: a brief description of the man, his car and his movements. When Robin had eased up to the junction of York Road Jonathan Pettigrew had hurriedly noted down his registration number. Two things, though, were in Robin's favour and would slow down the inevitable visit from PC Plod. The first was that Mr Pettigrew's eighty years told greatly on his sight. The second was his virtually unintelligible writing. His incorrect index would serve to hinder Police progress rather than aid it. It would also fail to link the car with an Automatic Number Plate Recognition list at Peldon Rise.

Nevertheless, Robin Bradford's whole world was destined to come crashing down around him like a giant Jenga block. Exactly when was simply a matter of time.

***

When Robin came down from his invigorating, purging shower, Lizzie was sitting at the dining room table with a burger and fries for them both.

"This is for me I take it?" he asked pleasantly.

Tapping away at the computer, his girlfriend looked up briefly and smiled. "After everything you do for me, I thought I'd treat you!"

Tapping his belly, he smiled back. "Oh well - any excuse to put off that diet I s'pose!"
Once again he was left at home to ponder his day's debauchery. Lizzie had work to do cleaning those caravans on Canvey, so Robin had the much maligned task of catching up on paperwork.

CHAPTER 10

13 A

Despite the Saturday morning drizzle and cold winter's bite, Alan Bigran marched doggedly along York Road in his light blue Post Office shirt and grey cargo shorts, parcel in hand. A sense of purpose in his gait, with his head dipping like a piston he closed in on Flitch Crescent.

Alan treated his round like a military route march: all that was missing was his brick laden Bergen and mock assault rifle, and every day he would push himself harder trying to cut off some extra seconds. His haste had cost him dear today; he had missed the plain brown parcel addressed to Miss Helena Landsvig. Cursing his own incompetence, he descended the red-tiled steps that led to 13A, and teased a pen from his pocket in readiness. A quick signature was all he needed and he would be off again, making up lost ground. He swung the brass lion into life and stood poised, clip board ready. The basement door gently peeled away before him, catching him unaware.

“Miss Landsvig?” Patience was not Alan’s forte. “Miss Landsvig! I have a parcel for you... Hello!” As the door halted abruptly against the corridor wall, Alan stepped inside cautiously and called out again. The dimly lit hallway stretched before him as he tentatively proceeded.

The ever vigilant Jonathan Pettigrew crept down the stairs behind him. “Oi! What you up to?”

Alan spun round, clutching the parcel tight to his chest. “Bloody ’ell, Mr P! You scared the bejesus out of me.”

“Oh, it’s you, Postie! Sorry! I thought you was somebody up to no good. I was coming back from the garage with me paper and milk and saw a head disappear down the steps. You can’t be too careful nowadays. Her three doors down was burgled last Tuesday week, you know.”

“When I knocked the door just opened,” said Alan, his heart still skipping erratically.

“Ain’t seen her yet today. She normally goes into town around ten-thirty on a Saturday, to do her food shopping. Comes back on the twelve twenty-two bus.”

Alan looked at Jonathan Pettigrew for a moment, as if to say ‘are you serious’! His knowledge of the woman’s movements bordered on stalker class.

“And her pesky cat’s been at my door begging for scraps since last night.”

“Will you sign for her parcel?” Alan asked, keen to get on his way.

“Sure thing, Postie, give it here!” A few swift strokes of

the pen, and Alan Bigran was away, back up to street level.

Jonathan continued down the hall to where a faint light shone into view. As he entered the room his eyes widened at the sight of such wondrous and intriguing machines. Panning around, his eyes came to rest on Helena's mutilated torso. The putrid miasma of death hung in the air, and he took a hankie from his jacket pocket to cover his face.

"What on Earth! Oh dear me, you poor, poor girl!" and he calmly retraced his steps to the front door and went in search of help. His many years working at Sutton Road Cemetery left old Pettigrew unfazed by the gruesome scene at 13A. He promptly went back to his house and called Southend Police Station. Minutes later Sergeant McEwan arrived with WPC Vicky Ward and PC Paul Semple, accompanied by the usual entourage of lights, sirens and squealing brakes. PC Semple took up sentry post on the top step, arms neatly folded across his chest, collar turned up against the rain.

***

Sergeant Macca and Vicky Ward headed straight for the 'Dungeon', as directed by the unnervingly placid neighbour. The beam of Sergeant Macca's cosh-like torch cut swathes of light through the dark hall until he found the light switch. Pettigrew had instinctively shut the murder room door to prevent Helena's cat from entering as it purred its way round his feet. The first thing to greet the two officers was a heady stench like tainted meat, which instantly made the WPC gag. She quickly composed herself, though, and

they both stood gazing in silent horror at Helena's lifeless body.
"Looks like another tom, Vicky."
"Judging by all this gear hanging about the place, I reckon you're right."
"There are some sick fuckers about!" Sergeant Macca squirmed as he took in the various objects scattered around.
"You're not kidding." WPC Ward was rigid, eyes fixed on Helena. "Better get onto Ambrose's mob again." She pulled the collar on her luminous green coat close to her mouth and contacted Headquarters. "Can you pass a message onto Vincent Ambrose that we have another dead brass on our hands!"

***

Standing guard at the front of 13A, PC Semple glanced at the grubby black Focus as it turned into Flitch Crescent and halted at the makeshift barrier. Robin Bradford had planned another visit to the flat, and was astounded to see the police already there. He panicked when he saw the PC approach and desperately sought reverse, grinding his gear box unsuccessfully. Semple approached the flustered driver and pointed out the obvious road closure.
"You need to back out, Sir! Then next left into Richmond Road. That'll put you further up the Crescent. Oh, and get your tax sorted pronto!"
"It's in the post, promise!" Robin had gone cold, and at the same time was sweating profusely.
"No worries, Sir! Be on your way now!" and PC Semple returned to his post. Lacking even basic psychology,

he couldn't fathom why Joe Public always looked so guilty. Only a bloody tax disc!

***

Retreating from Flitch Crescent in a blind panic, Robin backed straight out into York Road without looking. A car coming towards him had to brake sharply to avoid him, letting out a deafening squeal as the tarmac chewed through its rubber tyres. Missing Robin's rear end by inches, the car mounted the kerb and came to a halt. The irate driver remonstrated loudly and profanities ensued.

PC Semple headed for Robin again, wishing to point out his errant driving style, but he was off in a flurry, stricken with thoughts of capture. He headed for East Beach in Shoebury, a place of quiet and solitude; he could gather his thoughts and assess his next course of action from there. So many questions he needed answers for. How much did they know? How did they get there so fast? If he was placed at the scene, he would surely be arrested for roughing up a whore! For now, all he could do was sit tight and pray.

***

Back at 13A Flitch Crescent, Vincent Ambrose and Lucy Hockley had arrived simultaneously, exchanged pleasantries and descended into the dark basement. Sergeant Macca and WPC Ward left the flat in their hands, and reconvened outside with PC Semple. Jonathan Pettigrew approached Sergeant Macca, clutching his red diary.

"Good morning, officers!" Sergeant Macca's seniority, visible on his uniform and in his professional approach was evident, so Pettigrew addressed him personally. "I reported the situation to your station this morning at 09.40 hours." He thumbed through his notes as he spoke.

"Ok, Sir! And your name is?"

"Pettigrew, Jonathan Pettigrew. I'm an ex Staff Sergeant in the Royal Anglian Regiment."

Macca was used to dealing with ex-military types. Some years back there had been a notable garrison in Shoeburyness, Southend's sibling district, and many of the young men stationed there had taken up residency in the local area with the more than willing females.

"I have some other information which I believe will be of interest to you, Sergeant!"

"Sorry, Mr. Pettigrew!" Sergeant Macca's apology was superfluous, as old Pettigrew hadn't drawn breath long enough to allow him to speak. "I am Sergeant James McEwan, and my colleagues here are PCs Semple and Ward."

"Good morning to you all, again!"

"Not sure about the good part!" PC Semple quipped, promptly receiving a sharp dig in the ribs from Vicky Ward.

"What do you have for us, Mr Pettigrew?" asked Macca.

"Well now, let me see! First of all, late afternoon Thursday the lady had a visitor - a male around fifty years old; about five-ten, and portly. I spoke to him briefly after what seemed to be a loud altercation with her downstairs. He assured me that everything was ok.

His girlfriend had had an accident. Though she seemed to have a lot of boyfriends," he paused. "He was driving a black Ford Focus, registration number X181 ZFT, or XL51 ZTF. Not sure exactly, but it was parked over there. He came back about ten the same night, but I didn't see him go in - just saw the car again."

"Thank you, Mr Pettigrew," said Sergeant Macca. "That's very helpful," and he gestured to WPC Ward to pass on the information to Vincent Ambrose downstairs.

"Also, strange thing was he put something in the waste bins over by the garage." continued Pettigrew.

Just as she was on the point of leaving, Vicky Ward was stopped by PC Semple.

"What!" she said impatiently.

"Ma'am, a black Focus!"

"Yes, what of it?"

"There was a bloke here earlier in a black Focus. He looked well stressed when I approached him. I thought it was odd to get so wound up over a spent tax disc."

WPC Ward shook her head in despair.

"How the hell was I to know?" he bleated back.

"Pop to the garage!" she said, changing tack.

"Why?"

"See if they sell some bloody intuition, will you!" she barked sarcastically. "And while you're there, tape off the bin store and make sure no one goes near it - Numpty!"

***

As Vincent Ambrose made his way with Lucy towards the gruesome room of torture, he remained half a yard behind her. Ever the scoundrel, Vincent's motives were not born out of apprehension, but merely so he could check out Miss Hockley's 'tush'. The astute young Scene of Crime officer was already on his case, though. She had caught him ogling her several times before.

"You'd do better to concentrate less on my derriere, and more on the crime scene, Sir!" Then she gave him a deliberate wiggle, which embarrassed the normally composed Vincent.

"I was looking at the walls actually to see if..."

Lucy cut him dead. "Of course, Sir! Whatever you say!"

When they entered the dungeon in their crinkly white over-suits, latex gloves and blue over-shoes, Lucy seemed perplexed. "This is blatantly not the same killer," she claimed boldly.

"What makes you say that, Lucy?" Vincent had naturally assumed that with two prostitutes butchered in a week, the evidence pointed to a serial offender.

"Well now, the last girl - Katya - her attack was a rash and wild affair. But this, this is something altogether different."

As they drew nearer Vincent could see that Lucy's observations were well founded. The body was laid out almost ritualistically, legs bound and spread and arms in a similar pose, with deliberate cuts and markings adorning the torso. 'Mistress' Helena's corpse lay face down in a pool of sticky crimson blood, her once immaculate hair matted and tousled. The straps holding her PVC corset together had been sliced from the nape of her neck right down to her buttocks, exposing her slender tattooed trunk. Criss-crossing her back were countless deep lacerations, carved in an almost symmetrical fashion. Lucy edged closer, peering deep into Helena's gusset.

"My God!" she exclaimed. "I was wrong. Look, the knife handle! These details weren't released to the Press were they? So it must be the same guy!"

Vincent strained to see over Lucy's shoulders as she pushed aside the tassels on Helena's knickers.

"You know what this means, Vincent!"

"Enlighten me, Sweetheart!"

"This means that our man has now got a taste for blood. His craft is evolving. The first murder was sporadic and reckless, whereas this..."

Vincent interjected. "He's honing his skills isn't he? And playing out his fantasies!"

"I'm afraid you're probably right, Vincent. This is a calculated, deliberate execution."

"And if we don't find him and stop him, there's going to be more!" Vincent put his head in his hands. "Fuck, Lucy! You need to work swiftly, Girl, and get me some leads. I can't chase shadows; I need something to follow up. Please be thorough!"

"I can only give you what's here. It's an exact science, Vincent - not a frigging magic show! I'll try my best: you know I will."

At that very moment WPC Ward walked in, bearing her message from Sergeant Macca.

"Vincent!"

"Yes, Vic! I hope it's good news - I certainly need it."

"Possibly, Guv. A neighbour has some helpful Intel. Sounds like he may have a vehicle id as well. A partial index for a black Ford Focus that was hanging around before the murder. And PC Semple had a run in of sorts out the front ten minutes ago with a guy in a black Ford Focus."

"Outside? Are you kidding! Lucy Love, are you ok if I get on?" There was a sense of urgency about Ambrose's tone. He was seriously under pressure now. A potential serial killer on his patch could have unimaginable consequences for him.

"Guv, the neighbour also said the man dumped something in a wheelie bin."

"Have you looked yet?"

"No Guv, just roped it off. Thought it best if we didn't contaminate the scene. Let SOCO do their thing."

Vincent edged his way past WPC Ward, and towards the exit. "Lucy, can we arrange a post mortem for around three o'clock?"

"Should be fine, Vinnie."

As she and Vincent Ambrose left, Vicky teased him over Lucy's familiarity. "Ahh, how sweet! 'Vinnie'. She laughed and repeated, 'Vinnie!'

"Jealous are you Vicky!"

"Me, Guv!" Vicky blushed and looked away with a coy expression on her face. "No boss, no!"

"So you wouldn't care to go out on Wednesday evening then for a bite to eat, or something?"

"No, Vinnie!"

"Ok, Vicky! Your loss, Hun." Vincent, the player, looked disappointed at her rebuttal.

"Thursday's good, though!" and smiling, WPC Ward took off across the road to meet up with PC Semple.

"Thursday it is, then." Vincent Ambrose had been briefly distracted, angling for WPC Ward's affections, but when he saw the road cordon and Black Maria, he

came back down to earth with a jolt. Sergeant Macca was talking on his radio as Vincent approached.
"Both index numbers he gave us have come back blank, Mate. The first one doesn't exist, and the second is a purple Fiesta registered to a nineteen year old girl on the Isle of Wight."
"Shit!" He banged the gate shut as he struggled to keep his composure.
"We're running a comparison check - see if we can find a near match. Possible he had false plates I s'pose!" Sergeant Macca was trying to appease his friend and colleague.
A dejected Vincent Ambrose called his cohorts Brian and then Nicky on his mobile. "Need you in straight away. We have another prostitute due in the morgue in a few hours."
Both protested momentarily, as they had family commitments, but it was pointless. The job always came first: they knew that. Brian said his farewells to his wife and set off for the Station. Nicky made a flask of tea and some sandwiches wrapped in cling film and placed them next to her elderly mother's chair. She was asleep, blanket over her knees, so her daughter kissed her gently on the forehead and quietly left the house.
Back at the scene Vincent Ambrose carefully lifted the lid of the huge wheelie bin. A busy weekend had ensured it was now full. He turned over a couple of bags and then caught a flash of grey sweater covered in splatters of blood. Lifting it out carefully and bagging it up, he replaced the rest of the rubbish and returned to 13A. As he passed WPC Ward, both grinned a little self-consciously, and looked down. "Have I missed

something?" asked PC Semple, not wanting to be left out.

"Wouldn't be the first time today, now would it?" Vicky Ward retorted acidly.

Semple felt like a factory tea boy on his first day at work, only menial tasks to do and the butt of everyone's jokes. Considering himself distinctly downtrodden, he was all the more desperate to prove his worth.

***

Scrupulously adopting William Mumford's modus operandi, Lucy took out her Dictaphone and began to dictate her observations of the traumatic scene. "The room is laden with sexually orientated paraphernalia, including torture racks, swings, whips and other beating implements. Our victim's arms and legs have been immobilised by metal restraints. I estimate her time of death to have been about twenty-four hours ago. She has approximately forty lesions to her back, and around half a dozen to each of her arms and legs. There is one long slash from coccyx to nape. The knife which is believed to be the weapon used to kill her has been forced inside her vagina, as in the case of Katya Lesniak." Lucy began to photograph the body, taking care to scrutinise each wound.

"Her wrists have suffered very deep cuts, assumed to be from struggling with the shackles." Lucy's study concluded at Helena's head, which was slumped forward off the end of the makeshift bench. "Her skull is smashed in just above the crown, and bone fragments are visible." She lifted the head to reveal a wooden truncheon hidden by the thick tangle of black hair.

"Ah-ha! Below the victim's head, previously concealed by her hair, is a small, wooden, phallus-shaped truncheon, presumably a sex toy. This object is about eighteen inches long, with a leather type handle. There are traces of blood along the shaft."

As Lucy studied the weapon, thoughts of its sexual usage washed over her and she shuddered. At that moment, the all-too familiar figures of the black-suited Corpse Bearers shuffled into the room. Their arms crossed, as if in some ritual of mourning, they stood silently waiting for Lucy's command. "Two minutes, Guys - nearly done!" She felt nervous of the ghoulish twosome, watching them cautiously from the corner of her eye. After snapping a few more pictures, she beckoned them over. As they gently teased the pathetic mutilated body from the bench, the sound of skin breaking away from dried blood was the only noise to disturb the unholy silence of Mistress Helena's dungeon.

CHAPTER 11

WHO HOLDS THE KEY

Robin Bradford sat in his car drumming the steering wheel, deep in thought as the unrelenting rain pattered against the windscreen. The occasional sweep of the wiper's arm cleared his view as he stared aimlessly out at the foamy waves lapping the beach and then retreating. How he wished he could follow them out to sea, way beyond the horizon. He felt trapped.

Soon Essex Police would be beating a path to his door. He knew he had left too many traces. Now he deeply regretted filling Helena with his lustful seed, but all he could do was sit tight and pray they didn't link him to both girls.

***

Vincent, Nicky and Brian stood transfixed in front of the whiteboard. Names, pictures, times: somewhere in this list was the man they so desperately sought. Soon

Lucy would be wading through yet more files, reports and pictures. Vincent felt as if he was drowning in a great sea of evidence, none of which helped, or seemed to make any sense. Worse still, they now had a chief suspect but no idea who he was. Could the black Focus be the key to all their problems?"

"Nicky, get back on the CCTV. Pull up anything you can from the last incident and cross reference it against any images you can find local to York Road. Brian, get on to William Mumford: put pressure on him to rush this one through."

***

Lucy had finished at 13A and was back in the chill of Mumford's lab. Despite the ambient temperature being no different from the office area, she always felt less comfortable in the morgue. The polished, stainless-steel surfaces deceived her brain and convinced her it was cooler. Helena's corpse lay face up now, and Lucy could see the full extent of the butchery. The killer must have gloated for hours over her dying body. This assault had been premeditated, calculated, and deliberate, the trademark disembowelment dominating all the other, ancillary wounds.

"Blunt force trauma would appear to be the cause of death. Time is difficult to establish, but would speculate between seven and ten Thursday evening. Had the deceased not died from the head wound, she would certainly have bled to death. Most of the cuts to her back are superficial, perhaps symbolic, but the cuts to the wrist would certainly have proved fatal." Lucy surveyed Helena's body in search of fibres and hair samples. "Several hairs around the torso and a couple inside the victim's underwear; also residue in the vaginal area, possibly semen." She carefully collected various items of interest and bagged them for further analysis. William Mumford came into the laboratory and put his arm around Lucy's shoulders. "How's my debutante?"

"She's good, William - somewhat better than this poor girl. Same MO to some extent as the other one, but this was a much more controlled execution. She was tied up and tortured for several hours, and whoever did this spent quite some time cleaning and bleaching the flat. There was no evidential material anywhere. Not so thorough with the corpse, though!"

"How so, Lucy?"

"There are hairs and fibres again."

"They hold the key to this puzzle, Lucy!"

Lucy stopped him in his tracks. "Key! That's it. That's what's been nagging at me all afternoon!"

"I don't follow."

"There were no flat keys anywhere... so whoever did this either had keys, or took hers!"

"Needles in haystacks, my dear! Needles."

***

Robin Bradford watched the kite surfers zigzagging across the bay and wished he could turn back the clock. He leant down to retrieve his private phone, wanting to double check his history was clear. As his head dipped below the seat, his eye caught the gleam of Helena's keys, nestling in the door pocket next to his fuel receipts. He carefully lifted them out with his right hand and studied them thoughtfully. A single brass-coloured key was dwarfed by the multitude of dangly bits adorning the ring: a small brown ceramic bear wearing S and M gear, a large chrome 'H' and a 'Find Me' tab all jangled together noisily. Robin opened his door and walked purposefully towards the shoreline. He threw the keys as hard he could, sending them flying towards the little white horses that topped the waves. It was almost as if this act had cleansed him of the heinous crimes and moral failures. After a few seconds of deliberation he walked back to his car and carried on with his day, as if nothing had happened.

***

Lucy began the arduous task of testing and logging all the samples from Helena's flat and post mortem. The pubic hairs and stale semen sample taken from around the victim's vagina were a definite match, though Lucy's job had been made somewhat more difficult by the overriding presence of bleach and other cleaning products. Better prepared this time, it would appear that the killer had gone to great lengths to try and eradicate all traces of their existence. Even so, forensics being the invaluable tool that it was cut straight through these veiled attempts to disguise their visit.
Lucy eased the slides across the projector screen one by one, cross referencing them against the six samples from Katya's flat. When she reached the fourth she exclaimed, "Yes! William... William!"
"Yes, my love! What ails you so?" Always the lyricist, Mumford's love of words graced his every conversation.

"Sample four from Katya... it's a match with the samples from the new girl, Helena!"
"Good, good! But do we have any more clues as to his identity?"
"I'm afraid that's down to Vincent Ambrose, Sir - not us!"

***

Back at the station, Nicky was on the phone to her colleague from Chelmsford. She had remembered a black Focus being on the list of cars highlighted by Victoria Avenue's camera. "Can you go back to the cars on the first case for me? I need a reg. from the black Ford Focus which turned into Winchester... ok. ... Yes... If you could, please. Call me straight away if you have any luck."
The wheelie bin had yielded a blood-stained top, matching the DNA for Sample Four. The CCTV footage at the local garage forecourt was slightly less conclusive, failing to show portly Robin Bradford withdrawing money from the garage cash machine some fifteen minutes before dumping his top in the bin. If it had, both the garage and the ATM CCTVs would have given him away, also leading them right to his door via his bank account.

***

Vincent found himself sitting in front of the Media for the second time in a week. He wouldn't escape so easily this time: the Press were baying for blood, and they had Vincent Ambrose in their sights.
"Two prostitutes murdered in a week, Inspector

Ambrose! Do we have a serial killer in our midst?" asked one of the journalists.

"How close are you to catching the killer?" posed another.

"Do you have a suspect?"

Vincent lost his cool. "We are pursuing every avenue we can to apprehend this dangerous criminal. All I can say at this stage is that we hope to make an arrest very shortly."

One of the braver journalists pointed out that Vincent Ambrose had said exactly the same thing almost a week ago.

"I'm sorry, but that's all you are getting for now!" and he stormed from the stage under a barrage of comments and camera flashes. The image splashed across every paper just hours later would haunt him until he finally got to grips with his nemesis. Meanwhile news came through from Lucy and William that it was indeed the same man present at both crimes. The DNA matched, the car was around the fringes both times and the style of execution, albeit crafted the second time round, was identical.

***

Despite knowing that his world was collapsing around him, Robin Bradford also knew that within days he would once again be soliciting the services of a massage parlour. Lizzie grew more distant daily, and their sex life was almost non-existent. Ironically she seemed to have become needier of his closeness over the last few days, just not the sex. He resigned himself to thinking that he too had changed since his visit to Anja; he had become withdrawn and unsociable. Lizzie, on the other hand, never seemed to be away from the house unless she was working. Yoga classes and visits to wine bars with Maria were cancelled, in favour of staying at home.

He chanced his arm with Lizzie again that night and was typically, but tactfully rebuffed. The insatiable thirst for sex was never far from his thoughts, and he was already planning another encounter.

CHAPTER 12

MARIA

Lizzie's phone rang unexpectedly and unnervingly around midnight, waking them both instantly. "It's Maria, at this time of night! What the hell...!" She pressed the answer button cautiously. "Maria?"

"Lizzie, please come round... there's this bloke!" She was clearly distraught.

"What bloke? What are you on about?" Lizzie was still bleary-eyed, not compos mentis.

"He's an ex and he won't leave me alone. Please come round!"

Maria couldn't tell Lizzie who he really was, or her friend would almost certainly disown her. The 'friend' was actually a Regular who had become smitten with 'Marina' and taken the bold but foolish move of following her home some weeks earlier in the hope of convincing her to let him become more than just a client. She had rejected his advances several times over the previous days, but this time was different. Fuelled up with alcohol and randy as a stray dog, he wasn't prepared to accept her rebuttal.

"Give us ten minutes! Just stay inside away from him till me and Robin get there."

"Robin?" Maria's heart sank. Out of the frying pan into the fire, she thought. The last thing she needed was to be indebted to that ignorant fat oaf.

"Well I'm not coming on my bloody own...Robin will deal with him!" She cancelled the call and scurried around the room for something to wear.

"What the fuck is going on, Lizzie?" seethed Robin.

"Grab some clothes and your keys... I'll explain on the way round to Maria's."

The very mention of the name filled him with both excitement and dread. But if she needed his help that could only strengthen the hold he already had over her. Despite Robin's blatant oafishness towards her friend, which Lizzie could never fathom, she knew she would need his help and support to tackle Maria's problem. Once she was safely buckled in, she grabbed his hand and made him promise to be careful - not go off half-cocked and end up in a skirmish. She'd seen it so many times before. Wade in and ask questions later!

As they rounded the end of Maria's road, Lizzie could see the guy still banging on Maria's door and once again warned Robin to stay calm. Before she had finished her spiel, Robin was out. He abandoned the motor, door open and engine running. His anger was running too, positively overheating. He let off a salvo of abuse at the dumbfounded Romeo, who now switched his attention to Robin. The guy was the epitome of stupid, and his limited vocabulary consisted mostly of 'fucking', 'tosser' and 'wanker' as he defended his bizarre, bullish behaviour towards Maria. She stood in the doorway petrified, but for reasons Lizzie was unaware of. One tell-tale word from the punter about her profession and she would be answering to Lizzie, not him.

"Keep your fucking, grubby mug away from her or you'll be sorry, you scum bag pikey!" Robin was right in his face and determined to exercise his authority over the hapless drunk.

"Who you calling 'pikey', Mr High and Fucking Mighty!" came the stout reply.

"You'd best run off home to your mum before I slap your arse!" Robin edged closer to the bloke, trying to intimidate him, whilst avoiding the now flailing arms. What the reveller lacked in size he certainly made up for in enthusiasm. They do say it's not the size of the dog in the fight, but the size of the fight in the dog! He didn't seem too intimidated by Robin's brash threat, and promptly shoved him backwards. One of the inevitable curtain twitchers made a hasty call to the local Cop Shop and was assured that help was on its way. Unfortunately for the half-cut pisshead, Robin's sheer body-weight won the day and he sat astride the gobby drunk, choking him with his own shirt collar. Lizzie pulled at Robin's jacket to try and restore some order, while Maria did her best to keep out of the way.

The nosey neighbour leant from an upstairs window two doors down and bellowed. "I've called the Police, you know!"

Robin's pent up rage began to subside, his blind fury dissipating as he rose to his feet and brushed himself down. "Now look here... you just keep away from her! Do you hear me?" Robin was wagging an accusing finger.

In an almost surreal turn, the lout had also risen to his feet, but was screaming 'assault!' in Robin's direction. "I want 'im nicked: he's a fucking madman!" he shouted.

As the argument continued and tempers once again began to simmer over, two police officers arrived on their mountain bikes and stepped boldly between the warring factions. The sight of the uniforms was enough to make both parties retreat a pace or two and bring the level of debate down. After a quick chat with all concerned, the plods removed Robin and the punter to one side and tried to unravel the story behind their rough and tumble. The drunken client protested his innocence and ranted incoherently about Marina this, and him that. He was still adamant that he wanted Robin charged with assault, but Robin stayed cool as a cucumber, trying desperately to avoid a little trip down to the station.

During the altercation Robin had managed to snag off the guy's eyebrow piercing, which was showing faint traces of blood. The pisshead had managed to wreak revenge by dragging his nails across Robin's cheek, scratching him like a girl. The lanky officer walked over to his colleague and intimated that the other fella still wanted to press charges for assault. Robin flipped instantly and burst between the two coppers who stood in the way of him getting at the bloke. Grabbing hold of his sparring partner's lapels, he began shouting at him again. "Press charges! You little piece of shit... I should rip your fucking head off!" Lanky grabbed hold of him and wrestled him to one side as the drunk made a lunge at Robin now that his tormentor was safely restrained. The second officer immediately cuffed the lad and pushed him against the railings. Meanwhile, Robin was getting the same wrist treatment from the other plod.

"Right then, you pair of goons... enough warnings! You can have a trip to Southend Nick!" one of the officers stated.

Despite Robin's pleas, the officers would not relent. A couple of the more disgusted neighbours had now stepped forward and offered to give witness accounts. Vans were summoned and the two fighters were soon tucked safely on board, heading for the Station to get processed.

Both men were taken straight to interview rooms and subjected to a thorough cross examination by the keen 'Peelers'. Soon tempers had eased, and they were sent through individually to have their DNA samples recorded. The amorous drinker took his Caution with a pinch of salt, happy to be able to boast of his latest accolade. Robin sat outside the room and listened intently to the performance given by his adversary. He was desperate to avoid a swab being taken and began to make all sorts of pleas and excuses. The louder he protested, the more determined Lanky was to have him processed. The cycle cop duo led him into the room and plonked him down opposite the Custody Officer, Sergeant McEwan.

"Sergeant McEwan will take over from here, Fella! If

you have any further questions, please direct them to him." And the pair left Robin to stew with Sergeant Macca.

"Look, is this really necessary? I mean, it was only a little fracas in the street. Surely you can see this is all a bit OTT?" Robin tried to shrug off the incident with a smile.

"Sorry, Sir! Standard procedure now, Sir. Could you please sign this form to acknowledge acceptance that we will be taking a DNA sample, and that it will be held on record."

"Do I have to?" bleated Robin.

"In the light of your behaviour tonight, Mr Bradford, I should consider yourself very lucky. The quicker you sign it, the quicker we can get you out of here!" This warning shot was sufficient to silence him: he was desperate to get out of the Station.

As Sergeant Macca led him out of the room and into the foyer, Semple and Ward happened to be passing. Robin saw PC Semple first and recognised him from Flitch Crescent, instantly looking down and away. He made his discomfort obvious, though, attracting the policeman's attention. PC Semple looked at Robin Bradford, and then did a double take as he and WPC Ward rounded the corner of the corridor.

"I am sure I know him from somewhere!"

"From where?"

"Not sure, but I've seen him recently on one of our jobs. Can't place him at the moment, though."

Sergeant Macca handed Robin Bradford an information leaflet on DNA sampling and invited him to sit in the chair. He placed two small containers on the

counter behind a makeshift screen and removed their lids; from the desk drawer he took out two large sealed packets, containing what looked like large cotton wool buds. As he opened the first he addressed Robin.
"Have you ever had this done before, Sir?"
Robin shook his head to indicate a negative reply.
"It's a simple, harmless, and of course painless process, which you are legally obliged to undergo. I shall take two samples with these," showing him the spatula type swabs as he spoke, "and place the contents on the surface of these dishes. They will then be sent off for analysis, and be kept on your file for future reference."
Robin's heart sank. Surely this wasn't happening to him!
"The swab is rubbed on your cheek where it collects saliva..." The sergeant put on a pair of latex gloves as he went through the spiel, and motioned to Robin to open his mouth. Having stroked the swab back and forth across his gums, he rubbed the contents onto the dish's shiny surface. Sealing it carefully shut, he then repeated the process, and finally he tagged both pots.
"That's it, Sir! Take these with you, Sir - you may find them helpful!" As he rose to escort Robin from the building he handed him a couple of leaflets, one on Victim Support, the other on Anger Management.
Lizzie had been waiting patiently in the lobby, but far from being supportive she gave him a barrage of verbal abuse and stormed out, leaving him dumbstruck in her wake. He followed on behind her like a naughty child, double-stepping to try and keep up.

CHAPTER 13

STRESS RELIEF

Rather than shy away from the obvious links with two dead prostitutes, Robin Bradford decided he would shelve all his calls for the day and indulge in a little stress management course of his own. It would undoubtedly involve him cavorting naked with a hired hand. With Lizzie forecast to be on Canvey all afternoon, he thought a bit of 'home help' might be in order. Perusing the back pages of a free paper, he found just what the doctor ordered.

'Estelle's Ebony Delights'

No-Holds-Barred Adult Fun. Tie and Tease a Speciality

Visit us- Visit U

Generous Recession Bust - ing Rates!

Robin was suitably impressed with the allusion to big breasts, and particularly with the reference to cheap rates: all this debauchery was hitting his pocket hard. That wasn't the only thing hard in his pocket now ei-

ther. With all the tension from the morning's charades, he needed a sexual de-stress. Preferably followed by a good hard fucking session, he thought! He sat in his car pondering whether or not to risk bringing a brass back to his house. After all, this wasn't just your average take-away he was contemplating! His decision to go ahead was either very brave or very stupid. At his wit's end with Lizzie, he couldn't care less whether he was caught or not now; she would either have to put out, or shut up if he got it elsewhere - her choice. The familiar scrabbling under the seat soon produced his trusty mobile phone, ready for use. Pausing briefly, he made the bold step, and dialled Estelle's number.
'If I get her round for about two, I'll have about an hour with her, easy. Then that'll give me an hour or so to chill out before Lizzie was due home from being a different sort of scrubber!"
"We are sorry, but the person you are calling does not accept withheld numbers." The automated voice encouraged the caller to hang up and try again.
"Damn...damn!" He touched the phone to his forehead and paused. He'd had his heart set on a visit from the busty black Estelle, she sounded so alluring. Robin assured himself that he would be safe calling from his 'pay as you go' phone; it was virtually untraceable. With this thought for comfort, he re-dialled.
"Hello! Estelle's." Like all prostitutes that tout for business, she was cagey with her calls. Holding back and allowing the man to solicit her avoided entrapment by the local Fuzz.
"Hi! It's Mr ... Smith. Would you be available for a home visit this afternoon?"

"Yes, I'm free all afternoon! What time are you thinking of?" She had a very sexy phone voice and used it to the max.

"Could you come to Leigh-on-Sea for one forty-five? I would quite like an hour-long appointment, so how much would I be looking at?"

"I can make it for then, no problem. And I would be looking for a hundred pounds for the hour -providing you are not after any special services!"

Robin thought hard before he accepted her terms, as Lizzie's possible return was playing on his mind. As for 'specials', they had got him into enough trouble as it was! So he decided to opt for a good old straightforward 'rutting' session with the lovely top-heavy hooker.

"Definitely not after anything out of the ordinary, Darling!"

"If you would be kind enough to give me your address please, I will book you in."

"Of course!" He gave over his home address with a pang of guilt and regret, which was very quickly nullified by erotic thoughts of his pending encounter. Just as he was about to delete her details from his mobile, his work phone rang unexpectedly. He switched the other one off and threw it hastily back under the seat, as if the other caller could see him and his deceit.

'Incoming Call... Lizzie Mob' the screen read. "Bollocks! What does she want?" Cursing aloud, he stretched out his hand to take the new call. Completely changing his tone, he answered passively, amenable to whatever her wishes might be. "Hi, Hunni! What can I do for you?"

"Can you go to the supermarket and get some stuff for tea before I get home? I thought we could have a cosy night in with one of my home-made lasagnes."
"Oh, for Christ's sake, Lizzie! That's a bit much to ask, actually!"
"Why? You told me you'd cancelled all your appointments and were going to veg out at home!"
"I just wanted to relax here - hide away for a bit. The last thing I want to be doing is traipsing round the bloody shops!"
"Oh please, Robin! I really wanted to make a special effort for you... I think it's important we spend some quality time snuggled up in front of the TV with a nice home-cooked meal."
Very far from impressed, Robin made it blatantly obvious he was displeased. But to shut her up, he reluctantly agreed. Doing the maths in his head as he spoke, he realised his shower and freshening up slot had just gone out the window.
"Look, I can hear in your voice you don't want to go, so I'll leave work early and go myself. Or we can just eat later than normal. I'll touch base with you later."
"I said I will go, didn't I!" But it was too late; the dejected Lizzie had hung up on him. He slammed the phone down on passenger seat. 'Fuck you, you fucking go then!' He snarled to himself.

***

Robin vented his frustration at Lizzie's interference by banging his arms on the dashboard. Grabbing his keys from the ignition, he stormed out of the car and headed to his front door. He took his jacket and tie off whilst looking himself up and down in the hall mirror. What had he become! Why couldn't Lizzie just be a proper lover to him! Then he wouldn't need to satisfy his lust elsewhere. Covering the matrimonial bed with a picnic blanket pricked his conscience just a little, but he never batted an eyelid when he placed the lotion, oil and condoms on the bedside table. He glanced back to admire his handiwork, only to see Lizzie staring right back at him; he swiftly laid the photo frame flat. Busty Estelle certainly wouldn't be bothered by his infidelity, but he shuddered slightly, momentarily uneasy at his betrayal.

One forty-five came and went as Bradford paced the lounge, occasionally parting the curtains to peek out at the street. Just before two o'clock a black sports Mercedes with its top down cruised towards the house with a black woman in sunglasses at the wheel. She was the epitome of cool and class in her expensive car and designer clothes: business must have been good. She parked up right outside, which made him curse. He watched the car roof glide slowly back into place, and then saw her step confidently out of the Mercedes. Pushing her glasses up onto her head, she scanned the road looking for his house. Robin felt his excitement build as she strode towards the door. She wore a short, tight, low-cut red dress, which barely covered her huge breasts. She looked like she would topple over as they double bounced towards him. Her thick black belt defined her hips and gave her a perfect hourglass figure. A black pearl necklace matched neatly with the belt, calf length boots and chunky earrings. Estelle's hair was slick and tight, similar to how Lizzie wore hers.

Robin shot through the hallway to the front door and flung it open before she could even knock. "Come in quick... before anyone sees you!" He let her pass him, and then surveyed the street to make sure no-one had seen her enter. Shutting the door, he directed her straight upstairs. Allowing her to go first gave him the chance to perv over her shapely arse, and he could tell from the lie of the thin material that she wore no underwear at all. He liked what he saw and was looking forward to enjoying this ebony beauty's ample charms.

"Make yourself comfortable!" he said, gesturing towards the bed. "Would you like a drink or anything before we start?"

"Could I trouble you for some water, My Love? It's awfully hot in here." Duly obliging, Robin went down to the kitchen.

When he returned, Estelle stood before him stark naked. Her voluptuous body glistened in the half-light that crept between the drawn curtains. "Wow!" Robin nearly spilled her water. He had expected a little more pomp and ceremony to the disrobing, but was suitably pleased.

"Would you like to get your hands on these babies?" She asked as she seductively caressed her massive black breasts.

"Oh, yes please!"

"Then you better be a good, patient gentleman for me. Now lie down on the bed and take them boxers off. Face down - that's it!"

Robin lay flat on the bed with his neck twisted to watch Estelle as she rubbed his lotion into her palms. As she knelt by his side, he could feel the warmth of her body pressing at his thighs. Estelle leaned across his back and began sensuously massaging his shoulders, moaning as she teased down his spine towards his buttocks. All the while he could feel her hard nipples dragging along his flesh as she stooped over him.

"Oh, that's good, Estelle! I need this sooo much!"

"You're tense, Mr Smith. We'll soon work that off you, now won't we!

"Mmm!" was all he could manage as she ran her hands back up his flanks towards his strong arms.

***

Lizzie unlocked the first caravan on her list and returned to the Corsa's boot to retrieve some more cleaning equipment and chemicals. Her mind couldn't escape from Robin's earlier selfishness.

"Fuck it!" Slamming the boot down and re-locking the caravan she got back in her car intent on heading home.

"If he can't be bothered, I'll bloody well go myself! Quick change of clothes at home and some fresh lippy first, bound to see someone I know and I don't want to look like Mrs fucking Mop!"

The winter residents watched her stropping and cursing as she left the park. Clasping her phone to her ear, she dialled Robin's number repeatedly but without luck. Robin's phone sat silently illuminating on the dresser adjacent to his naked frolic.

***

Robin turned over and Estelle placed her firm black breasts around his rampant tool. Squeezing more lotion in the crevice between her tits, she slowly eased them up and down along the length of his cock.

"Oooh that's nice, Mr Smith! You like?"

"Damn right!"

"You want to fuck me now?"

"Yes, I do!"

None of the aggression that Anja and Helena had suffered surfaced during his wild ride with Estelle. This time, a mellow Robin Bradford was quite literally lying back enjoying his sensual wanking.

"Can we go without a condom... please?"

"It will cost you an extra fifty."

"Fine, fine! Just do it."

"Go for it Angel!"

Estelle brushed her hard nipples past his lips and straddled his eager phallus. "Oooh! You're a big boy, Mr Smith, big in my tight pink lips!"

"Mmm! Come on, Baby... fuck me hard now!"

***

Lizzie closed in on Leigh, momentarily being held up at the lights just a few streets away. Trying Robin's phone again, she left him a message this time.

"Pick up the phone, you grumpy sod! Call me back as soon as you get this. I'm going to the supermarket myself, so you don't have to worry."

***

Estelle's buttocks slapped hard on Robin's legs and she bucked her head wildly, moaning loudly for effect. Grasping her large brown tits, Robin grunted as he spurted his hot semen deep inside her warm 'money box'.

"Oh, My God! That feels so fucking good!"
"You like Estelle then, Mr Smith?"
"God, yes! You're so hot!"
Estelle gleaned as many compliments as she could while she cleaned herself down, getting her clothes together when Robin went into the en-suite. With his penis in the basin, he began to wash himself with Lizzie's flannel. Smiling broadly he thought, "that'll teach the frigid cow!"
Back in the bedroom, Robin fanned out Estelle's money on the bed. Cupping her buttocks he pecked her warmly on the cheek.
"See you again soon, I hope."
"Yes, Mr Smith, very soon! You are a good generous man." Slinking her way out of the bedroom, Estelle headed for the front door. Robin made her wait as he checked left and right: nothing but a skip lorry.
"Go on Girl, you're safe to go... go on, look lively!"
She paused for a second in the hallway to kiss him on the cheek, before darting out to her car and easing off down the street.

***

Around an hour later Lizzie came sauntering in looking pale and distracted. Robin picked up on her mood straight away, and assumed it was because he hadn't offered to get the supplies that now hung from her hands in carrier bags. Closing in for a forgiving cuddle, Robin was greeted by a familiar perfume, but not one of Lizzie's fragrances. His senses acknowledged it, but try as he might, he couldn't place it. Lizzie half-heartedly received his embrace before scuttling off to shower. He followed her to the bedroom full of remorseful chatter, but she remained impervious to his attempts at conversation.

When she was safely in the steaming shower, Robin retrieved his mobile from the bedside and saw all the missed calls Lizzie had made during his sordid liaison with Estelle. He rang through to his Voicemail to retrieve her message, and became instantly concerned when he realised that Lizzie should have shown up almost an hour or so before she had.

'Still, fucking good job she didn't get home earlier, or she'd have been even more pissed off!' he thought.

CHAPTER 14

BACK TRACKING
A couple of weeks earlier.

Lizzie stormed out of her house clutching Robin's keys and her gym bag, conscious of the hour ebbing away. She lurched out of his parking space and zigzagged down the road, trying to steer the car with one hand and prime the sat nav with the other.

"Add new route. Bollocks! Where's the bloody paper?" Pulling over to the kerbside and rummaging in her handbag, she found the crumpled note bearing the address and started to navigate the sat nav menu. As she pressed the button to 'add a new route', it put her onto a screen to enter the new details. Staring back at her was the last entry that Robin had made, accompanied by the distance and expected arrival time. This revelation was a complete contrast to Robin's account from earlier that evening.

"Lying bastard! He said he was in Westcliff!" she exclaimed. She surmised that her already unfaithful boyfriend had been up to his old tricks again. She changed her plans instantly, heading now in the direction of Peldon Flats with the dulcet tones of her onboard hostess guiding the way. Then she rang Maria.

"Maria, Luvvy, I'm so sorry but I'll have to cancel tonight. An emergency's come up at the Park, and I have to go sort it, Babe."

"OK Liz, no worries! I'm shattered anyway. I'll catch up on the Soaps instead. We can always go next week."

"Definitely. Catch up tomorrow!"

"Bye!"

Shortly after hanging up, Lizzie reached her destination and reversed her car into a bay at the far end of the dark, shadowy car park where she could see door number 34. She waited patiently for about ten minutes, all the time stewing over Robin's infidelity. After a while she pulled the hood of her top over her head, stepped from the car into the chill of Peldon's courtyard and made her way across the open expanse of paving to the stairwell. When she pressed the bell of Number 34 her heart was pounding so hard she thought it would come right out. Eventually, Katya came to the door and eased it open against the security chain. As soon as she saw the pretty blonde, she knew Robin had reverted to his promiscuous ways again. She thought quickly and delivered her alibi.

"Help me, please! There's a strange man chasing me!"

Lizzie's apparent distress easily fooled the gullible Polish brass.

"You come in quick, and I shut door! You be safe here... we call police, yes?"

Lizzie looked Katya up and down distastefully, her facial expression beginning to change; no longer the victim she had professed to be seconds earlier. "Who are you? Why has my boyfriend been visiting here? My God! I get it...you're a fucking tom! If it ain't bad enough the bastard is cheating, he's paying a fucking slut with money we ain't got! You cheap, nasty little whore!" Within an instant, Lizzie had become a wild raging animal. Katya, dumbfounded and trapped, was understandably terrified. She bolted for the kitchen, and grabbing a bread knife from the worktop she brandished it at Lizzie with intent.

"Pierdol się! Fuck you, Lady! Go from my house, I not do wrong. Go, or I cut your throat for you!" Waving the blade under Lizzie's nose did the trick. She backed away towards the door, still spitting venom. Katya, now full of confidence, edged her closer to the front exit.

With her back to the front door and nowhere else to turn, now it was Lizzie who was trapped. She gasped loudly as the seriousness of her predicament hit home. Reaching to her side she grabbed a large umbrella with her left hand and swung it violently towards her assailant. She struck Katya on the arm with enormous force, causing her to drop the knife to the floor. Katya screamed in agony, turning to flee as Lizzie struck out again, the blow glancing off her temple. Stumbling slightly, she regained her feet and shot into the bedroom, desperately trying to wedge the door shut with her body. Lizzie grabbed the knife from the floor, ran the full length of the hallway and hurled herself at the door, catapulting Katya backwards. The Polish girl fell

by the bedside and lay groaning with her arm buckled under her back. Towering over her, totally out of her mind, Lizzie hacked and thrust until at last her rival fell silent. Sitting on Katya's legs, she wiped the blood from her face then, blinded by rage, stood up again, plunged the knife into Katya's stomach with both hands and sawed her way downwards. The blood and guts spilled from her like nothing Lizzie had ever seen, and she was instantly awash with guilt and nausea.
"What the fuck have I done?" she gasped, as the severity of her actions began to sink in. But then she looked at Katya, dressed like a tart, and was consumed by hatred and fury. She attacked the very place that had been the source of so much anguish - her vagina. Forcing the knife in right up to the hilt, all Lizzie felt was relief that her rival was no more. She rose to her feet victorious, the object of her brutal assault slain at her feet. Stepping over Katya's lifeless body, she slipped on the blood-soaked floor, bracing herself against the wall as she struggled to keep upright. The urge to be sick surfaced again, so she ran for the bathroom and leant over the sink, desperately trying not to vomit. Then the overwhelming desire to abscond took hold, so she fled the flat and skulked off into the night, guilt-ridden but joyous.

***

After removing her blood-soaked hooded top, Lizzie drove at speed back to Canvey, knowing the Camp was the only place she could clean herself up without question or hindrance. On arriving at the Caravan Park, she saw Benny the Security Guard locking up his office ready to tour the site on his hourly inspection. She called to him as he turned to walk clear of her car. "Benny! Could you leave the office open, Mate? I left my phone in one of the vans. I'll shut it when I leave, Hun!"

He duly obliged. "I'll see you tomorrow night, my little darling!" With that he was off, whistling his way into the night.

Lizzie parked inches from the steps of a caravan well away from any prying winter residents. Darting up to the door, she unlocked the van and then pulled the door tightly closed behind her. This was the first time she had properly drawn breath since massacring Katya's young body. She looked wildly around, drew all the curtains and switched the lights on. Tears formed in her eyes and her breathing quickened as she re-lived the horror of her actions. Every time she shut her eyes Katya lay there, lifeless and mutilated. She held out her hands, the blood still fresh under her nails, and wept.

After removing all her clothes, Lizzie showered in piping hot water. But no matter how hard she scrubbed, she would never be clean of the blood she had spilled that night. It would stain her soul, haunt her sleep and ravage her dreams. The smell of death hung in her nostrils. She re-dressed and stuffed her tracksuit in a black bag, hiding it under the lounge seat and planning to take it to the incinerator the next day when the coast was clear. She locked the caravan and headed back to Benny's office. He was still out on his round, so she took the keys for the Lost Property cupboard and went in search of some clothes. All she could find was a grubby tracksuit, which most certainly was not her usual choice of colour or style, but in her situation anything would do. She daren't risk going home before Robin went to bed: she was far too stressed to deal with him now. She wouldn't be able to hide her guilt or anguish, so it was best she waited for him to go sleep before re-entering the house. Lizzie parked near Hadleigh Castle, whiling away her time watching the dog walkers and courting couples disappear into the night. She tried desperately to compose herself, to gather her thoughts and work out what to do next.

At around eleven thirty her phone rang, startling her out of a brief sleep. It was Robin, presumably trying to hunt her down before he turned in. She pressed the key to silence the ringing and stared intently at the screen until it eventually stopped drumming and the light went out. True to form, a few minutes later a text landed from Robin saying good night. She knew that within half an hour he'd be sound asleep, snoring grunting and passing wind like he always did. Soon she would be able to sneak back in and try to sleep herself.

CHAPTER 15

A LITTLE TIED UP!

The days and nights blurred into one for Lizzie as she became more and more introverted, struggling to come to terms with her own vile actions. Haggard and heavy-eyed, only copious amounts of caffeine helped blot out the images of hideous carnage that dominated her dreams. Every time she tried to sleep it ended the same. She would relive the butchery at Peldon Flats and then wake with a jolt: even Robin commented on her sleep patterns, saying that she was nearly as bad as he was. She just could not shake off the memory of what she had done - or what Robin had done either. Their relationship was at an all-time low, his infidelity impacting on both of them. The only thing that kept Lizzie together was the anger that rampaged through every waking moment. The thought of Robin mauling his slut ripped her to the core. If she wasn't thinking of Katya lying dead in her flat, she was thinking of Robin and his sordid secrets. She was on his back like a rash, and he had no idea why. She checked his every move, poring over his phone records, scrutinising his computer history and occasionally following him when she could. She knew that sooner or later he would indulge again, and she intended to catch him red-handed.

When he came down that fateful afternoon after his post coital shower, Lizzie was seated at the computer. Robin naively thought she was catching up with idle chat on one of her countless social networking sites. She wasn't: she was searching the computer's cookies and caches for signs of his sexual activities. Her understanding of computers was leaps ahead of his, and she used it to her advantage, spying on her blissfully ignorant boyfriend. Before Robin came down she had discovered a wealth of porn sites and chat rooms that he had visited. Then she stumbled on it - Mistress Helena and her dark dungeons. She was scribbling down the contact details just as he wandered downstairs.

Lizzie swiped his keys again, and then made her excuses to leave the house. She rang the mobile number from the car but no one answered. Helena was already indisposed: she was still tied up in her own dungeon. Employing the same tactics as before she searched through the sat nav's last entry and found it large as life - 13A Flitch Crescent! Lizzie was no mug and had already been right through the landline and mobile's menus. Finding nothing, she'd guessed Robin must have another phone somewhere. The only hiding place he had left was his car, which would also explain why he had become so protective of it lately. She parked up about two roads away from their house and conducted a detailed search. The boot produced porn and contact magazines hidden in the spare- wheel compartment, as well as condoms and wipes. There was even a bag with women's underwear in it, which she assumed he either wore himself, or had purloined on his travels.

"The fucking smutty pervert! Wait till I get my hands on you, Arsehole!"

Venturing back to the front of the car, she knelt down on the pavement and leant in, blindly swiping her hand under the seats. Amongst the litter and coke cans she found his much prized mobile. She put it on the passenger seat and carried on scouring the vehicle. There seemed to be nothing more to be found, so she plonked herself back in the driver's seat and shut the door ready to start checking his Call Register. As the door banged shut she heard the rattle of metal in the door pocket and switched the interior light on. Squinting in the dim light, she caught faint glimmers of shiny metal winking back at her from the pocket. Her fingers met with a key-ring and she swiftly plucked it from its hiding place. The bondage-clad bear and the chrome letter both pointed to Mistress Helena, but why would Robin have the keys to her house or flat? There was only one way Lizzie could get answers for the countless questions that plagued her, and that was to ask Helena herself by paying her a visit. She began looking through Robin's phone calls and texts, but the evidence against him was so overwhelming that she soon gave up.

Her temper now at fever pitch and her heart palpitating faster than ever before, Lizzie called in sick at the Caravan Park. With her diary free, she could follow the trail to Helena's house. The sat nav hostess guided her along the front, past the pier and up into York road. The journey to Flitch Crescent was harrowing for Lizzie, and she struggled to contain her emotions. From time to time tears graced her cheeks, but more often than not profanities stole the day. She gripped the steering wheel so tight that the veins in her hand stood out like purple road maps.

She pulled up abruptly just past Helena's steps, sending Jonathan Pettigrew's dustbin flying. With so much weighing on her mind, her concentration was lost. She pulled her hood tight across her face and waited till the next-door curtains stopped twitching: Jonathan Pettigrew had given the car and its occupant only a cursory glance before going back to his documentary. When Lizzie was sure the coast was clear she sprinted from the car, clutching Helena's keys, and disappeared down the basement steps. She knocked and waited, but nobody came. She knocked again before tentatively trying the key in the lock. The key inched its way into the barrel and then eased the latch to one side as Lizzie applied a steady pressure to the tab. The door creaked open slowly, and she stood nervously on the threshold. Somewhere inside she could just make out what sounded like faint cries of distress, and her anger turned to fear as she worked her way down the hall to where a chink of light penetrated the darkness of the hallway. She pushed the door open in front of her and was met by the dimly lit dungeon. She could see Helena tied up over a bench in the corner and edged cautiously towards her.

"Please help me! Please, I beg you!"

"My God, what's happened to you? Who tied you up?"

Shocked, Lizzie was distracted from her mission, her anger temporarily quelled.

"A client, he...hit me! Things got out of hand. Help me, please! I have been here for hours."

Weak and pitiful, Helena snivelled and wept. Her words were barely comprehensible. She had no idea who her visitor was, nor did she care. Clueless as to this stranger's connection with her captor, she was just elated that a saviour had heard her desperate cries for help and come to set her free.

"This man, what did he look like?" Lizzie started to remember why she had come calling. The anger began to surface again as she realised this was probably another of her lover's 'bed post notches'.

"Vat!" exclaimed Helena. "Vy ze hell does zat matter? Just set me free - PLEASE! I really need to go to hospital. Vill you call ze police for me?" she begged.

Lizzie stepped a bit closer to Robin's victim and posed the question again, this time with much more conviction and menace. Helena cringed back in panic, tugging at her chains, trying to get away from Lizzie's overbearing inquisition.

"I'll ask you one last time! Who the fuck was your client and what did he look like?" Lizzie snarled.

"I don't know! He just booked me today, I have never seen him before... Smith! Zat's it, Mr Smith!"

"Smith! You thick bitch! Every other punter must be Mr Smith!" Lizzie was spitting as she spoke, exasperated by Helena's ignorance.

"I don't know! Zat is all he told me, honest!" Helena screamed back at Lizzie now, frustrated and frightened. "Please, just help me!" she begged.

Picking up the wooden phallus that Robin had used earlier, Lizzie threatened Helena with it. "You will tell me, or I'll smash your fucking head in! WHAT did he look like?" She showed her intention by smashing the phallus into the bench by Helena's head. Lizzie had long since lost all sense of reason: all she saw in front of her was the whore who had committed the cardinal sin of shagging her boyfriend. Shaking with distress, Helena described her last client to Lizzie, praying for compassion.

"Enough! I get the fucking idea! That fucking..!" A bone-crunching thud followed, "man, is my..." and then again Lizzie drove the wooden cosh hard into Helena's skull, "... fucking boyfriend!"

The eerie sound of timber striking flesh and bone echoed around the chambers as Lizzie lost control. The blows continued to rain down on Helena, who was unable to even raise a hand to her face for protection.

Helena buckled forward and slumped face down on the bench. Lizzie struck out repeatedly until she was convinced the whore was unconscious, then she dropped the wooden cock on the bench and headed off in search of a knife. Her now ritualistic desire to mutilate her victim's body with slashes needed to be quenched. This time her work would be more symbolic and crafted, not haphazard and random like Katya's slaughter. On the kitchen worktop lay a large serrated bread knife, still bearing crumbs from the bread it had sliced earlier that day. Lizzie wiped it across some kitchen roll and studied the sparkling blade with a maniacal grin, then returned to the victim to carve her mark once again. Sitting astride the body, she began her demented chant. 'He loves me... he loves me not!" With each line of the verse she would drag the knife mercilessly through Helena's soft pink flesh, watching as the blood filled the cuts and wept over the skin. Inching her way down the body, slicing, carving, Lizzie stared straight through Helena in a semi hypnotic state. She plunged the knife into her chest and dragged violently down towards her midriff, laying her stomach open with all her guts on show. She grabbed a handful of intestines and let them spill through her fingers like seaweed on a sunny beach. Then she laughed hysterically for a minute or so, squelching the tubes between her fingers and thumbs. "Do you think my Robin would like to fuck you now, my pretty little whore?" She spun through a wealth of different emotions: hatred for Helena, contempt for Robin and elation at her triumphant defeat of yet another of her so-called boyfriend's conquests.

After a while, some sense of reality began to surface in Lizzie's mind. Regaining her composure, she went back to the front door, chained and then bolted it. She needed time to clean away every trace of her visit. Washing her hands in the kitchen sink first, she peeled off all her outer clothing and footwear and put it in a bin bag. Then she set the bag down in the hallway and headed for the shower. Spending an eternity under the hot steamy water, she scrubbed all the blood and brutality from her fresh pale skin. Stepping from the shower onto a towel, Lizzie cleaned the walls meticulously and pulled a large wad of matted hair from the waste guard. She put the hair, guard and towels in another bag ready for disposal, and then flooded the shower tray with bleach.

Searching through Helena's flat, Lizzie was unable at first to find some clothing to cover her modesty. Then ambling round the flat swamped in one of Helena's tracksuit combo's, she blitzed, bleached and cleaned every surface and corner that might bear testament to her presence. With everything else done, she heaved the swollen black sacks out of the flat - forgetting to close the front door in her rush to get to Robin's car - and promptly snagged one of them on the hand-brake, sending its contents tumbling into the passenger seat. "Bollocks!" Pushing the various garments into the passenger foot well, she fired up Robin's jalopy and drove off into the night.

***

In under an hour Lizzie was back on Canvey and winding her way through the caravan park yet again. She sat shivering on the lounge seat, knees brought up to her chest, drinking tea. She spent over an hour deep in thought, pondering the events in 13A's basement and trying to convince herself that her actions had been justifiable. Before she left the camp she bundled all the clothes and sacks into the site incinerator behind Billy's office, watching as the flames licked and danced around the last traces of Helena's existence. Then she made her way back to Leigh-on-Sea.

Wandering through the hallway of her house she entered the bedroom. The silence was broken only by Robin's deep, rumbling snores, battering her eardrums. Lizzie stripped and lay on the bed next to him. Her anger flaring again, she raised a pillow to Robin's unconscious body. Clutching it tightly in both hands, inches from his face, she contemplated suffocating the dribbling, snoring oaf that had ruined her every waking moment. In seconds she could rid herself of this demon - snuff out his life - and her alter ego was urging her on with a deafening voice.

'Do it Girl, do it! Suffocate the lying bastard!'

CHAPTER 16

ESTELLE

Lizzie swung into their road and halted abruptly as the driver of the skip lorry jumped from his cab, walked to the side of his vehicle and started to unload the skip off the back. He turned to look at Lizzie and smiled, knowing he was holding her up.

"Hurry up, will you!" Lizzie shouted her annoyance.

"Quick as I can, Love!" he answered with a dopey smile.

"Cut out the 'love' crap, and just get moving!" Arsehole! She muttered under her breath.

The skip driver just loved the impatient Lizzies of this world. Taking his time whilst perfecting the art of looking busy, he clambered back and forth, netting and chaining. Then at last he climbed into his cab and pulled away from the driveway with a grin, tooting and blowing Lizzie a kiss. "Pillock!" she said, and then smiled at his audacity. But as his lorry swept round the front of her car she saw Estelle turn and kiss

Robin on the cheek. Then he quickly shut the door and went back inside. Lizzie stayed motionless, watching the leggy black tart climb elegantly back into her fancy black sports car. "What the fuck!" she exclaimed as she watched her pull away. Suddenly consumed by rage, she put her own car into gear and began to follow. "Let's see where you go, Bitch!" Shelving her plans to change clothes and get food in, Lizzie pulled out after her and the pursuit was on.

Estelle drove out onto the London road and headed for Southend, with the very irate Lizzie hot on her heels. After what seemed like an eternity, Estelle turned onto the main drag and pulled up into the car park of a large new apartment block near the Sea Front. After walking away from her car, Estelle clicked the alarm into life and entered the foyer. Lizzie parked beside her and bolted for the door, seconds behind her.

Just as Estelle was about to let the security door go she saw Lizzie approach her. "Sorry, Love! Here you go!" and she unwittingly held the door for her pursuer, allowing her free access.

"Cheers!" Lizzie managed a stifled thanks and followed Estelle to the lift. As she stepped in behind her, Estelle pressed Floor Three and waited.

"Sorry, Love! What floor?"

"Erm, Three, please!" she replied promptly, having already seen Estelle's choice.

"Oh, that's my floor too! Are you new here?" asked Estelle with a smile, "I haven't seen you before."

"No - just visiting." Lizzie's terse replies were enough for Estelle to realise that conversation wasn't on the agenda with her fellow lift passenger.

"Third Floor!" The tinned voice of the lift announced their arrival. "Doors opening!"

Estelle swanked out of the lift and went straight to her door. Lizzie cautiously followed, looking around aimlessly, as if lost. Estelle wasn't about to offer any more help to the mardy stranger, so just put her key in the door, clicked it open and pushed. Right at that second Lizzie hit her across the back of the head with a fire extinguisher and quickly followed her falling body through the doorway. Swiping the keys from the lock, she sat on top of Estelle and pulled her head up off the ground by her hair. "Who... the...fuck...are...you?" bashing Estelle's pretty head back down on the floor with each word as if to enforce her authority and desire for answers.

"Stop, please! You're hurting me!"

"Not... until...you ...tell...me!" Again thrashing her head downwards.

"Estelle, I am Estelle! Stop it, I'm bleeding! Please stop!" Estelle begged.

"What was you doing at my house, you slut!" Lizzie's spindly frame summoned enormous strength to subdue the much larger black prostitute, adrenalin coursing through her like electric energy.

"He paid me. I'm an escort - it's just a job. I'm sorry!" Estelle knew she wasn't a match for Lizzie's determined assault and offered no resistance, hoping that the other woman's pity and her own honesty would save her from the onslaught.

"How many fucking times?" Lizzie's saliva was flying everywhere as she completely lost control, clawing and swiping at Estelle like an animal. "How many? Get up, you cheap, nasty whore! Get up!" Estelle rose unsteadily to her feet. "Get in the Lounge!" Lizzie demanded. Holding her head, the black girl tentatively moved through to her lounge. "Take your clothes off, I want to see what makes my man so fucking horny." Lizzie spat the words out.

"No! Get stuffed, I ain't doing that."

"Why? Coz I haven't paid you? Is that it? Do you only get your kit off for money?" and Lizzie left the room. Estelle cautiously followed her out into the hallway hoping to retrieve her handbag, which had fallen from her shoulder when Lizzie struck her with the extinguisher. She bent down, opened it quickly and grasped her mobile phone, sighing with relief - just as Lizzie emerged from the kitchen. Estelle had already flipped it open and started to dial, but as her finger hit the second consecutive '9' she felt a burning sensation in her wrist. Her fingers went cold and unresponsive as the phone fell from her grasp. She tried to grab at it again but her hand wouldn't move, and the phone hit the floor and smashed into pieces, with the battery and back case scattered across the tiled surface. She saw the blood gushing from her wrist and spun quickly to see Lizzie's haunting grimace as she stood over her with a large kitchen knife. Holding it aloft; she began taunting Estelle.

"Have you got a 'hands' fucking free', Bitch!"

Any chance of Estelle calling for help had gone. "Oh, My God! What have you done to me? It's just a job... for Christ sake!"

"Tough! You'll get no pity from me, you cheap little whore! Not one little, tiny morsel." As Lizzie spoke she leant right in close and waved the blade inches from Estelle's face.

Estelle was sobbing uncontrollably, her head smarting and bleeding from the earlier onslaught.

"Now, get into the bedroom and take your clothes off, Tart! I'm going to enjoy your body too, but I don't think you'll like it quite as much as fucking my man."

The weak and dejected call girl protested, then refused to co-operate. Lizzie grabbed her by the hair and literally dragged her kicking and screaming to the bedroom, where she told her to lie on the bed. There was nothing she could do but lie there helpless, pleading with Lizzie, hoping for leniency.

"Please show mercy. It's just business. Just business! I don't know who these men are."

"What? And you think that makes it better! Trust me, it fucking doesn't! Now do as you're told and get your clothes off...NOW!"

Reluctantly Estelle began to remove her clothes, struggling to ease them off with her one good hand. The red dress slipped over her head easily, exposing her full and voluptuous figure, which did nothing but enrage her captor. "Oh, look at you in all your glory! Bet he liked them nice big titties, didn't he! Did he paw all over you, did he?"

"Please don't hurt me anymore! I'm begging you!" She clasped her hands together and winced with pain as the gash to her wrist poured yet more blood, dripping onto her breasts and knees as she prayed for her ordeal to be over. "I have money... you can have it. Take it! Take my car, anything! Please!"

"Lie down on the bed!" Despairingly Estelle complied,

knowing that resistance was futile and that compliance was perhaps her only hope of survival.

“Ooh, look at that sexy black body! All young, curvy and fresh.” Lizzie was now much calmer in her voice and actions, each move cold, calculated and deliberate. “Did he feel you up, grab at you! Grope your nice arse and tits, did he? I bet he did, you’re just his type of girl - you have a pulse! Well at the moment anyway!” Lizzie suddenly struck out at Estelle, driving the knife into her abdomen. Then she jumped on the bed, knelt full-weight on Estelle’ body, and began to slice at her naked torso, carving random lines back and forth. Her spine-chilling laughter echoed through the flat as she exacted her revenge on the helpless hooker. She slashed and swiped, satisfying her blood lust more with every stroke. Estelle started to choke as the blood filled her mouth and nostrils.

“Please...forgive me!” her voice weak and her will fading, the young woman’s eyes rolled back as she prepared herself for death. There would be no forgiveness from Lizzie. Crazed and demented she tore at Estelle’s body. With a final deft swipe she severed the main artery in her victim’s throat, sending blood splashing and bubbling everywhere. When the last wisps of air had drained from her lungs under the weight of Lizzie’s tiny frame, she climbed off the lifeless body and walked to the end of the bed. Parting Estelle’s knees to expose the vagina still tainted by Robin’s semen, Lizzie thrust the knife deep into her. Driving the last part of the handle up with her palm, she stood back to admire her craft: grinning satisfied with her handiwork. Then as a last act of defilement she spat on Estelle’s stomach.

"Fucking bitch! Not so sexy now, are you!"
A moment of panic swept through the murderess as the scene etched itself into her mind. 'Got to get cleaned up,' she thought as she made for the bathroom. She spent ages scrubbing and washing every exposed part of her body before leaving the room, tap still running, washing away her existence from the sink and plug. She knew the forensics boys would be sure to search every inch of Estelle's luxurious apartment seeking out that which was lost - clues! She stopped briefly, just as Robin had done, to look at herself in the hall mirror. Quickly snapping out of her reverie, she went to the kitchen and got together all the cleaning products she could carry. By the time she left that flat there would be no trace of her ever having been there. She was fast and thorough, leaving nothing to chance, even stopping to wipe her spittle from Estelle's body. She grabbed a tea towel from the kitchen, placed the keys on the sideboard and left, wiping the handle as she went. Travelling down in the lift, she stroked the buttons and door with the towel as it ground to a halt. Just as she was about to get into her car, she stopped and had one last look back up at Estelle's flat before driving off. As she drew up to the gates they peeled open in front of her majestically, as if heralding her retreat. Then, with a small puff of blue smoke from the exhaust, Lizzie left the scene of slaughter, justice done.

CHAPTER 17

A GIRL'S MAKE-UP

Like most of us, Lizzie Fenwick had skeletons neatly tucked away in the closets of her mind. Not the usual stolen kisses from a friend's boyfriend, or High School shoplifting secrets: hers were far more sinister. At fourteen Lizzie began her journey into womanhood, and a string of school girl crushes and playground snogs saw her neatly over the threshold into her fifteenth year. The kisses became more intimate now, the gropes and the caressing edged towards more sexually charged encounters, but she remained a virgin.

Lizzie was one of the last in her year to reach sixteen. Sweet Sixteen! Her mum and dad, who had separated years before, lectured and battled to keep her safe from the clutches of the local boys' illicit advances. Her sister had become pregnant at fifteen, leaving a cloud over the family and over her own life. Her education ruined and her prospects bleak, she was left to face a life of chasing benefits and meal tickets. Painfully aware of the dire consequences of a teenage pregnancy, Lizzie vowed never to fall foul of the same trap. Her mum also knew only too well about the perils of raising children alone, and her struggles to find the next dinner, or a fiver for the electric meter were a constant reminder.

Despite always knowing her father's love, Lizzie never saw her father's money. When the marriage failed he turned to drink, and inevitably his world collapsed beyond repair. The first thing to go was his licence, swiftly followed by his job as a carpenter. Regardless of his own failings, Malcolm Fenwick always championed the moral stance, brow-beating Lizzie until her ears felt like they were about to start bleeding. "Don't go down the road I took, Lizzie! You're destined for better things, my girl! Me and your mother made some really bad mistakes when we were young, and you must learn from them!" She listened attentively to his advice: she had no choice. She was always chaperoned to and from parties or gatherings, and any boy who showed an interest was given the third degree by her dad, who usually persuaded them to move on to a softer target.

Lizzie managed to get herself a decently paid job at a care home in nearby Benfleet. Despite the drudgery of working around incontinent pensioners, she loved it. The old girls would fuss and mollycoddle her and the old men would tease her rotten about 'what they would do if they were forty years younger'. She loved the attention, and soon grew into a caring and considerate companion for her favourite residents. The staff at the

'Lazy Daze Care Home' were a good bunch too, sharing jokes and doing everything they could to make the days go quicker and boredom free.

The best of the bunch was Maria, a confident glamour puss who lived solely to attract the men and solicit compliments. She was the complete opposite of Lizzie in every respect. She was sexually active for a start, having a string of young lads and mature men regularly pawing her. She would let the old farts in the care home cop a feel, and always wore provocative and revealing clothing to gain their favour. Her rewards were many and varied, with the naive old codgers buying her presents of makeup, chocolate and jewellery. Lizzie often caught her in compromising positions and would shy away to another room, embarrassed by her outrageous ways. Some of the more generous residents even received a rather exuberant and indulgent bed bath on a regular basis.

Over time, Lizzie and Maria became inseparable, pubbing, clubbing and eventually courting their men side by side. Lizzie was still always yards behind Maria. She would only go as far as heavy petting in the front seat, while Maria would be in the back with her bloke, her knickers round her ankles. Eventually Lizzie relaxed like her counterpart, and consented to full sexual intercourse. Like a lot of late starters, once Lizzie had 'tasted the cake' she couldn't stop eating. Within a year of losing her virginity she had eagerly devoured more than a dozen conquests, and at the tender age of nineteen Lizzie and Maria had earned the dubious nickname of the Margarine Twins. Every male in a ten mile radius of Leigh-on-Sea who wanted a good time and an easy lay would try to date one of the accommodating pair.

Life at Lazy Daze got just as interesting for Lizzie, with Maria egging her on to follow her example. The resulting tips and perks funded their night time exploits and they enjoyed a carefree crack. Like all rollercoaster rides, sooner or later it would have to hit the buffers. That day came in August 1988. The previous care home manager, who had enjoyed the odd perk himself from the girls, had decided to move on to pastures greener. He was immediately replaced by a fifty-something 'Thatcherite' spinster. The only thing she loathed more than men was the harlots surrendering their honour out of wedlock. She clashed with both the girls on her very first shift and they quickly realised the road ahead wasn't going to be smooth. Lizzie knuckled down and got cuter with her conduct, whereas Maria took a head-on course with the new manager. She refused to ease up on her wayward antics, continuing to wrestle with her at every corner. Heated verbal altercations between the cardigan-wearing, slipper-shod matron and the flirty floozy soon became a regular feature of the long day and night shifts.

The final nail in Maria's coffin came late one evening as the sun was disappearing behind the building-dominated skyline. She was just finishing giving Mr Clemence his 'bed bath', taking due care to wash his erect penis very thoroughly, when the old maid burst in, seeking help with a bed wetter. Taking a very dim view of the antics of the cheeky young Maria, she dismissed her on the spot - though not before Maria had relieved the old man of his twenty pound note. "They told me when I started I had to work a week in hand, so what's your problem, Frigid Knickers, you miserable old bag!" She tracked down Lizzie before she left and asked her to go too, but Lizzie brushed her aside, saying she needed her job. Maria slunk off into the night, blowing the old girl a kiss as she watched out of the window.

Lizzie was hauled up before the management committee and warned in the strongest possible terms that 'this misconduct must cease forthwith!' or she would suffer a similar fate to her best friend. Lizzie bit her tongue and bided her time at the now 'Not So Lazy Daze' Care Home, staying for a couple more years before finally moving on.

***

Maria wasn't so fortunate: in fact her life was set to sink to the very bowels of Hell. Like many others in the late eighties, Maria dabbled in recreational drugs, despite her friends' vocal objections. She began a relationship with Lee Codling, one of the local lads loosely connected to their social circle. His reputation as a 'wrong un' had carried far and wide throughout South East Essex, and Lizzie hated him. More to the point, he was a petty dealer: not hard-core, just friends and family - originally born out of the need to get cheaper deals for his own use. He plied Maria with the fruits of his labour, ecstasy, acid tabs and weed. You name it, they took it. Initially Maria only dabbled in the low-grade fixes, but as time passed her need for a bigger buzz outweighed the risks, with the tame weed and pills no longer providing the euphoric highs she sought. The jobless pair began to snort and inject more serious gear, looking for utopian and psychedelic adventures.

Maria and Lee moved into a squat near Southend town centre after about six months together and contact with Lizzie began to peter out. Lizzie hated Maria's new friends, and the rancid flat even more. She knew Maria was slipping into fathomless depths, but was powerless to stop the pitiful decline, and took to visiting the flat only if she knew that Lee was out. She couldn't stand his bravado and 'Great I Am' attitude; worse still she knew he was slowly breaking Maria's spirit with his cocktail of heavy-grade narcotics. Jobless Maria was a shadow of her former self now. Black-circled, sunken eyes and gaunt features transformed the once pretty, cheerful face; her hair was unkempt and bedraggled, her clothes grubby and torn. She wouldn't have looked out of place in a town centre shopping mall selling the Big Issue. Lee enjoyed a modicum of success with his drug dealing empire, but sadly for Maria his proceeds went straight up their noses, or got cooked up and pumped into their veins.

***

Lizzie was nearing the end of yet another grave yard shift at the care home when the reception desk received a call from a pay phone at the end of Maria's street. The caller wasn't known to Lizzie but the message they carried was clear.

"Is that Lizzie Fenwick?"

"Yes, who is this, and how did you get my work number?"

"It don't matter who I am! I'm a friend of Maria's - that's all you need to know. She's in a really bad way, and she's asking for you. You've got to come and help her... please?"

"What's wrong with her? Why are you ringing me?"

"You're the only one who cares enough to save her from that bloke. You better get to the flat before it's too late. It's urgent or I wouldn't have rung!"

The young female sounded genuine - and moreover, desperate. The voice was quickly replaced by the long dial tone that signals the end of a call, and for a moment Lizzie was confused and unsure what to do. With less than fifteen minutes of her shift left, she decided to sneak off early and head up towards Maria's pathetic excuse for a home. Her trusty beige metro flashed through the streets of Hadleigh with only urban foxes and milkmen for company. The drunken revellers had long since gone, leaving their scattered cans, kebab wrappers and pools of sick for the early traders to step over as they raised the shutters.

Lizzie parked as close as she could to Maria's flat and crept towards the door. Several loud knocks later, and all she had managed to achieve were the curses of a middle-aged neighbour, rubbing sleep from his eyes and challenging her parents' existence. Understandably, the residents of this middle class suburb took exception to the waifs and strays that frequented the squat. Pushing her hand through the letter box, Lizzie swept her palm back and forth, probing till her fingers traced the nylon cord. Pulling it up gently and quietly, she prised the key through the flap and placed it in the lock. With a hint of trepidation, she entered the squalor of Maria's humble shack. Clutching her handbag tight to her cherry red leather jacket, she traversed the hallway, anxious not to touch anything and risk staining her clothes from the grimy pit that housed her closest and dearest friend.

As she closed in on Maria and Lee's room, if it could be described as that, she could hear the sound of someone vomiting and then choking on the aftermath. Crossing the last few yards at double speed she ventured in. What she saw was a scene of such squalor and degradation that it would stay with her indefinitely. How could her friend, once the life and soul, and envy of all, have sunk so low in such a short space of time! Maria lay on the festering, piss-soaked mattress with her knees pulled up to her chest in an almost foetal position. She was writhing in agony. Wave after wave of puke gushed from her mouth, drenching the bed and showering the floor. Lizzie gagged just watching the horrid scene; her stomach had never been strong. Maria made eye contact and mouthed, 'Help me', as the next torrent of bile surged outwards again.

Lizzie stepped over the mess and bent down to comfort her friend. "Hospital!" Maria knew the situation was dire, and was pleading with Lizzie to call for help. Next to Maria was her boyfriend Lee, his body convulsed with violent spasms, lifting him right off the sheets. On the table next to him were three syringes, two empty and one filled with a brown, syrupy-looking liquid. Lizzie knew instantly what it was, and what it meant. Lee still had a tourniquet tied tightly round his arm, the bruises and needle marks confirming her worst fears. Unlike Maria, Lee lay on his back, eyes wide open and rolled back in their sockets. The whole room carried the acrid smell of desperation.

Lizzie knew she had to get Maria away from this vile leech; he wouldn't stop until they had both lost all shreds of dignity and hope. She wasn't prepared just to sit back and watch him do that to her best friend. She wanted Maria back to being her familiar confident self, not the hollow shell that Lee had transformed her into. She picked up the remaining syringe in a piece of tissue and stared at it for an eternity: could she; dare she? The veins in Lee's arms stood out, plump and inviting. He was already teetering on the brink of the abyss; it would only take a little nudge for him to plummet to the depths of Hell. Lizzie was convinced the contents of the third syringe would alter the balance of power and release Maria from his clutches.

Touching the needle point to his skin - nervously, cautiously - Lizzie pushed. The skin flexed inward under the pressure at first, taking her by surprise; evidently more force was needed to puncture the outer layer. As if inciting her or giving her a signal, Maria vomited again - violently, full of pain and anguish. Lizzie was more determined than ever now; the psychological deadlock had just been broken. Slowly the tip punctured the flesh of Lee's arm and sank gently along the shiny metal shaft. When the trickle of blood formed around the needle, Lizzie knew she was in. Her thumb pressed firmly on the plunger as the liquid death seeped straight into Lee's body. For a split second his eyes rolled back and engaged with Lizzie's. Like a rabbit in the headlights, he was painfully aware that her actions heralded his departure from this world, but he was powerless to stop her. His body was already paralysed by the first wave; all he could do now was slip away quietly as the poison's inevitable coma drifted over him.

Satisfied that Lee was totally incapacitated, Lizzie cleared Maria's mouth and put her in the recovery position. She kissed her tenderly on the forehead and told her to wait patiently until she got back. "Wait for me, Maria! Don't go, stay with me PLEASE!" Praying for her survival, Lizzie fled to seek help.

In a rundown call box at the end of the road, the panic stricken friend desperately tried to see through her tears to dial 999. Once confident that the Emergency Services were on their way, she returned to the squat. By the time the ambulance crew arrived at Maria's home, Lizzie knew that Lee would have passed well beyond their reach. The double dose of sweet poison had sealed his fate and likewise secured Maria's hopes of rehabilitation.

***

During the weeks and months that followed, Lizzie was never far from Maria's bedside. Her life began to re-emerge and flourish as her friend nursed her through the trials and tribulations of beating her drug addiction. Maria's recovery was not without its hurdles and hiccups, but both remained strong, determined and focused.

At last the day came when the saviour and the saved stood shoulder to shoulder, arm in arm, watching the misty morning fog clinging to the Thames. Neither spoke, both of them basking in the glory of their rekindled relationship. Maria was now deeply indebted to Lizzie, something for which she would always be grateful and always be humble. Once naive and shy, Lizzie Fenwick had somehow scraped through to womanhood and learnt to show whole-hearted love. More significantly, she had learnt that she was capable of anything - even murder - if it threatened herself, or those close to her. Despite her small stature and demure looks, Lizzie Fenwick was a cold-blooded, calculating killer. Heaven help anyone who crossed swords with her.

CHAPTER 18

THE LIGHT BULB MOMENT

Vincent escorted Vicky Ward to their table and pulled back her chair as he eyed her appreciatively from top to toe.

"Who said chivalry was dead!" cooed Vicky as he filled her glass with wine. Chiming their glasses together they toasted a 'Cheers' and Vincent sat watching as Vicky studied the menu.

"You know what you want already, Vince?" she asked.

"You! That's what I want, Vic." He smiled raising an eyebrow.

"Funny! I don't see that on the menu," she replied, blushing briefly before grinning like a Cheshire cat. "Well, at least not until after dessert anyway!" With a cheeky wink, she turned away and beckoned the waiter over.

During the course of the meal the innuendos flowed freely, as did the wine. Vincent certainly knew how to spoil and charm a girl. If the cheesy lines failed, at least the vino would loosen her clothing. Vicky spooned her pudding seductively into her open mouth and teased the food off slowly, lingering for a second to let out a moan of appreciation. Vincent looked on transfixed as she intimated sexual skulduggery.

"Oh, Vince... I want you too!" Then she erupted in a fit of laughter, followed swiftly by Vincent. "I can't do this saucy stuff, Vince!" she protested. "Let's cut to the chase - we both know what's going to happen next." Vicky stood up as she spoke and walked round to his side of the table. "I'm going to powder my nose; you're going to settle up, collect my coat, then order a taxi." She nibbled his ear and then his neck, and strode off to the Ladies.

He didn't need telling twice. "Waiter!" and he was up, waving his hands as if writing.

***

As they got into the taxi the driver asked where they were heading. Vincent looked blankly at Vicky.

"Don't you know your own address Vince?"

With the driver enlightened they headed for Chalkwell and the warmth and privacy of Vincent's bachelor pad. Vicky lifted his hand and placed it on her bare thigh, sliding it up just under her skirt line. The driver took a crafty peek in his mirror and they both giggled again, like a pair of fresh faced teenage lovers. Vincent carefully worked his way up her thighs, and was now gently teasing her mound through her silky knickers, whilst kissing her passionately on the neck and open cleavage. Increasingly aroused and oblivious to the per-vy driver's stare, her knees were parting a little more every few seconds. She could feel his throbbing desire bulging through his trousers and was anxious to get back to the comfort of his flat.

As Vincent fumbled for his door key, they enjoyed a passionate embrace on the doorstep. Vicky pushed him back against the door and kissed him full on the lips, her tongue gently teasing his. "Are you gonna get the door open, or are we gonna do this in the street?" Vicky knew what she wanted and she wanted it now. When he opened the door she virtually pushed him up the stairs, eager to satisfy her lust. He sat on the edge of his bed and Vicky stood between his legs, pressing his head between her breasts. "Now for the real 'dessert!' she said, running her hands over his broad back. "You get undressed while I go and get myself ready for you. Where's the bathroom?" Vincent pointed to his en-suite and began to unbutton his shirt as Vicky disappeared.

The phone rang just as he slipped his trousers off over his feet. "Ignore it!" she shouted from the bathroom. Eager to please, he cancelled the call and removed his watch, but even as Vicky stepped out from behind the en-suite door and leant seductively on the frame, Vincent was distracted once more by his buzzing mobile. Vicky's womanly curves were sheathed in his blue satin robe as she sauntered to his side. Turning her back to him, she began to slide the robe from her shoulders. He sat transfixed, salivating, mesmerised by her seductive movements. The phone rang again. "Oh for pity's sake!" she laughed, "This doesn't happen in the movies."

"Let me just answer it and get rid of them. Sorry, Babe!" He leant over and picked up his phone.

"Vincent? It's Macca." Vicky began to tease her hand into his boxer shorts, feeling the hardness of his cock.

"Yes, Macca? I have to tell you it's not very convenient right now. Can't you call me in the morning?" Vicky leant forward and began kissing her way up his thighs, while stoking his firmness. "What!" he exclaimed suddenly. Leaping to his feet, he inadvertently knocked Vicky flying backwards.

"Careful, you bloody great oaf!" she said as she rocked forwards and got back up still chuckling, blissfully unaware of Vincent's new burden.

"Oh, My God! Where?" Vincent went white, and Vicky stopped laughing and froze. "Same MO?" Vicky realised now that this wasn't going to be good news. "Give me twenty minutes, Mac! And yes, you did hear Vicky's voice. And I would very much appreciate it if you kept schtum!" Vincent scrambled into his clothes as Vicky looked on horrified.

"Not another one, Vincent!"

"'Fraid so! I'm terribly sorry, but I'm gonna have to leave you. Make yourself at home, and I'll phone you in a couple of hours when I know the SP." He lurched from the room with his jacket over his shoulders, fumbling for his keys.

"Vincent! You've been drinking!" she hollered after him, but he was gone.

Putting the dressing gown back on, Vicky wandered downstairs and raided the fridge whilst the kettle hissed in the background.

"This wasn't the sort of bloody spooning I was imagining... but, hey-ho!" she bleated as she stuffed another spoonful of gateau into her mouth.

***

Vincent blasted along the Seafront. The speed cameras flashed away at him as he veered from side to side - squinting, trying to refocus with the alcohol slightly fuzzing his view. As he neared the pier he flicked on his grill lights and sirens, and the drunken rabble parted left and right to avoid him. The bustle and noise halted for an instant as the car surged past, and everyone stood watching, eagerly anticipating the drama they associated with the Blues and Twos. He passed by as swiftly as he'd come though, and conversations were resumed and eyes diverted elsewhere. The buzzards ceased circling with no feast to gaze upon.

As he neared the seafront apartment he slowed down, scanning the properties, looking for the victim's gated block. He needn't have bothered because in the distance the blue lights from the local Bobbies' cars shone around the buildings, bouncing back and forth in the glass reflections. A uniformed officer was manning the gates and directed him in. Hot on his heels came William Mumford and Lucy Hockley, parking behind him, and all three entered the building in silence.

Vincent Ambrose stepped from the lift, flanked by William and Lucy. They were then directed to the apartment by a solemn looking plod. Vincent was crestfallen, his unblemished reputation now threatened by the death of a third prostitute in as many weeks. He was desperate for retribution; he so badly needed to nail this evil fiend before he had another Ipswich or Whitechapel on his hands. Even as it was, the whole country's Media were already camped out in the lively seaside town, so when news of the third killing broke Vincent expected a feeding frenzy second to none. He was already fending off a handful of persistent pressmen, and didn't relish the spotlights being trained on his furrowed brow.

The crime scene was similar to the previous two in every respect. William Mumford deduced very quickly that it had only one major difference. This place had not been used for a sexual encounter, just the butchery. Had the killer followed her home? Had he broken away from his usual pattern of behaviour? The contents of Estelle's handbag were scattered across the hall floor and the keys dumped beside them. The bedroom was much more homely, with no signs of all the traps and trimmings that go with an illicit boudoir. The decor was functional, not tarty, and there was an abundance of family photos dotted around. This was a home not a brothel!

Mumford's supposition was right: Estelle had enjoyed a fruitful business relationship with a local B&B manager. If she wasn't doing house calls, she would work well away from her own doorstep in one of his rooms. Choosing not to air her dirty linen in public allowed her to project a classier, albeit elusive persona. Allowing her neighbours to believe she was a prominent local businesswoman suited Estelle just fine. Those pressing her for more details would be greeted with a fabric of lies, half-truths and evasive replies. Despite her somewhat vague identity amongst them, her neighbours held her in the highest regard. When news broke of her death and her dark professional secrets they would be astounded on both counts. Only one resident, Rashid, knew the truth about the curvaceous black tenant. Like the B&B owner, the rent for Rashid's lavish apartment was paid for with Estelle's most readily available currency, sex. Unlike money, this timelessly valuable commodity was always at hand. Estelle had used her feminine charms expertly and often, always getting what she wanted with a cheeky wink and a smile, if not more.

Lucy Hockley carefully sidestepped all the discarded knick-knacks and went straight for Estelle's gusset. Parting her thighs gently, she searched for the knife that would confirm her as the third victim. "Afraid we have number three, Gentleman!" she stated, in an almost matter of fact way. "But I just don't get this business with the knife," she added. "Why there? Surely if you had enjoyed her sexually, that's the last place you would desecrate!" Lucy was puzzled, but no more so than Vincent or William.

"Have you considered a profiler Vincent? Maybe he could answer some of Lucy's questions."

"The last thing I need right now is some nerd throwing predictions and a load of wild geese my way. I have enough to deal with as it is! 'I see a man! He's troubled!' I can't be doing with all that mystic bollocks."

"Surely you would welcome any help you could get right now?"

"Lucy! Have you ever worked with one of those twats?"

"Yes, I have actually. While I was in my second year at university, we were seconded to a lab in Cambridge.

They had a guy there called Alvin Lythgo. I have to say, he was absolutely bloody marvellous."
"Really? Look, for now take this place apart and give me facts. I'll have a chat with Him Upstairs and see how he feels about 'Mystic Lythgo'. Can't see him being too keen, though!" Smarting as he was, Vincent wasn't his usual amiable self. William sensed his growing antagonism and intervened.
"Listen, Vincent! I know you're under a mountain of pressure. But take comfort from the fact that Lucy and I are on your side. We want to help in any way we can. Her suggestions are well-meant, Old Fellow! How about she has an 'informal' chat with this Lythgo - off the record, so to speak?"
"I suppose it couldn't do any harm. Strictly off the record though!"

***

William and Lucy set about deciphering the clues in Estelle's apartment, scrutinising and bagging the smallest fibres and particles. All they seemed to unearth was copious amounts of bleach in the bathroom, very little else. Lucy removed the sink waste and carefully bagged the spiral of interwoven hair. Estelle's coarse black follicles were entwined with Lizzie's brunette locks, but this and certain other clues would be overlooked in favour of focusing on Robin Bradford's samples. Blinded by the fact he had been present at all three killings, they forged ahead regardless.
Estelle had dragged Lizzie's hair band from her scalp during the fracas, and promptly snagged it behind the radiator, speckled with blood. Lizzie had fragmented

one of her neatly manicured nails as she struck out at her subdued victim, leaving the shard caught in Estelle's silky bed cover. Together with the hair sample from the sink, this surely would have cast doubt on Robin's guilt, but they had other distractions. After all, Robin's fresh semen and pubic hairs were still dribbling in and around the corpse's neatly trimmed bush. They were so sure these would be a match for Sample 4 that the rest was almost a formality. There was no doubt in anyone's mind: the evidence was overwhelming.

***

Vincent Ambrose's breakthrough came a few hours after his visit to Estelle's, as Lucy Hockley stood in the lab sampling the new swabs. Following Robin Bradford's arrest over his kerbside squabble with Maria's punter, his details lay waiting in the system. All it needed was a new entry of his DNA profile and...

"Bloody hell!" Lucy scrambled to the printer. "William!...William, quick! Have a look at this!"

William Mumford came hurrying out of his office and into the lab, where Lucy was standing looking shaken but excited. Pushing his glasses up his nose, he began to inspect the slides she was now placing on the light board. "Yes, Lucy! Samples from Katya and Helena? We knew they would match, so where's the fire?"

"No, William! Don't you see? Look in the left hand corner. This is a DNA match from the Police National Computer Data Base!"

"But there must be a mistake. We've run this profile a dozen times, haven't we?"

"Yes, but this sample was taken at Southend Station recently by uniformed officers involved in a dispute between two adult males. Look again!"

She handed him a sheet with Robin Bradford's name emblazoned across the top, complete with his address.

"Jesus H Christ! Have you told Vincent yet?"

"No, I thought you might like to be the bearer of the good news - after all, it is three a.m!"

"I don't think he'll be too bothered about the time, young Lucy! Best you get on the phone to him. It's your find, so you'd best take the glory!"

CHAPTER 19

COLLAR AND CUFFS.

Vincent felt that every conceivable avenue had been explored and re-explored. No-one was going to solve the case tonight, so he gave the order for his crew to fall out. "Reconvene here tomorrow morning at eight-thirty please, People!" Vincent ambled out of the Station towards his car his hands in his pockets, kicking at leaves and deep in thought.

Glancing at his watch, he let his mind drift back to Vicky and earlier on in the evening. He gave a wry smile as he put the key in the ignition. 'Bless her!' he thought. 'She must be safely tucked up in bed by now'. Making a mental note to text her when he got back, he sped off towards home. At three in the morning, very little stood between him and his bed sheets. Stepping inside, Vincent chucked his keys in the fruit bowl and loosened his tie. From the corner of his eye he caught a faint glimpse of movement.

"Who the fuck's there!" he shouted, raising his fists like a Queensbury Rules fighter, then bounded up the stairs towards the intruder.
"Err... how many naked girls have you abandoned tonight?" came the quick witted riposte from his scantily clad dinner date.
"Bloody hell, Vic! You scared the living shit out of me... you're lucky I didn't stick one on ya! I thought you'd have been long gone."
"Two sugars in mine. Oh - and nice and strong!" Vicky sauntered back off towards his bed.
"Cheeky mare! When I get up there you'll get more than two bloody sugars, I can tell you!" and Vincent went to put the kettle on. Moments later he was making his way back up, brews in hand, hoping this time for a different kind of rough and tumble from the one he'd expected when he first came in. Vicky was hiding under his duvet trying to get warm with just her head poking out, grinning wildly. Vincent put the teas down by the bedside and leant forward for a kiss.
"No chance!" Vicky edged away from him, briefly teasing. "It's going to take more than that to crack this ice maiden, Hunny! Leave a girl cold, and expect to pick up where you left off - I don't think so!" She turned her back on him, smiling like a naughty child.
"Ok, Vic! Your call, Babe... if you want to miss out on this!" and taking off his shirt and playfully flexing his muscles, he began to loosen his trousers, with Vicky watching his reflection in the dressing-table mirror. He yanked his belt free in one deft jerk and swung it around his head, rattling the lampshade. Then he placed his hands on either side of his waist and start-

ed to tease off his trousers. “Dum da-dum --- da dum da dum!” Mimicking a stripper, he slowly peeled his pants down to his feet.

“Phwooooar!” said Vicky, playing along with him. Suddenly he snagged his pants on his foot and shot across the bedroom. Vicky bolted out from under the covers laughing hysterically as he stumbled around the room trying to regain his footing, and they collapsed together in fits of laughter.

“I meant to do that!” he said blushing wildly.

“My arse, you did! If only I could've videoed that! Sod the two hundred and fifty quid, it would have gone straight on the station intranet.”

Their merriment was cut short when his trouser pocket started to blast out the Sweeney theme again. “Oh, for pity's sake! What now?” Vincent was exasperated at the thought of yet another missed opportunity to sample Vicky's charms.

“Sorry, Vic, it's the forensic team.” Vincent told Vicky cupping his phone with his hand, he then took the call. “Vincent speaking. This'd better be good at this time of the morning!”

“Sorry, Vinnie! It's Lucy Hockley.” Vicky sat on the bed mouthing ‘Vinnie’ at him and making kissing gestures, ridiculing the oblivious Lucy yet again. “We've got a match on Sample Four!”

“Well, I guessed you would!”

“No, I mean a named match!”

“You're joking! But how?”

“Some of your boys lifted him on a Breach of the Peace a few days ago and when Estelle's samples were run through, the swabs came up with a match.”

"Give me twenty minutes and I'll meet you at William's lab!"
"See you in a while, Vinnie!" and Lucy was gone.
"See you in a while, Vinnie-Winnie! Kissy, kissy!" Vicky enjoyed the tease, but knew how important it was for Vincent to catch the culprit.
"Sorry Vic, Love... You understand don't you?"
"Of course I do! But just keep away from Lucy-Wooosy, or I'll rip your balls off." Laughing she drew in close for yet another parting kiss.
"Now, now, WPC Ward! Any more of that and I'll have to detain you immediately!"
"Bugger's chance of that happening - your phone would ring."
"Ha-ha! Now give me another snog and I'll see you at the station tomorrow."

***

Full of optimism, Vincent breezed cheerfully into the lab. Finally a case was coming together: now he had a name, he could rally his resources, mount his evidence and then strike. He would deliver a swift, calculated assault on Robin Bradford within forty-eight hours. The diligent copper would assemble a team of Essex's finest and execute a massive raid with armed officers just as the day was breaking free from the night's shadows.
Lucy and William proudly showed off their new found evidence, all the pieces finally bonding together, or so they thought. The subtle irony of Sample Seven, the latest discovery from Estelle's flat, was that Lizzie's DNA lay side by side with Robin Bradford's in the lab, just as

the couple did in their bed that night. But all the trio could see was Sample Four. The DNA matches from all three scenes, the witness reports, and the blood soaked clothing: it all pointed to Robin Bradford.

***

The next morning Vincent called an emergency meeting with his faithful aides, Nicky and Brian. When he had their full attention, he prised a photograph of Robin Bradford from an envelope. Holding it tight to his chest in a moment of almost theatrical suspense, he extended his arm towards the white board.

"Guv?" Nicky looked on surprised; Brian stood silent, mouth open. "Is that a suspect?" she asked.

"No it's not 'a' suspect... it's 'the' suspect!" Vincent revelled in his moment, showing off to his underlings.

"But how and when did all this come about?" quizzed Nicky.

"Last night there was a third girl found dead. Her name is - well was - Estelle Mandichi. When forensics ran the new swabs through their computer it 'pinged' our man here. His name is Robin Albert Bradford, forty-eight years old, and he co-habits with Elizabeth Fenwick at 162 Hadleigh Crescent, Leigh-on-Sea."

"Elizabeth Fenwick? She owns one of the cars that came up on CCTV during the Peldon enquiries." Characteristically alert, Nicky was quick to contribute her knowledge to the pool.

Vincent continued. "Correct, Nicky, but it would appear she has two cars registered in her name. She seems to use the second car, a Vauxhall Corsa. This guy Bradford is about five-eight, with greying hair and

quite obviously enjoys his food! He has no distinguishing characteristics - no tattoos etc. Brian, I want you to familiarise yourself with his file. In half an hour I want you out of the station and fronting a six-man observation team. Nicky will take over tonight at eight with a fresh crew and different cars, so spend your time getting to know him better. I want to know what he's been up to, what he eats for breakfast and when he takes a shit! Nicky, as you'll be on the graveyard shift, you can leave off at one o'clock and get some rest. Then back in for seven-thirty so Brian can do a half hour debrief."
He delivered his orders with military precision.
"Nicky, access his home phone, mobiles and internet usage, if you can. Also get on to his network provider and trace all calls in and out as far back as you can. Preferably for at least one month. Under no circumstances are you to pounce till I give the nod. We're looking to lift him from his pit tomorrow morning, early doors! Everybody clear? Good! Any questions? Right then, crack on!"

***

Brian began briefing his colleagues as soon as he left the room. They headed off in three different cars and made their way towards Leigh-on-Sea, where Robin Bradford was having his breakfast. Nicky started to mull over the mountain of paperwork pertaining to Bradford's case. "Oh, and by the way... did you have a visitor last night!" laughing aloud at her saucy rhetorical question.
"Doesn't news travel fast round here! And yes - I did."
Brian sat about one hundred metres away from Robin

Bradford's door, with his second car parked discreetly at the end of the road facing in the same direction as Robin's Focus. The third car was approximately six hundred metres away in a siding abutting London Road. They estimate that the average person will spot a tail within ten minutes, so Brian and his cronies planned to change the lead car periodically; also, changing vehicles on rest breaks or shift changes helped to maintain their anonymity.

***

Robin moved to his computer, oblivious of the street staking going on outside. He'd managed to sort out a few appointments for the day, and was preparing papers for a newly acquired Spanish apartments. Fresh on his books, 'Casa las Rotas' would be high on the agenda for his day's sales pitch. If he could secure a few tenants, the owner would be elated and maybe allow Robin access to some of his more prestigious properties. Stuffing the papers in a case, Robin grabbed his keys, swigged the last dregs of his coffee and went out to the car.

Slipping nonchalantly over the threshold, he unwittingly set in motion a chain of events that rattled round the whole district. Brian clicked away on the camera, creating a pictorial account of Robin's every move: close-ups of his face, his keys turning in the door - no stone left unturned. Brian's driver Chris radioed through to the other two cars to alert them to the movement outside Robin's house. All three cars' engines simultaneously fired into life as they waited patiently to start their pursuit.

***

Robin lifted the tailgate and put his case in the boot. He took off his jacket and placed it on a hanger behind the driver's seat, revealing a crisp white shirt. Little did he realise as he climbed into his shabby old car that all eyes were on him. The engine spluttered and coughed, sending a cloud of black fumes billowing over the pavement. Robin pulled out of his parking space and coasted the few hundred yards to the end of the street. Brian's car gained momentum and was on his boot just as Robin eased left at the junction and headed for London Road.

"Visual on the suspect's car!" Rick and Terry were in the second vehicle and radioed their sighting through as Bradford kangarooed out of his road.

"Hold off, Tel, till we get to London Road. Keep back a few hundred yards - we don't wanna spook him!" Brian was understandably anxious that his posse should not be spotted.

"Will do, Bri!" Terry didn't need telling - he was adept at following - but he let Brian have his moment of authority.

"Sasha, it's Brian! We're nearly on London Road now, so we'll be on top of you in seconds. He's indicating right. That's a right towards Westcliff, Everyone!"

"Eyeballing him at the junction now, Brian." Sasha was paired with Yusif. They were the chalk and cheese of the cavalcade. He was just over five foot tall and nearly as wide, whereas Sasha was a leggy six foot three even in her flat black work shoes.

Chris patched through to the other drivers as they

neared the town centre of Southend. "Terry, Rick, can you come by me and take over as lead car? I'll peel off at the roundabout and double back up behind Sasha."

"No worries!" came the reply from Terry's car.

Just as they overtook Brian at the roundabout Robin suddenly pulled over into a bus lay-by.

"Bollocks! I think we've been rumbled, Brian."

"Fuck's sake, you goons! You've only been on him twenty yards."

Sasha cut in with the good news just as the bickering started. "Guv, he's only reading a piece of paper. I'll plot up on the roundabout over Queensway. I can't lose him from there. Go down to the Queensway Car Park roundabout, and then we're covered!"

"Good call, Sash!"

They reset their position just as Brian and Chris came back onto the roundabout. Robin pulled out behind Brian and indicated left towards Sutton and Southchurch Road.

"He's on your tail, Brian. You go right ahead, and I'll pick him up again!" Sasha was quickly establishing herself as race leader and soon had Robin in her cross-hairs.

The toing and froing went on well into the afternoon as Robin bounced from client to client. His day had been very fruitful, securing eight places out of the available fifteen. He'd already earned more today than in all the previous four weeks put together. He was on a roll, and still with his potentially most lucrative purchaser to visit. If this went on, he'd be back on his feet in no time!

***

Asif Aggi was a very wealthy and prominent businessman involved in the import and export of sportswear from the Middle East. He would occasionally purchase large blocks of Time Shares from Robin and use them as bait or reward for his numerous suppliers and retailers. He was a persuasive and genuinely quite generous man, who could get his employees to work their fingers raw under the promise of reward. He had frequently benefited in the past – usually in female form - from deals done with Robin. In return for his custom, Robin would take him to dubious night spots with dancing girls, and treat him to a little one-on-one. This tactic usually had the desired effect, loosening the purse strings on many a drunken occasion. Knowing Robin from those more affluent days, Aggi now took pity on his fallen comrade.

Eager to secure a deal, Robin parked alongside his old friend's swish house near Thorpe Hall Golf Club and pressed the buzzer on the gate. The gates peeled back gracefully and Robin edged in. Brian could only sit opposite and snap Robin's progress from the safety of a side street. Asif came to the door in a long flowing white robe and embraced him warmly, kissing him on both cheeks: not Robin's ideal greeting, but Asif Aggi was the fabled cash cow that he badly needed to milk. By the time Robin stepped into Aggi's house, Brian was scrolling through pages of Intel on Robin's accommodating host.

"Asif Gadar Aggi, forty- six; born in Sudan to Ramish Aggi, an oil tycoon. The family came to the UK in the early 90's when Ramish was executed by a rival business syndicate. His mother fled the hostilities and set up here with a cool four-point-eight million in the bank. In 1994 she died, leaving the family fortune to one Asif Gadar, the only child. When my parents die, I'll be lucky if I escape paying for the funeral, let alone coming in for any money!" Brian spoke into the radio, informing the whole network of police.

"That's the way the cookie crumbles, Old Mate!"

"Cheers Chris, most fucking helpful!"

"What do you think a millionaire businessman wants with a tin-pot, timesharing, prostitute- murdering twat like Bradford, Brian?"

"I'd go with my first hunch here, Chris, and say... Timeshares!"

"Ha, bloody Ha!"

***

Robin and his esteemed business associate sat drinking iced tea from glass beakers in silver filigree holders. "I know they aren't in your league Asif, but for staff and hospitalities these would be far better than any of your managers and their families could usually afford," he explained as he indicated the photos in a glossy brochure.

"Mr Robin, please spare me the sales bullshit you bombard the old couples with! I'm a man of honour and integrity and, I feel, so are you. So cut to the chase and give me figures!"

Sighing and stroking his chin, Robin scratched his pencil over the page and rattled at his calculator.

"Come on Mr Robin, don't be shy!"

"I can do each unit for seventeen and a half K per annum, but that's without service charges and utilities."
"And how much for the service charges, My Friend?"
"At a guess, three thou two fifty. Maybe three K, if you're lucky."
"I'm always lucky, Mr Robin. I was blessed by the Almighty."
"God?" Robin wasn't sure how to respond.
"Not God! Have you learnt nothing of my life in all your visits? I was blessed by my father: he's the Almighty! Only he could have bestowed such wealth and happiness, My Friend."
"Oh, I see!" Caught out by his client, Robin felt embarrassed by the prank-playing businessman.
"I'll take them, Mr Robin!" With a click of his fingers, Asif summoned his servant and right hand man to his side. He whispered briefly in his ear, and the aide swiftly exited the opulent drawing room.
"But I will pay twenty K for each, yes?"
Robin was unable to hide his delight. "One unit or two?" Feeling cheeky, he pushed his deal just that little bit harder.
"One or two, Mr Robin? I want all seven! Now, would you prefer cash or cheque?"
Robin choked on his ice tea, before gushing, "Cash!"
"Mandip, bring in my case, please!" His butler-cum-servant promptly obeyed, returning with a black leather briefcase.
"You drive a hard bargain, Mr Robin!" Asif placed fourteen neatly-packaged bundles of twenty-pound notes on the table. "I know you're not enjoying good fortune at present, so I wish to indulge you a little for

your hard work and constant care of my affairs. Will you allow me this honour?"

"But of course! What do you have in mind?" Robin was faced with a pleasant dilemma. Firstly, he knew Asif Aggi would be mortally offended if he didn't accept his hospitality: it was customary in his world to reward those around him. Secondly, it would surely be a lavish gift- they always were. Robin had previously enjoyed swanky London restaurants, whores, weekends away and even Asif's Ferrari for a few days.

"On Saturday night I'll have my driver collect you from your home in my limousine and take you and your lady to Covent Garden. My friend has opened a new restaurant there. What do you say Mr Robin?"

"That's most generous, Sir. Normally I would be more than happy to accept such an invitation...but..."

"Speak up, don't be shy! We are old friends Mr Robin."

"Well, for one thing, it's my cousin's wedding on Saturday, which frankly I would happily miss. It's more Lizzie; we're not doing too well at the moment. I don't wish to sound ungrateful, but she's the last person I would want to be looking at over a meal."

Asif rose from his seat and Robin courteously followed suit, stuffing the money into his case. He put his arm around Robin's shoulder as they headed for the grandiose hallway. "My friend, in times such as these there's only one thing to put a smile on a man's face. I'll arrange for my best girl to be prepared for you. You must go to her now. Is that suitable form, Mr Robin?"

"Oh, God - yes!"

"Mr Robin, I have some advice for you too. Take some time to spend with your lady Elizabeth. I remember her charms very well, and a man must have harmony in his house." Despite having a string of beauties holed up all over Europe, Asif was a dedicated family man and still found comfort and solace with his wife Ameria.

"Thank you, Asif! I am truly indebted to you for your gracious and generous gift, as well as for your wisdom." Robin's flannel bubbled over as always. Asif could stick his advice where the sun didn't shine, but he would gladly partake in a little 'time out' with Asif's whore - and relieve him of his cash into the bargain. Returning to his car, he slipped through the gate clutching his case and new appointment details. Brian sat opposite the huge black gates, his head dipping slowly as the boredom and late shifts played havoc with his concentration levels.

"Bri!... Brian! He's on the move again!"

"What! Who? Was I asleep?" The disorientated Brian drifted back into the world and remembered the importance of their duties. "Look sharp then!" For Brian, covering his own shortcomings by barking at others was par for the course. Freshly alert, he started snapping away again at Robin as they all prepared for the next round of 'follow my leader'.

***

Robin back-tracked on his journey towards the town, pursued by an entourage of hide-and-seekers. Blissfully unaware of his tails, he guided his car up Victoria Avenue through Cuckoo Corner and along the A127. When he reached Progress Road he swung left and anchored up near Belfair's Wood. Once again the posse following had to take evasive action and plot up en-route, waiting for him to re-pass them. Sasha held back three or four hundred yards behind him.

"Bollocks!" Realising his error, Robin cursed out loud and then promptly turned back towards Eastwood. This immediately isolated Sasha and Yusif. They couldn't turn around fast enough without alerting Robin to their presence, so they sat tight and waited for him to pass by, hopeful that one of the other cars would pick him up before he was out of sight.

Brian, Chris and the others went into meltdown. They were stranded several hundred yards away, facing acres of traffic and staring in the wrong direction.

"He went left, Yusif! Left here!" Sasha was waving her arm frantically, trying to get her point across.

"Shit! I've lost him, Brian! Shit! Shit!"

"Please don't tell me that, Sash, for fuck's sake! Ambrose will have my bollocks for paperweights!"

The three cars scoured the back streets and side roads between Belfair's and the A127, hopeful that they would stumble on their quarry. Brian was having kittens, cursing and sniping at everyone else's incompetence.

"Brian, I've got him! He's sitting in his car near the petrol station. Outside the parade of shops."

Terry was first to reignite the pursuit, navigating back to the forecourt and settling in to watch Robin through the shrubbery. Sasha pulled up alongside with Yusif and was immediately subjected to a barrage of complaints as her colleague shared his story. Brian and Chris took up sentry watch in the parking bays fifty yards from Robin and began their painstaking photographic reportage of their suspect. Meanwhile, Robin Bradford was reaching under his seat to retrieve his mobile, so he could dial the number for Asif's obliging tom.

"Shit, he's got another mobile!" Chris spotted it before Brian, but Brian soon had it safely snapped on film.

"Chantelle?" enquired Robin.

"Yes, speaking!"

"Asif Aggi has given me your details; I believe you're expecting me?"

"Indeed I am! You must be Mr Robin?"

"Yes, that's right."

"Well, you'd better come up! It's the white door to the left of the entrance to the hair salon. When you buzz, I'll come down for you."

"Ok, thank you! I'm outside now." Robin stowed away his phone under the seat and left the car.

"Must be going to the newsagent," Sasha called across to Brian.

"Certainly not a client living in those flats," Brian reflected.

"Guv!" Terry chipped in from the second car.

"Yes, Tel!"

"That door he's at - it's a knocking shop. My mate raided it about a month ago; rolled over two brasses. It was being fronted by some Arab, I think."

"Jesus Christ! You'd better call in to Ambrose, Guv!" Sasha was pressing Brian. "He's just come out of an Arab's gaff in Thorpe Hall."

Brian rang Ambrose immediately, but went straight to his Voice Mail. He was "In Conference" with the Big Cheese upstairs, probably getting a dressing down for his inability to fill the cells with a suitably gratifying range of offenders, Brian thought. Top of the list would be the three-time killer. Luckily, Ambrose was now in a position to deflect his boss's onslaught by offering up Robin Bradford's details as a kind of olive branch.

"What now, Brian?" Terry was keen to push forward.

"Fucked if I know! He's probably in there now stabbing the poor cow."

***

Robin followed Chantelle upstairs and was led into the lounge area. From the outside the place looked like a typical tenement hovel, but inside it was decked out in sumptuous fabrics, lavish furniture and fine objets d'art. When Asif came calling he could close the door behind him safe from prying eyes and bask in sensuous luxury, pampered by girls who attended to his every whim and fancy. Chantelle was the exact opposite of her Sudanese counterparts, busty and leggy, but blonde. Asif had a passion for blondes, hand picking them from numerous clubs and parlours across Europe. He would ship them in, pay them generously and treat them like princesses.

This one had been cherry-picked from a London lap dance bar. Brought to Southend, she was showered with clothes and luxury cars, and further rewarded with an envious wedge. Sometimes she would only do two or three tricks a week, but never missed Asif's Friday Night Special with Dolores, the other resident tart. Greed and boredom had led Delores to solicit services elsewhere, hence the attention from the Essex Fuzz. Asif showed her the back of his hand, then the door. She was replaced within hours by another leggy blonde called Alesha. Alesha, Chantelle and all the other girls in Asif's stable looked as if they'd just been broken free from a toy shop's blister-wrap.

Asif's wife was well aware of his infidelity and accepted it: it was part of their way. He likewise turned a blind eye to her choice of gardener, tennis coach and gym instructor - always a fit, twenty-something Adonis with a washboard abdomen and orange perma-tan.

***

Outside, Brian had hit the panic button. Sasha and Yusif had moved in a little bit closer to Robin's car and parked up. Terry stayed where he was in the petrol station forecourt, which afforded him a good view of the shop frontage and the windows of the flat. Now he was patiently watching the undrawn curtains for signs of activity. Ambrose was still unreachable, so Brian took it upon himself to lead the charge and make all the decisions. Sit tight, or kick the doors in? He knew Ambrose was planning a dawn raid, but 'no one' could have foreseen Robin's visit to another parlour so quickly. Sasha left the comfort of her unmarked car and cruised past Robin's car on foot, glancing in at the windows as she passed. Reaching Brian's car, she plonked herself down in the back and put in her own two penn'orth.

"His car was unlocked, Guv. There's a mobile on the driver's side floor next to the paper he was reading. I could get it...what do you think?" she asked.

"No chance, Sash! He could be out any minute - it would be suicide!"

***

Inside Robin was faced with a choice of his own, Chantelle having just introduced him to Alesha.

"You choose!" she said.

"Choose! Are you serious?"

"Of course you choose! Me or Alesha?"

Like a kid in a sweet shop, Robin's eyes darted back and forth perusing the beauties. There was very little in it, so Robin deliberated for some time, not wishing to offend either girl.

"How can I choose between you two when you're both so goddam hot? This is unfair!" What a dilemma to be faced with, he thought. "You're both so ravishingly sexy, I can't possibly choose. Come on, help me out!"

"Then toss for it!" Chantelle winked at Alesha, sharing the saucy innuendo.

"Doesn't that make a mockery of me coming here? I could have stayed at home and done that!"

Chantelle broke the deadlock with a mutually satisfying compromise. "I'll tell you what, you go and get started with Alesha, and if no one calls in the next ten minutes or so, I'll join you both. How does that sound?"

Robin was more than happy with that suggestion, so off he sloped to the bedroom with the debutante Alesha to begin his pampering session.

***

"Guv, there's a blonde bird in the front window, all decked out in sussies. She's just closed the curtains. Robin Bradford was in the background!" Terry reported his sightings to Brian and awaited further instructions.

"Ok Tel! Keep me posted if you see anything else."

Sasha commented that Robin Bradford was sure to be otherwise engaged for a good few minutes, thus leaving the coast clear to scour his car.

"Alright, Sash - but be double quick! I'll try and get hold of Ambrose again." Brian was unconvinced, but in his naivety allowed himself to be railroaded by Sasha. He tried to reach Ambrose again, but to no avail, so decided to leave a message this time.

"Guv? It's Sasha... I've rung my own phone from his mobile and deleted the number from his call history. We can get Technical to run a search on it. The paper just has this address on it... do you want me to give the boot a once-over?"

"No Sasha, just get clear ASAP!"

"But what about the case he stowed in there?"

"Hang on, Girl... Tel, are you there?"

"Yes, Bri."

"Any signs of movement in there?"

"No mate, not a titter."

"Sasha... Go for it - but be fucking quick!"

She exited the front of the car and rounded the back, gently prising open the tailgate. The case was nestled on the left hand side next to some brochures, so she pulled it clear and slid the catches outward.

"Jesus!" She reeled backwards as the huge bundles of cash filled her vision.

"Guv! There must be over a hundred K in here... in cash!"

"Fuck! Get away from there, sharpish!"

Sasha returned to her seat next to Yusif and sent Robin Bradford's number through to the Station's tech boys. Silence reigned at the scene for over an hour: no movement, no communication. Brian had heard nothing back from Ambrose and was getting very concerned. He knew Robin Bradford was inside the flat, almost certainly crucifying another of Southend's illustrious masseuses. He was also keen to move things along, as his shift was drawing to a close, but the last thing he wanted was to hand over the reins and lose all the credit. Without the backup of Ambrose, Brian was at a loss.

***

Nicky hadn't been able to concentrate on home life with all the drama unfolding around the district, so she had come into the station early. She took up the mantle with Robin Bradford's personal phone and cross referenced all the information the tech heads had gleaned. All the girls or madams had received a call from his phone prior to meeting their grizzly fates. Then the second and most damning news came through. Satellite mapping evidence had put the phone's location within yards of Katya and Helena's murder sites at the time of death. The only glitch was with Estelle; it didn't show up either in her flat, or anywhere in the area. However they took comfort from the fact that her records tied her up at Robin Bradford's house. Contact had been established between the two parties via his call records too. They could only surmise that Robin Bradford had inadvertently left his phone at home when he followed her back to her own accommodation.

"Brian, it's Nicky back at the station."
"Hi Nick! What's the coo?"
"Good news! The number you gave us from Robin Bradford's other phone has been linked to two of the addresses in question via global positioning data."
"Well done! Any news yet on where Ambrose is?" Brian was desperate for feedback before he made any more moves.
"Yes, apparently he's playing golf at Belfair's with 'Him Upstairs.' Sounds ominous, doesn't it!"
"Belfair's! Shit! - that's only just round the corner. Listen, you get sorted with a car and get over here. I want the chopper scrambled and hovering overhead. I also want an armed response team out here pronto!"
"Are you bloody serious? ... If you fuck this up, Ambrose will hang you out to dry by your bollocks!"
"Yes I'm sure! But without Ambrose to make the call I have to step up to the plate. Sasha, you and Yusif go round to Belfair's and find Ambrose. I don't give a shit who he's playing golf with... get him now!"
"Brian, it's Nicky again. I've just found Ambrose's mobile phone on his desk, so he's definitely out of reach."
Sasha and Yusif headed straight off in search of their boss. Belfair's was less than a mile from where they were all holed up. As they entered the car park they could see the Super's shiny gold Lexus wedged in the corner, next to the first tee. Barrelling into the club house, Sasha demanded to speak to Vincent Ambrose.
"I'm afraid he's out on the course, Officer...there's no way of contacting him. He could be anywhere!"
"We need a buggy then! How long has he been out there for?"

"About an hour I'd say. Go to the last tee and work your way back round the course, that's your best bet!"

***

Robin Bradford had taken his time with the vivacious Alesha, enjoying her slinky and sumptuous body. Chantelle breezed into the room and was greeted by the sight of Alesha gesticulating at her to be quiet. Robin lay on the bed stark naked, snoring his head off. They both shared a joke at his expense before slipping out of the room into the lounge area.

***

"Nice shot, Sir!" Vincent Ambrose knew the merits of sucking up to his boss, especially in his current position.

"I understand you are one of us as well Vincent?"

"One of us, Sir?"

"Yes, William Mumford is in my Lodge and mentioned your association with the London Masonry." The Super had not only flourished in the Force, but excelled in Freemasonry too. "I think it's time you considered a couple of changes, Vincent. First of all, I think you should drop that tuppenny- ha'penny golf club you joined last year with all those tiresome 'Green fee' types, and come along to mine."

"But there's a two year waiting list, let alone the astronomical fees, Sir."

"Speculate to accumulate, Dear Boy! Anyway, Gregory, who runs the membership list, is in my Lodge too, I'm sure we could swing a few favours."

"And the second thing?"

"Your choice of Lodge. Too many low ranking officers and undesirables. If you want to elevate your status in the Force, you would be well advised to take a sideways leap of faith. Mumford and I have discussed it at some length and would be happy to propose and second your move."

"Sir... I'm flabbergasted! I would consider it a great honour." Vincent loved his Masonic roots, but knew only too well how the likes of his boss worked. He didn't relish the thought of hobnobbing with him and his cronies, but the subliminal messages were far too obvious to miss.

The silence and tranquillity of Belfair's was shattered by a low thundering rapidly approaching from the north. Vincent knew instantly what it was. The helicopter's drone resonated in their ears as it flashed past and banked sharply, heading back due north towards the A127. Vincent felt for his phone, sensing something was terribly amiss. "Damn!"

"What's the matter, Vincent? Can't you call up and get that bloody thing away from the greens? It's putting me off my stroke!"

***

At the exact same time, Sasha and Yusif came swerving into view right in the middle of the fairway, like a couple of circus clowns, legs and arms flapping in all directions as the cart zigzagged the Course.

"What the Hell! Who are these buffoons! Don't they know who I am? I say! Get off the pitch! Bloody green fees!" The Superintendent was less than pleased by the constant stream of interruptions and distractions plaguing his game.

"Guv! Guv!" Yusif bellowed from the buggy as they neared the tee. Vincent looked on in horror as his stony-faced boss stood glaring at the hapless duo.

"What the blazes are you doing? You're supposed to be tailing Robin Bradford!" he said, ushering the pair to one side out of earshot.

"Sorry, Guv! Robin Bradford is laid up with another tom, and Brian is getting ready to lift him!" Sasha was clearly out of breath and distraught.

"Please tell me you're fucking joking!"

"That's what the chopper is doing... and he's got Armed Response on the way too."

"Jesus Christ, the feckless idiot! What's he trying to prove?" Vincent went purple and jumped on board the buggy.

"Yusif, you stay here and caddy for the Guv. Sasha, get me round there now. Where are they?"

They left in a whirl, leaving a speechless Yusif standing like a lemon at the Super's side.

"Come on, Lad!" he boomed, totally oblivious of the melee. "Grab my clubs! Did you see that last drive? Straight down the fairway like a missile."

***

As the helicopter thundered overhead Robin Bradford yawned and sat up in bed alone, wondering for a minute where he was. "Girls! Girls?" Neither replied: they were gazing out of the lounge window sipping red wine as the chopper circled. When he entered the room, now fully dressed, they both looked round at him. "Sorry girls, I fell asleep. It was so peaceful in there, and you'd well and truly worn me out! What's happening?"

Feeling relaxed with the girls, he leant between them to look out the window too, knocking Alesha off balance. She promptly discharged her wine all over his fresh white shirt.
"Oh, My God! I'm so sorry. Here - let me clean you up! I'm so, so sorry - I really am." But her frantic dabbing at the stain just seemed to make matters worse.
Robin was seething. "Leave it! Just leave it!" he bellowed, and grabbing his effects he stormed towards the door.

***

Meanwhile, Vincent and Sasha ran across the car park towards her car and she grabbed the radio from the dashboard. "Give it to me, Girl - quickly! You just get me round there as fast as you can."

***

Robin burst out onto the street just as Vincent pressed the call button. Brian shouted to all that could hear him..."Go...Go...Go!"
Weapons raised, the Armed Response team stepped slowly forward in formation, screaming various instructions at Robin Bradford. "Hands on your head! Lie down ...flat on the floor! Don't move...!"
He stood rooted to the spot, hands drifting slowly skyward.
"Fuck me, he's covered in blood!" Brian was elated, convinced he had just caught Robin Bradford literally red handed. "Take him down!" he screamed at the gun-toting coppers, then raced past Robin towards the flat, amidst the dust churned up by the still-hovering

helicopter. "Call an ambulance!" And he rushed into the stair well that connected to the upstairs flat.

"Brian!" Vincent Ambrose tried in vain to halt his underling's advances, but the chaos was already being played out a few streets away. As Sasha swung into the junction facing the cluster of shops, Vincent could see Robin Bradford face down on the pavement, Mr Heckler and Mr Koch ensuring he stayed prostrate and silent, hands cuffed behind his head and feet zip-tied together. "Oh, my Lord! What have you done, Brian?" The fallout from Brian's actions could only land on Vincent, regardless of whether he had sanctioned them or not. Brian was merely a pawn in the game of chess between Robin Bradford and Vincent Ambrose.

Brian led the visibly shaken Alesha and Chantelle out into the street, their skimpy lingerie barely covering their embarrassment, and only fuelling everyone's desire to stare at them. Vincent stood scowling at Brian and motioned to the armed guard to bring Robin Bradford up onto his feet. Both policemen now knew that no murder had taken place.

"But his white shirt is covered in blood!" protested Brian.

"Try House Red, you prat! Wrong sort of claret, I do believe! We have no choice now but to take him back to the Nick... you call the dogs off, you incompetent arse!" Glancing up at the helicopter still buzzing around the scene, Vincent could barely hide his anguish.

Brian and the others shepherded Robin Bradford into a waiting prison van. Soon it was weaving its way through the rush hour traffic, the Armed Response

Unit tight at its rear, weapons still drawn. Meanwhile Vincent Ambrose was trying to work out how he could salvage a collar from the mess that his colleagues had dumped on him.

***

Vincent and Sasha stood waiting in the Police Station compound, hushed and fraught as the van swung in and ground to a halt at Ambrose's feet. Terry and Brian pulled Robin Bradford from the steel-gated vehicle and led him up the long ramp to the Station's rear doors. One by one the policemen snaked their way past Vincent, some offering vague apologies, others passing by in sombre silence. The long knives were drawn, arses started to get covered, fingers were already being pointed, and no-one wanted Ambrose's teeth marks in their backsides. Brian steered a dazed and bewildered Robin Bradford through the corridors and towards the Duty Sergeant.

"Robin Bradford, arrested on suspicion of the murder of three prostitutes."

"Put him in Cell Four!"

The foyer was deadly quiet except for Robin Bradford's echoing profanities and his repeated protestations of innocence.

CHAPTER 20

RED TAPE

Robin Bradford was left stressing and festering in his eight-by-eight. He couldn't begin to fathom why such force had been used to lift him. After all, he fumed, he had only given some brasses a back-hander. He paced his cell endlessly, stopping frequently to bang on the door and shout obscenities at anyone who passed. When the Duty Sergeant appeared, Robin demanded his right to make a call, which was reluctantly granted by the rule abiding officer. Robin tried to get through to Lizzie, but there was no answer. "Damn!" With few other options available to him Robin called on his associate and generous business colleague Asif.

Asif was not best pleased to hear of Robin's plight, but promised to help him anyway: nothing to do of course with the one hundred and forty grand in cash now in Police possession. The Arab duly called Lizzie and left a message. About twenty minutes later she was confronting the Desk Sergeant, demanding to see her boyfriend. "Take a seat, Madam! Someone will be along shortly." She stamped her feet and banged the counter, but he had seen it all before. "Do yourself a favour and park your backside over there, Lady, or you'll be getting the cell next door to him!" Lizzie bit her tongue and dutifully sat silent next to all the other undesirables gracing the waiting-room.

The minutes merged into hours as Ambrose's team assembled page upon page of evidence and information. He knew they needed to be water tight or Robin Bradford's brief would turn them inside out. Everything fell neatly into place, no stone left unturned as the Boys in Blue made ready their literary assault. Paperwork ruled this domain: each document was painstakingly prepared, perfect and precise. Few doubts crossed Ambrose's mind as he sought the help of the Crown's legal team.

Asif had instructed his own solicitor to assist Robin in his hour of need and, more importantly, obtain the release of his funds. Raymond Stimpson sauntered into the Station, brushing aside the advances of any lowly PCs. Marching purposefully up to the Duty Sergeant, he handed him his card.

"Stimpson here, to see Mr Robin Bradford!"

"Yes, Sir! If you'll take a seat, someone..."

"I think not, Sergeant." He cut the minion short. "If I can't see Mr Bradford immediately, you had better have a very good reason, or your Curriculum Vitae will need to be polished and ready."

The sergeant clocked Stimpson's determination and promptly called upstairs to Vincent's office. Cupping the phone tightly, he spoke to Nicky. "We've got some airy-fairy suit at the desk, throwing his toys out! You'd better get Ambrose down here sharpish."

Nicky barged straight into Vincent's office and gave him the bad news. "Who is it, do you know?" He asked.

"Stimpson... Raymond Stimpson."

"Oh well, that's me fucked then. He could get Adolf Hitler a barbecue for his cell, the smarmy tosser!"

"That good, is he?"

"Damn right he is! You'd better order Robin Bradford a taxi now - save the wait! Shit!"

***

Back down at the desk the Duty Sergeant reluctantly gave Raymond Stimpson the news. "Vincent Ambrose, the senior office handling the case, will be down to see you shortly, Sir. In the meantime perhaps you would like to take a seat."

"I would like to take them all - preferably to the Civic Amenities tip!" Sizing up what was available, Stimpson elected to stand, rather than soil his Saville Row suit on the row of torn, sick-stained chairs. Smoothing his lapels down and checking his watch, he stood waiting impatiently for the arrival of Vincent Ambrose. Lizzie rose from her seat and approached the lawyer as he gazed with distaste at his surroundings.

"Are you here for Robin Bradford?" She asked him.

"And who might you be, Madam?"

"I'm Lizzie Fenwick, his fiancée. Is there any news on him? Can you get him out?" Lizzie was pale and sweating profusely: out of concern for her man, so everyone assumed. That was an aeon away from the truth. In fact she was all about self-preservation - and destroying Robin into the bargain.

"Ahh, Miss Fenwick! My client Mr Aggi has told me about you. He holds you in very high regard. As for the plight of your husband..."

"Boyfriend!"

"Sorry - boyfriend! I would like to refrain from passing comment until such time as I have had the opportunity to speak with him."

His jet black hair and swarthy skin gave him a Mediterranean look. Couple this with his slick attire, and you could well have mistaken Raymond for a Sicilian businessman.

Vincent Ambrose entered the fray and was instantly recognised by Raymond Stimpson. "Mr Ambrose! We meet again. I hope you don't still hold any grudges over the Anderson trial, Dear Boy!"

"Raymond, good to see you again! As for the Anderson debacle, if your conscience can let you sleep after that, then good luck to you!" Vincent Ambrose was still smarting from their last encounter. Stimpson had managed to secure the release of an armed robber Vincent had taken two years to nail.

"I'll take that as a yes then." Smirking wildly, Stimpson followed Ambrose through to the cells.

Lizzie tucked in behind the suits as they made off, but was quickly halted by the Desk Sergeant. "Sorry love, you can't go through yet."

"I'm not your fucking love!" Lizzie retreated to her sticky blue vinyl seat.

***

Ambrose put Stimpson in Interview Room Two and then stood by the door awaiting Robin Bradford's entrance. Bradford was shepherded in by two burly uniformed officers and plonked down in a chair, still cuffed. "I believe we can dispense with the restraints now, Gentleman!" They both looked for approval to Vincent, who nodded in agreement. "If I could have a few moments alone with my client, please."

"I don't think so!"

"Come now, Mr Ambrose! I have hardly come bearing any contraband. You have my word that nothing untoward is afoot."

"Five minutes!" he barked.

"How gracious, Vincent!" Stimpson's sarcasm did nothing to repair the rift between the two men.

"Now then Mr Bradford, if you would care to enlighten me, we can set about getting you home."

"Well..."

***

Fifteen minutes passed and Ambrose was still pacing the corridors outside. Stimpson came out into the hallway with a smug grin on his face. "So we are in court at ten sharp then, Vincent?"

"Yes, that would seem to be the case!"

"Well, I wouldn't bank on bringing my man back here. You have excelled yourself as usual. A catalogue of faux-pas and illegalities. You couldn't organise a 'piss up,' as they say. I bid you farewell... till tomorrow, Dear Boy."

Pompous, fucking idiot! Ambrose thought as he personally dragged Robin Bradford back to his cell. "Don't get too excited by your brief's news, Buddy! We've got enough rope to hang you ten times over."

***

Lizzie followed hot on Stimpson's heels, firing questions at him left, right and centre. "Miss Fenwick, there is nothing I can really tell you at this juncture. You must just be as supportive as you can, and God willing, we shall have him home for dinner tomorrow evening.

Back upstairs in the Station Brian had been called through to Vincent Ambrose's office.

"So Brian, what part of 'just fucking follow him' didn't you get?"

"I thought..."

"You didn't think, that's your bloody problem! Now that slippery bastard Stimpson is going to shit all down my neck in Court tomorrow morning! You make a mug of me over this, and you'd better put in a chitty for a transfer."

Brian skulked out of the room with his tail between his legs. Inside the office Nicky and the others began frantically dashing around trying to make out they were busy and not idling, whilst listening to his bollocking.

***

Lizzie could barely sleep that night as she tossed and turned, thinking of all the ifs, buts and maybes. Robin Bradford didn't get his forty winks either. Bewildered by the actions and accusations of Ambrose's team, he was at a loss to understand why they thought he had murdered three prostitutes. He knew it looked bad,

considering he had visited all three, assaulting two of them. But surely they had no evidence even of that.
As for Vincent Ambrose, his reasons for not getting much sleep were decidedly different; he had managed to track down Vicky Ward and was enjoying a passionate night. She went for him like a wild animal, determined to make her mark. Vicky wanted love and stability and she knew just how to get it. Vincent would melt in her arms like ice cream on a summer's day.

***

Next morning Lizzie sat in the gallery comforted by Maria, who incidentally had a vested interest in the case, praying that Robin would be sent down, in the vague hope that he would then disappear from Lizzie's life. Lizzie was trying her best not to crack under the pressure she was receiving from everyone involved, especially the whole Media entourage. Assembled below were Vincent Ambrose, Lucy Hockley, William Mumford and the rest of the team, waiting for their hard work to come to fruition. At last the Clerk of the Court walked to centre stage and addressed the audience, his booming voice echoing through the cold, barren air of the Courtroom.
"All rise for the Right Honourable Judge Cartwright!"
The babbling noise abated and the room fell silent as Cartwright adjusted his robes and sat majestically surveying the wooden stalls. "Please be seated!"
The Clerk began to read aloud. "We are convened here today for the preliminary hearing between the Crown and Robin Albert Bradford, who is charged with the murders of Katya Lesniak, Helena Landsvig and Estelle Mandichi between the seventh of January

and the fourth of February, 2010. It is not the purpose of the court to pass judgement on Mr Bradford today, Your Honour, but merely to establish the need to incarcerate him until such time as evidence may be presented in full."

"Mr Bradford, I have heard the case made against you today and it is my view that you are a dangerous man who needs to be imprisoned until such time as the Crown Prosecution Service can bring a full case against you. You are, on the evidence provided to date, a threat to the general public and we have a duty to protect young women from you." The judge had delivered a crushing verdict on Bradford's character. Lizzie wept hysterically.

"M'Lord, if I may address you briefly." Raymond Stimpson took the stage to deliver his well-practised response. "I put it to you, Your Honour, that Mr Bradford is not a dangerous man at all. The operation mounted against my client is at best flawed, at worst farcical. The senior forensic scientist states clearly in his report that the attacker is left handed. Mr Bradford is right dominant. The mobile phone evidence to determine Mr Bradford's location at the time of the deaths was acquired illegally, and I move for it to be struck out. Allegedly, Inspector Ambrose's team already had records of a phone that they had not yet discovered. How so? There is no physical evidence to place my client at the scene of Estelle Mandichi's death. He freely admits to sexual relations with all three victims, but I stress that the onus must be on Vincent Ambrose's team to prove that my client killed any one of them." With that, the noise level in the room jumped up a notch or so as the whispering intensified.

"Ladies and Gentleman!" announced the Judge, "I wish to retire to my chambers for a short interlude. Mr Ambrose, Mr Mumford and Mr Stimpson, would you please make yourselves available to me in ten minutes' time." Brian glanced at Sasha, who promptly shrugged back at him. Ambrose fixed his stare on Brian and mouthed 'Useless Arsehole' as he left to try and salvage his case.

The four mighty heads clashed within the confines of Judge Cartwright's chambers for nearly an hour, the gallery back in the courtroom waiting with bated breath. Even when they returned to their seats, the three were still unaware what action Cartwright would take.

"Would the Court please rise for the Honourable Judge Cartwright."

This time Cartwright was looking even more solemn, but removing his glasses with a sigh, and folding his hands together he delivered his judicious opinion. "I have no doubt that Mr Bradford has some case to answer to, but I am greatly vexed by the manner in which he has been brought before me today. The evidence that has been presented is without reasonable foundation and thus I have no choice but to issue instructions for his immediate release." The courtroom erupted into life as Ambrose leaped from his seat, with others echoing his concerns.

"Order! Order! I must insist, Mr Ambrose, that you exercise more restraint; otherwise you will find yourself in Contempt of Court. This case is now adjourned until the First of March. Court dismissed!"

A mixture of emotions was evident in the room when

the verdict was read. Robin Bradford punched the air in jubilation, while Ambrose's utter dismay was reflected in the faces of all his team. Lizzie didn't know whether to laugh or cry, as 'her man' rushed to embrace her, and Maria stifled the urge to punch him for what he had done to her and her best friend. A preening, smirking Stimpson sauntered over and offered his commiserations to his jousting partner with outstretched hand.

"Never mind, Dear Boy! We'll just chalk this one up to me, shall we?"

"Let's hope we aren't chalking up another murder between now and the next hearing. You'll have blood on your hands, Stimpson! Mark my words!" Vincent shouldered past Raymond Stimpson, leaving him in his wake to readjust his jacket and regain his suave composure.

"All fair in love and Courtrooms, Vincent!" But Stimpson's smug parting shot fell short of reaching Ambrose as the noise in the Courtroom rose to a crescendo.

Outside, the paparazzi surged around him. "No comment!" was all they got as he made a hasty getaway in his car. Meanwhile, Stimpson and Robin Bradford stood on the steps proclaiming his victory and innocence to all that would listen. Then Asif Aggi stepped from the crowd and congratulated Robin before delivering the killer blow.

"We need to speak urgently, Mr Robin! I have to reconsider my investments."

CHAPTER 21

THE DUST SETTLES

The following morning Brian walked into Vincent Ambrose's office, placed a white envelope amidst the clutter and retreated hastily towards the door.

"What's this?" asked Vincent.

"My resignation."

"Ok, thank you!"

Brian paused briefly in the doorway, waiting for Vincent to beg its retraction.

"Don't let me keep you!" was the last thing Brian heard before he packed his meagre belongings into a plastic container.

"Well, that's me done then, Guys!" Not one person stopped working to bid him farewell. He was as popular as the proverbial lucky dip's snake.

As the door finally closed behind him, Vincent Ambrose ventured out of his office. "Right, you lot, listen up! That miserable cantankerous old fart has re-

signed. Hopefully all the mistakes this case has been plagued with will follow him out the door. I want one hundred percent commitment from you lot - and more importantly no 'fuck ups'. We go back to Court in under a month." All around the room murmurs of agreement heralded his call. "Terry, I want you to step up to the plate and take over Brian's role."
"Cheers, Guv! I won't let you down."
"Cut the arse licking, Terry! I know you won't - that's why I picked you! Sasha, I need to see you in my office please!"
"Guv?" She looked anxious at his request.
"Come on, don't look so worried!"
Someone at the back of the room shouted, "Reckon you're gonna get the same as poor old Vicky Ward!"
"I don't need promotion that bad, Guv!" Sasha turned to the crowd and mimicked oral sex, which sent frenzied applause and laughter buzzing round the room.
"Close the door behind you please, Sash." Vincent settled in his seat and motioned for Sasha to take up residence opposite him.
"I don't want the mistakes you've made during Brian's reign to cloud your thoughts. You've shown great promise and ingenuity. Keep it up! However, you mustn't allow your cavalier attitude to surface like it did yesterday before Robin Bradford's arrest. If you need to think about whether it's right or wrong, chances are it's wrong. He let you down by not keeping you in check. You remind me of a younger version of myself..." He continued his sermon for a few minutes before reiterating his praise.
"Thanks for the feedback, Vincent! I appreciate the chat."

Vincent followed her out of the room to a chorus of catcalls and whistles. She wiped her hand across her mouth and imitated spitting, while Vincent adjusted his flies in allusion to sexual misconduct. Once he was safely back in his office and out of earshot, Chris called across to Sasha

"Did you get the 'pull your socks up' speech or the 'you remind me of a younger me' speech?"

"The latter, smart arse!" she smiled.

***

Maria knocked on Lizzie's door, hoping to offer a shoulder of support to her friend. "How are you bearing up girl? ... You look like shit!"

"I feel like it too! But seriously, I'd rather not talk about it just yet. I'm going out of my mind with worry."

"You haven't been yourself for weeks Lizzie - even before all this surfaced. You know you can talk to me about anything, don't you?" Inside, though, the last thing Maria wanted to do was coax Lizzie into a one-on-one about Robin. She might say, or do something to trip herself up and face an unwelcome verbal assault from her mate, or worse still a physical altercation.

"When the time is right, Maria, I will - I promise. Just not now...ok?"

***

Robin sat at the table, pushing his cereal aimlessly around the bowl with his spoon. When Lizzie returned to finish her coffee he thought it would be best to come clean about his shameful behaviour over the last few months.

"I know I've made massive mistakes, Liz, but I'm willing to make every effort, do whatever it takes to get us back on track. I owe you big time for my failings."
"Go on..." she maintained a frosty air, but encouraged him to continue. He thought that reconciliation was possibly on offer, so blurted out his grizzly details.
"I've been visiting call girls and massage parlours since the bankruptcy. I know it hit us both very hard, in different ways of course. But since you've been working so hard to bankroll us out of this shit pit, you've been tired all the time, and I feel neglected."
"It's more than that, Robin! You have no idea of the pressure I've been under. I've lost everything too. Friends, my home, even my mum's jewellery had to go to bail you out!"
"I know I was out of order: I took a gamble and it didn't pay off. What more can I say? I was a fool!"
"Too bloody right you were!"
"Just give me a chance, and I will prove myself, I promise!"
"I don't think I can ever forgive you, Robin. You have no idea what this has turned me into. I feel so much resentment - rage even!"
"Look, don't make any hasty decisions yet. Wait till after the court case. When I'm found to be innocent of these trumped up charges, maybe we could go away somewhere. Start afresh?" Robin was desperate for Lizzie to believe him, to believe in his innocence. The irony was; she was the only person who knew he was telling the truth.
"Listen Robin, this isn't going away overnight, and I'm not making any promises. Let's just see what hap-

pens!" She seemed to melt a little as the conversation petered out.

***

Ambrose was throwing orders at his team from all angles: 'fetch this', 'check that', 'go and speak to this person, that person'. With one of the most vital pieces of evidence taken from them, his crew needed to work like Trojans to rebuild the case, desperate to restore their advantage. Every piece of Robin Bradford's technology was seized, legitimately this time, and systematically pulled to pieces in search of a hidden clue or link.

Eventually the pieces began to slot back in one by one. The sat nav placed him at two scenes; the computer verified his interest in Helena, as did hair samples from Estelle found during a forensic sweep at his house in Hadleigh Crescent. Neighbours came forward to corroborate Estelle's movements at his home, and Jonathan Pettigrew identified him from a catalogue of stooges visiting Helena. All this, together with his cash withdrawal from the garage, meant he was well and truly hung. Robin Bradford didn't know it, but Ambrose was sitting pretty.

The final nail in his coffin was the dog walker in Shoebury who witnessed him throw the keys into the Thames. The following morning she re-walked the same stretch and plucked the keys from the muddy silt. The 'Find Me' tab led her to a key holding company in Romford, who tried in vain to reunite the keys with their owner, Miss Landsvig. Eventually the persistent calls to her flat were answered by a policeman, who filtered the information back to Nicky at the station. The dog walker also fingered Robin Bradford from a line-up of potential villains.

Barring a miracle, Robin Bradford would be enjoying a long and uneventful stay at HMP 'Hard luck'.

His only salvation was that he had managed to resurrect his business dealings with Asif Aggi. This had set him back on the road to success and nicely lined his pockets. If his entrepreneurial skills continued to flourish, his confident and progressive attitude to work would soon see him and Lizzie enjoying their former luxury lifestyle. He just needed to get the better of the Judicial System.

CHAPTER 22

BUSMAN'S HOLIDAY

Lizzie Fenwick was battling hard with mixed emotions. She had once loved Robin dearly, but struggled now with his horrid infidelity. She would balance her own vile actions by telling herself that it had been this that drove her to murder the three cash-hungry sluts he had bedded. Some days she was totally in control, on top of her game; other days saw her reclusive and introverted. Robin had really gone to town in his efforts to redeem himself. Lizzie was bombarded with gifts and meals, and the shabby old Corsa was replaced with a shiny new Fiesta - all funded by his new- found business wealth. He paid her compliments at every turn and helped out around the house wherever he could. Most mornings would see him in the kitchen preparing breakfast and coffee for Lizzie, usually taken up on a tray for her to enjoy in bed. He had been considerate to a fault, especially in the bedroom. Rarely would he press for any more than a peck or a hug, (which was all that she was prepared to agree to as yet). He told himself that Lizzie was softening, her frosty exterior melting slowly away, and he was convinced that she would soon give in to his sexual demands and consummate their relationship once more.

***

With all this trauma to cope with, Robin Bradford needed to escape for a while. Foreign travel was strictly prohibited because of his alleged misdemeanours, so he resolved to spend his time at one of England's countless caravan parks. Tapping into his vast customer and client base, he managed to blag a free midweek stay for him and Lizzie at a site close to the seaside town of Weymouth. With its horseshoe shaped beach, clusters of shops and endless Sea Front hostelries, Weymouth was not unlike Southend. All it needed was a mile long pier. A veritable home from home, this suited Robin down to the ground: he was after all, a creature of habit.

Understandably Lizzie wasn't thrilled at the prospect of a few days and nights cooped up in a forty foot caravan with Robin, let alone the constant reminder of her work days.

"Couldn't you just have got a chalet or something? For Christ's sake, Robin... you couldn't organise the proverbial piss up!" she moaned.

"We've been through the mill lately, Liz. We owe ourselves a break - even if it's only this," Robin pleaded. "Come on, what do you say!" He smiled at her.

"OK, then! But I can't promise I'll bloody well enjoy it."

Robin glanced at Lizzie with a familiar smug grin on his face. The old, confident, arrogant Robin surfaced again just for a second. Lizzie had been cornered; Robin had railroaded her into submission, and she was not best pleased.

***

Monday morning's usual drudgery as the world and his wife beat a path to Work's door was an aeon away for Robin and Lizzie as they heaved their bags into the hallway. Robin took an abundance of belongings to his car, and they stuffed and squeezed the mountain of things into the boot. The journey down to Dorset was long and tiresome, with numerous stops for food, drink and toilet breaks. Annoyingly, Lizzie was worse than most kids, suffering constant bouts of nausea. "At this bloody rate we'll be just in time to turn round and come straight home again!" Robin's frustration began to show, even more so after the thousandth, 'Are we nearly there yet?' from his listless passenger.

When the roadside sign appeared for the 'Blue Lagoon Holiday Camp Next Right' they simultaneously raised a cheer, and Robin veered off down a dusty farm track. The site seemed clean and bright with lots of people meandering around the maze of pathways. Sandal and sock wearing dad's herded flocks of children to and fro, as the mums followed on aimlessly in their matching waterproof coats, weighed down with picnics and blankets. The older kids zigzagged the pathways in their bright red buggies, plaguing the campers by pedalling furiously and swerving erratically round the countless pitches.

"How do you fancy that Liz? Us cruising round the site in one of those!" Smirked Robin.
"Not on your bloody nelly! You can hire one - I'll sit outside the caravan and read my book, or go and get my nails done!"
As they made their way to Reception, Robin wittered on about all the things they could do on their little get-away break. Lizzie still remained unconvinced. Once they had picked up the keys and navigated the endless rows of static caravans, the pair parked up and decamped. "Come on, Love, let's try and make the best of it!" Lizzie raised her eyebrows before heading empty-handed to their van, leaving Robin weighted down with bags like a pack horse. As he all but fell through the caravan door he sighed. "Great, so I'll be doing all the running, fetching and carrying then will I?"
"Looks that way, Robin!" Lizzie had already finished her fleeting tour of the rooms and cupboards and was now stashing her stuff in the master bedroom. "Best you keep quiet, or you can have the box room!" She shuddered at the thought of being cramped up with him, with little or no room to escape his snoring and flatulence. 'God! I hope they don't have Real Ale' she thought.
"If you start snoring Robin, expect to find me sleeping in the lounge!"
"Do you fancy going for a quick nose around before tea?"
"No, I bloody don't! These places are all the same," she snapped. "You can go if you want. I'll stay here and unpack."
Lizzie was left to try and fit all their possessions into

the miniature cupboard space. Surveying the trailer, she couldn't help but envisage being on Canvey, hard at work scrubbing caravans.

***

Robin was in his element with all the pretty young mums parading around in short skirts and tight tops. Despite the cool spring air they simply had to follow fashion. And as if that wasn't enough, he also had a bevy of 'eager to help' female resort workers to ogle. Every bust, backside and pair of pins on the camp got scrutinised by Robin's roaming eyes. Even though he was desperate to make amends with Lizzie, he couldn't wait to get into the Arcades and Clubhouse, where he could indulge in his favourite pastime of 'goosing'. He was well schooled in the art: a brush here and a glance there, subtle grazes of busts and bottoms, all followed up with an 'Oops, sorry Madam!" or 'Could I squeeze past?' The odd recipient of his lascivious ploys would chastise him; most naively accepted the apology, oblivious of the real connotations.

Regardless of his true character, Robin always came across as well-mannered, and most would say he was agreeable in the extreme. Only those who crossed him, or happened to encounter him when the mask slipped would see the real Robin Bradford, predatory and brutal, selfish beyond belief. He had a crafty way with the ladies, always managing to seek out the weak and vulnerable, or young and impressionable. If any of them showed a trace of interest, he would charm his way into their trust, insidiously poisoning their judgement until they succumbed to his advances. With his body ageing, but his mind still sharp, he had resolved to work smarter, not harder in his quest for extra-marital activities.

The Blue Lagoon held one such victim for Robin's craft and guile, unwittingly primed for his trap to be sprung. She didn't know it, but Robin was already homing in on her, weapon drawn, sights locked, and ready to strike.

Anna Knight worked most evenings at the Camp: thankless jobs mostly, like removing coins stuck in machines, emptying the trays of cash, and changing money for the army of kids that swept through the Foyer and into the Arcade. Sometimes if she was lucky, she got a shift on Reception or at the swimming pool. On his first night Robin had seen her arguing with someone he assumed, was her boyfriend. Despondent that Anna wasn't giving in to his advances, he had just ended their three week old relationship. Despite their short romance, Anna was understandably upset. Seizing his moment, Robin sidled over as the ex-boyfriend disappeared from view and offered some pearls of wisdom, words of consolation. "Plenty more fish in the sea, Girl. Don't upset yourself! There must be a queue of boys waiting to date a pretty little thing like you. I know I would be if I was younger!"

Anna was very similar to Lizzie to look at, slim, petite and with small pert breasts. She boasted a shock of flaming red hair and a host of freckles, which gave her the innocence and charm of a young schoolgirl. The Camp uniform hardly flattered her physique, but Robin's imagination led his mind's eye right through the drab disguise. He stroked his arm across her shoulder and upper arm, and then said his goodbyes. The desolate Anna soaked up his kindness; they exchanged names, and she gave him a grateful smile. She watched him as he walked off, thinking to herself 'what a kind and pleasant man'. Robin had managed to get his foot in the door now, and would sit back patiently waiting for the fish to take his bait. Fresh on the rebound, her actions were typical of a slighted young woman looking to rebuild her confidence and move on from her breakup. Robin's aim was to be her shoulder to cry on, her comfort blanket.

***

Following the tedium of the journey, the couple decided it would be best to hit the sheets and recharge their batteries ready for the next day's excitement.

"Nice big fry up in the morning and we can hit the Boating Lake. What do you say?"

"Can't wait!" Lizzie exclaimed sarcastically.

***

The next morning, full of egg and bacon, Robin tried in vain to coax Lizzie out of the caravan, but she wasn't having any of it. Undeterred he set off alone; set off in search of excitement, while Lizzie had the dubious honour of doing the dishes before settling down to her book. Robin had more on his mind than a jaunt round the lake; he was seeking thrills of a different nature. He was hell bent on bobbing about on young Anna. Try as he might, Anna was nowhere to be found all morning. Eventually he wound up back at their base for lunch with Lizzie, and suggested they might visit the Pool later on in the afternoon. Reluctantly Lizzie agreed.

They both enjoyed a good session in the pool, splashing and frolicking together, minds averted from life's perils and problems. Around four o'clock Lizzie waved the white flag and suggested going back to the trailer for tea, before venturing out to the Clubhouse later in the evening. They parted company, and Robin made off for the Gents' Changing Rooms. Later, as he was leaving the Showers, he caught sight of Anna sauntering towards the pool from the staff area. She was wearing a tight, bright yellow t-shirt on with 'Lifeguard' emblazoned across it, and royal blue shorts. The writing on her shirt gave Robin the ideal cover to stare, under pretence of reading it.

"Hello, Young Lady! How are you feeling today? Over your troubles yet?"

She blushed with embarrassment as she recalled the previous evening. "Oh, hi! You're the man who was so kind yesterday, aren't you?" Robin was duly flattered, mistaking her blushes for evidence of a teenage crush. "Yes, Robin! I should have stayed in the pool. You could have rescued me then as a return gesture!" A cringeworthy but suggestive comment, which didn't register with the naive Anna. The pair exchanged a few more words before she made her way over to the pool's Lifeguard Chair. Robin was slowly drawing this little water baby into his lair. If only he could keep Lizzie at arm's length, he might stand a chance he thought. Ironically, the couple's visit to the pool would turn out to be a real stroke of luck. By mid-afternoon on the Wednesday Lizzie had developed a chronic ear infection, headache and general feelings of sickness. She blamed the pool, assuming inadequate hygiene had caused her to be unwell. Unfortunately for her, it looked as if she would be confined to the caravan for a while, leaving Robin to roam the Camp on his lonesome.

"You may as well go down to the Clubhouse on your own: I'm staying put. If I don't feel better in the morning, we'll be heading home!"

Robin of course was eager to stay. "Let's see how you are tomorrow! We don't want to be too hasty now, yeah?" She mustered a nod of agreement and lay back down again.

***

Robin showered and shaved trying to look his best for the chase he knew was coming. He packed Lizzie off to bed with a cocktail of pills and potions and slunk off out in search of dalliance. He eventually found Anna in the Arcade and stood silently watching, waiting for a poignant moment to capture her attention. He casually fed the machines while keeping an eye on her every move. As she bent over to remove some rubbish from between the machines he darted across and cupped her buttocks, gently squeezing her cheeks.

"I see you're feeling much better!" he joked as she spun round quickly to see who had taken liberties with her.

"Oh blimey, it's you! You scared me half to death, you cheeky bugger!" Far from being offended, Anna was flattered by the older man's advances.

"You'll get me the sack doing things like that!" she said, glancing around the room to ensure no one had seen his playful grope.

"You didn't mind then, I haven't offended you?" he asked respectfully, whilst already knowing the answer.
"Not at all! It just caught me by surprise. I'm petrified of getting caught messing around on my shift."
"Why don't I meet you at the end of your shift? I could walk you home."
"That'd be good, but what about your wife? Wouldn't she be angry?"
"Of course she'd be angry, but only if she finds out. And I'm not about to tell her, are you!"
"No way! She might kill me!"
"So it's your choice. What time do you knock off?" Robin was keen to move up a gear now Anna had given him the green light.
"I finish at nine-thirty. But I don't have to be in till nine forty-five. You could meet me on the bench by the entrance if you like."
"Nine forty-five! How come so early?"
Anna paused, thinking carefully before giving her answer. "I've got college in the morning; I'm eighteen though, honest!" Robin read between the lines and assumed rightly that Anna was lying and probably still at Senior School. Regardless, she had told him she was eighteen, and that was good enough for him.
"So you'll meet me then?"
"Why wouldn't I?" Her anxieties just made her more vulnerable, and him stronger and all the more determined to bag his little gym-slip beauty.

***

The night dragged on endlessly as Robin and Anna both waited for the allotted time to swing round. He managed to stave off his carnal thoughts by propping up the bar and ogling the other girls who staffed the pumps. The minute hand drifted slowly down to the half hour and he duly sank his last few dregs of beer before sliding off out into the night, impatient for his encounter with the 'green' student. Anna arrived right on cue and the pair ambled along the leafy lane that led up towards the main road. Arm in arm they paused briefly to engage in a few pecks and gropes. Robin had hardly managed to get a decent feel of his young lover, when she announced it was time for her to get home.

"Can't you stay a bit longer?" he asked, resting his hand on her arse.

"No Robin, my dad will kill me. I could try and see if I can stay out longer tomorrow if you like?"

"Ok! But I can't guarantee I'll be able to escape the old bag's clutches."

"We shall both have to try our luck. Same time, same place?" she asked, unfazed by his inappropriate advances and obvious commitments.

"Deal! But you definitely need loosening up my little lovely. I'll bring us a bottle of Dutch courage if you like?"

"I'm not sure; I've never really drunk before."

A few more pecks saw Anna sprinting up the road towards home, desperate not to invoke the wrath of her father.

***

The next day was a blur for Robin as he paced the camp. He had convinced Lizzie she should stay one more night. Now he was wishing time away, longing for his next rendezvous with Anna to come quicker. As evening closed in, he steered Lizzie towards an early bed, citing an 'up and out first thing!' and homeward bound motive. Lizzie was only too glad to see the back of Robin, who had plagued her all day with his restless antics. Now, while his girlfriend's back was turned, Robin lifted a bottle of vodka and some cheap-brand Cola from the cupboard, and secreted it under the caravan in readiness for his departure. He was pretty sure the inexperienced drinker would be far less tense and much more agreeable once he had coaxed some spirits into her.

***

Daniel Knight looked up from the TV when Anna walked into the lounge. "Dad, they've asked me to do an extra hour at the Camp tonight. They've got one of those Race Night thingies on and are short- staffed. Would you mind if I did it?"

"Yes, Anna, I would! You've got School in the morning, and exams to think about."

"Please, Dad! I could do with the extra money - I've got Tasha's sixteenth birthday party to go to Saturday night, and I want to get a new dress. Please?" And she fluttered her eyelids and mustered her cutest smile.

"Well, alright - ten thirty! No later, or I will be down the Camp looking for you and harassing you in front of your mates, and you won't be going to any parties!" Despite his overbearing manner, Daniel Knight only had Anna's interests at heart, but like all mardy teenagers she wouldn't see it for years, if at all.

"Thank you, Daddy!" Hugging him quickly she rushed

off out to work, only this time she had secured herself an extra hour with a rampant reprobate. At a tender fifteen years of age, Anna was too young and naive to see through the likes of Robin Bradford and his lecherous, perverted intentions.

***

Anna had been hatching a plan of her own too. Not wishing to be outdoors on a cold and rainy night, she had talked her friend into giving her a trailer key, ironically only two pitches away from Robin Bradford's sleeping girlfriend. Robin found her at the clubhouse just after nine, and was keen to make sure all was still well for their meeting. She explained the change of plans and passed him the key, being careful not to be seen. He was elated: she would definitely be giving in to him, he thought. "Go and put the fire on! I'll be along in about twenty minutes." He didn't need asking twice, and was off to find their love nest straight away. He passed by his own caravan and paused to take stock of his actions, but the guilt soon receded and he sloped on by. He convinced himself that it was too late in the day to stop now anyway. Anna snuck out of the club a few minutes early and went into the staff room where she promptly dug out a light yellow micro dress form her handbag. Once the dress was on, she applied some more layers of make-up and refreshed her lipstick. She topped it all off with a few pieces of bling, and then made for the warmth of their caravan.

Robin had searched through the cupboards and found a couple of glasses. He poured a very generous measure of vodka into Anna's and a smaller one for himself, and then added some Cola. He had a quick taste of hers and reeled back instantly as the bitter taste rattled at his senses. He put the television on a music channel, dimmed the lights and lay back waiting for his temptress to arrive. Like some Lord of the Manor, Robin Bradford was eager to sample the maiden's wares.

Anna showed up minutes after nine thirty and let herself in, locking the door behind her. Robin sat on the sofa, drink in hand. After rising to greet her, he showered her with kisses before passing her the poison chalice. She seemed very tense as the old letch pawed at her fresh skin but soon, he thought, the medicine would be working. She gulped at the drink like it was going out of fashion, blissfully ignorant to its potency. "Blimey! That's a bit feisty isn't it?" Anna's first real tipple certainly hit the spot as she downed nearly all of it in the first swig. Robin watched her, happy in the knowledge that she would be putty within twenty minutes or so. His conquest was edging closer to submission, powerless to halt his advances.

"Another?" he teased, knocking back his own, creating the illusion he was matching her glass for glass.

"What the heck...Go for it!" she smiled, showing her cute dimples.

***

Twenty minutes and another two drinks later and Anna's world was getting heady. The room started to spin and her legs felt seriously weak. Robin even started to look more appealing as her beer goggles kicked in. He had only pushed for lingering kisses and little squeezes so far, but now the time was right to up the ante. “We both know why we are here, Anna, don’t we?” he said brushing his hands across her slender stomach.

“I guess so, but I’m really not sure. I haven’t done it before...I don’t know if I’m ready. If I’m honest I’m quite scared.”

“There’s nothing to be scared about, my little angel, I’m here to look after you. You’re in safe hands with me, I promise!”

“I don’t know! I’m feeling a bit queasy and the room’s spinning too. I actually feel a bit sick as it goes.”

“Best thing to do is we both have a little lie down and see how you feel. Yes?” Robin scooped her up gently in his big strong arms and carried her through the caravan and into the bedroom.

“I don’t feel well, Robin. I’ve come over all hot and my heart is racing!” Robin didn’t care, he was going to fuck this virtually paralytic teenager come what may, but he still needed to be seen as compassionate.

“Just nerves, my beautiful baby!” he cooed.

As Anna lay on the bed watching the room swirling round, Robin started to peel her dress off. She offered very little resistance, but that was more through incapacity than desire. He threw her dress on the floor beside the bed and began to remove her underwear, despite her vague and mumbled protests. With very little finesse or expertise he defiled the young virgin’s body, dragging her forcefully into womanhood. No tender embraces or intimate whispers, just cold, carnal, self-satisfying sex. The whole ordeal was excruciating for poor Anna. She lay silent and still as he stole her innocence, occasionally trying to push the brute back as his suffocating weight bore down on her. As for Bradford, he had gone into a trance, ignoring every moan and move, and he wasn't finished yet.

When he climaxed, he simply rolled over and sighed out loud. Anna lay weeping, streaks of black mascara weaving their way down her freckled cheeks. The considerate, affectionate Robin Bradford had long since gone. Now the oafish brute who had stolen her dignity sat beside her pulling on his trousers, and without so much as a word he dressed and prepared to leave. Looking him up and down, she knew she had misjudged him and had duly paid the price. She started to convulse as the vodka blighted her stomach, and rolling on her side she got ready for the inevitable surge of vomit, due any second.

"I'll go and get you a bowl! Just relax; I'll be back in two shakes." But Robin Bradford's patience had been worn thin by the young Anna's tiresome inexperience. She tried desperately to hang on to her dinner as she waited in vain for his return. The selfish monster had already flown the nest, leaving her alone. He had bolted at the first opportunity, back to his own trailer to get cleaned up and grab some well-earned shut-eye before the dawn retreat back to Essex. After countless convulsions and projectile vomits, Anna fell asleep.

***

Ten-thirty came and went as Anna's father paced the floors of his bungalow, alarm bells already ringing. Moving out into the street, Daniel Knight stretched and craned to try and catch sight of his daughter. At ten forty-five he rang through to Grant, the camp manager in a bid to assuage his ever- growing anxiety.

"Sorry Dan, but Anna left as usual at nine-thirty, Mate."

"Nine-thirty? Are you sure? She told me she was working till ten-thirty because you had a Race Night on or something!"

"The Race Night was Tuesday. Not only that, Dan, but you know we have a strict policy on under- sixteens working after nine-thirty."

"Well, where the hell is she! It's not like her to be late. You can set your watch by her normally."

"You sit tight for ten minutes, and I'll ring up to the Clubhouse. See if I can shed some light on her whereabouts. Alright?"

"No, I'm not fucking alright. But what else can I do!"

***

The only other person apart from Robin Bradford who really knew where Anna was, had already gone home herself. Her best friend Simone had been working on Reception that night and had willingly agreed to sneak Anna a key. She thought her friend was going to the trailer to try and resolve the problems with her boyfriend. No one else knew about the key or the connection with Simone, and as a consequence nobody thought to ask her. Most of the staff indulged in the practice of lending keys to their mates: all of them enjoyed a little kiss and cuddle now and again, even the older, married ones. If anybody needed a bolthole or refuge, one was always available. Perks of the job, if you like.

***

Grant spoke to the Arcade Supervisor and was assured Anna had left promptly at nine thirty.

"Dressed up to the nines, she was. Skimpy little yellow dress - almost certainly had a date, looking like that!"

Grant knew Daniel Knight very well, and he was sure his mate would take the news badly, so he tried to stall ringing him for a while as he tried to think where the little urchin might be hiding. The whole Camp was now either out and actively looking for Anna, or on the look-out at the numerous bars and clubs. Not wishing to spark widespread panic amongst the Camp's residents, the search was being kept low key and semi-covert. By Midnight, though, Daniel Knight couldn't be avoided any longer. Grant was standing at the reception desk phone in hand, brow-beating his staff in his efforts to find Daniel's wayward daughter when Daniel himself strode in, large as life and twice as angry. He let fly at Grant with a string of four letter words and veiled threats, which Grant soaked up without batting an eyelid. He was well used to irate guests remonstrating over this problem or that issue, and always remained calm, composed and professional.

"I know you've got the raving hump, Daniel, but I can assure you we're doing all we can to track her down. I suggest you try to keep calm, and let us work with you!" His compassionate and measured response soon had Daniel simmering down. Grant knew that Daniel was stressed up to the gunnels and didn't mean a word of his ramblings. "Mary, sort Daniel out a coffee, will you please? It sounds like young Anna was possibly going to meet her boyfriend. I'm sure she's just lost track of time and she'll show up real soon."

"They finished with each other two or three days ago, and he's gone to Liverpool to stay with his uncle for a few weeks, so she can't be with him! She's been quiet and secretive all week, Grant. Where the hell is she! What if she's done something stupid! I'll never forgive myself."

"If it's any consolation, Anna's been a picture of happiness around the Camp the last couple of days. No way has she done anything silly, but still, I think it's time we got the Police involved!"

Daniel took Grant's advice and rang Dorset Constabulary straight away. It was coming up to twelve- thirty now, and she was two hours late. No one had seen her for three hours.

***

"I'm afraid there's not a great deal we can do at this moment, Mr Knight. We're very understaffed tonight because of the Festival in town. Unfortunately, a lot of fifteen year old girls go astray for a few hours. I'm sure she'll be back soon - probably with her tail between her legs begging for Daddy's forgiveness! My advice to you, Sir, would be to go home and wait for her! I don't suppose it's the first time she has come home late is it?"

"Well no, but usually it's only half an hour or so at most!"

"We'll circulate her details and give you a call if anyone matching her description shows up. OK, Sir?"

"Not really, but what else can I say! God help you lot if anything happens to her!"

"That sort of attitude will not do you any favours, Mr Knight! I know you're upset, but keep it civil please. If she hasn't turned up by breakfast time, give us a call and we will scale the operation up accordingly."
Daniel was livid, his little girl was missing and they only seemed concerned with a bunch of drunks at the local Town Festival.
"Is that it?"
"What else do you suggest, Mr Knight?"
"I don't know... but..."
"Call us again at nine in the morning, Sir, and I very much hope she shows up in the meantime." Daniel managed no sleep that night, and had probably walked ten miles as he paced the lounge, pausing to look out of the window with every circuit of the room.

***

In the Bradfords' caravan Lizzie was toasting crumpets and Robin was busy whistling away to himself as he refilled the car with the mass of belongings Lizzie had dragged along. Nothing was going to spoil Robin's day, not even his menstrual wife. He had taken his frustrations out on young Anna, so was blissfully happy.
"What time did you get in last night?" Lizzie asked as she smeared copious amounts of butter onto the piping hot crumpets.
"About eleven-ish, I think. I had a few bevvies in the Clubhouse and watched some crap cabaret act."
If Lizzie had taken the time to read the Programme of Events, she would have known that he was lying. The previous night's entertainment was bingo, followed

by some atrocious karaoke: a skin of the teeth escape for the fork-tongued Robin Bradford yet again. Their breakfast soon disappeared, as did the Bradfords. Glancing at Anna's caravan as they left, Robin smirked to himself, pleased with his previous night's conquest. Yet another notch on the bed post for him, only this one was much sweeter, as it had not cost him a penny - less a few shots of vodka. Result! He thought.

***

As they passed through the gates and out onto the main road, Robin muttered his farewells to the 'Blue Lagoon Camp Site' and watched in his mirror till it was just a blot on the horizon.

"That wasn't too bad, was it Lizzie?" he quizzed. "Return visit next year?"

"Are you taking the piss?" she replied sternly. "As for coming back; I very much doubt it. Hopefully we'll be sunning ourselves on the Costa, or somewhere more exotic!" Lizzie was adamant the Blue Lagoon was off limits. She consoled herself with Robin's promises of 'better things to come'.

***

Daniel Knight was beside himself with worry; his precious daughter had been missing for over ten hours. The local police were just about to feel his wrath again as he prepared to launch into them with another verbal assault. Since he had lost his wife unexpectedly to a tumour two years earlier, he had naturally become over-protective of his only child, Anna.

For the Dorset Police, it was just another day at the office. Another teenage tearaway pushing the boundaries.

CHAPTER 23

'MISS'CONDUCT

Anna woke at around eight-thirty to the sound of crunching gravel as the Bradfords drove past her makeshift resting place. She was naked, cold and frightened, her face encrusted with dried sick, her hair matted and dishevelled. She slid the blankets off and eased out of bed, only to find herself standing in a pool of the previous night's sick. The flimsy yellow dress that had made her look so grown up the night before now lay ruined amidst the chewed food and acidic juices which had once been a hastily consumed meal. Her head pounded relentlessly; no amount of squeezing and stroking seemed to help soothe the agony.

As she stood nursing her ego, flashes of the night's ordeal began to drift back. As the morning sun broke through the net curtains it suddenly dawned on her that she'd been here all night. Her dad would go ballistic when she finally showed up. Anna shot into the small bathroom and washed the vomit from her face and hair, before hurriedly dressing in her work clothes. She stumbled out of the trailer and into the fresh morning dew, binning her prized dress as she passed the refuse store. Knowing she was in a world of trouble, the anxious teenager broke into a trot as she made her way towards the Camp entrance. Grant saw her flash past between pitches as he heaved gas bottles into his pickup truck. "Anna! Thank God you're safe! Where the hell have you been? Your dad's going mental with worry. And why are you in such a state? You look rough as a tramp!"

After yesterday's ordeal, Anna wasn't sure how she felt, nor did she have any idea how to deal with the predicament she was now in. She felt degraded and embarrassed, sickened by the thought of her own naivety. Robin Bradford had played her for a fool, and in the cold light of day she could see that only too plainly. "Jump in, Anna! We'd be better get you home - your Old Man is having kittens!" Grant rang ahead to Anna's house, just as Daniel was walking through to the hallway to ring Dorset Police again. Heart in his mouth he picked up the receiver and waited, silent and frightened for Grant to speak, fearing the worst. "Daniel, it's Grant from the park. I've just found Anna. She's ok, so don't panic. She seems a little shaken and is very quiet, possibly hung-over. I'm bringing her back to your house in my truck, so sit tight and we'll see you in a couple of minutes."

Daniel's initial anger subsided for the time being, as the safe return of his little cherub was paramount. As soon as Grant hung up, he called Dorset police to let them know that his daughter was due home any minute. He wasn't best pleased with the 'I told you so' comments he got from the Desk Sergeant, and made his feelings very clear.

While Grant travelled the short distance from the Camp to Anna's home her dad was standing outside in anticipation of her return, and as the truck eased to the kerbside he was already tugging at the door handle to greet her. He embraced her warmly, squeezing her tightly for what seemed like an eternity, all the time telling her not to worry, easing any fears of chastisement. "Whatever's happened, whatever you've done, we can sort it out. The most important thing is you're home - safe and well."

Anna couldn't control her emotions and heart ache any longer and promptly burst into floods of tears, readily confessing to her dad her foolish and gullible behaviour. When he found out that Robin Bradford had stolen his daughter's innocence, he became inconsolable. Grant led them both inside and at Daniel's request made another call to the Police. When he knew the two of them were ok to be left, he slipped quietly away to the kitchen to make that strong sweet tea, which cures all known traumas and ailments. At first the Police sent the two officers Daniel Knight had dealt with the night before, but when they heard her tale they insisted Anna came to the station to formalise her complaint.

***

Robin and Lizzie sat in the Services on the M25 with their overpriced, sub-standard breakfasts and lukewarm dishwater beverages, both oblivious to the drama unfolding back in Weymouth Nick. Lizzie was uneasy with Robin's overly buoyant mood, though. Why was he so happy? Not many things got Robin Bradford chirpy! She surmised he had strayed again, but supposition was all she had, not facts. "Eat up, Fenwick! I want to be home by lunchtime, Asif is taking me to the Casino tonight, and I'd quite like to grab a couple of hours' shut-eye before I go. Need to be on the ball for that!" Lizzie pushed the oil-soaked offerings around her plate, having eaten almost nothing. Unsurprisingly, her appetite had waned as she tried to surmise what Robin might have been up to. "Waste not, want not!" Before Lizzie could say yay or nay, Robin had purloined her bacon and sausage with one clean swipe and was greedily chomping away at them. "Pig!" was all she could bring herself to say as she got up from the table and marched off to the car.

Robin followed out a few minutes later, once he had had his fill. Plonking himself down in the driver's seat, he let out a loud belch, quickly followed by a salvo of flatulence. "Oink fucking oink!" he grinned, looking at Lizzie. In return, she shot him a glance that said he was definitely pushing his luck. She despaired of his vulgarity, but knew that reacting too vehemently would just be a catalyst for more foul antics.

***

Meanwhile Anna sat in the police station sobbing her heart out, comforted only by her father's embrace. All she wanted to do was go home and have a shower, then try and forget the whole disgraceful episode. Sooner or later, though, she would have to come to terms with her own mistakes and misfortunes, if she wanted to move on. Deep down she considered herself culpable, but for the time being she was happy to roll along letting Robin Bradford take the entire blame. More than anything, she wanted to try and appease her irate father and divert attention from her own shame. Her embarrassment was far from over, though. Interviews, DNA samples and endless hours of waiting and being gawped at still lay ahead. The specially trained female officer used all her charm and expertise to make the DNA swabbing experience as emotionally painless as possible, but Anna still felt sullied and unclean.

After an invigorating shower, her tale was aired in a specially prepared child witness suite, where Anna and similar victims were offered an environment that was both relaxing and homely: somewhere they felt safe to divulge their awful encounters and tales of woe. Video imagery captured not just the conversation, but body language and emotions too, making it far easier to sort out the wolves from the sheep. Anna's version of events was altogether plausible, but both the officers involved suspected she was being somewhat economical with the truth. The difference in consequences between forced and consensual for Robin Bradford was vast, the latter being somewhat nearer the truth. Regardless of either conclusion, Robin Bradford was once again heading for a world of hassle.

***

When Robin and Lizzie arrived back at their house it was business as usual. Robin unloaded the car into the hallway while Lizzie began stuffing the washing machine with dirty clothes. Within minutes of the couple's return life in the Bradford home was back to normal. The usual constant bickering blighted the afternoon as Robin rested his weary carcass, leaving Lizzie to struggle alone with the chores. 'I've just bloody driven for four hours!' he would snarl whenever she berated his laziness. He managed to get in an hour's sleep before the drone of Lizzie's vacuum finally woke him. He bowled into the lounge carrying his trousers and shirt, asking Lizzie to press them for him. Her response was typically abusive and aggressive, so he resigned himself to sorting it out without her. "Guess I better iron them myself then, you moody cow!"

Robin spent an age preening himself in anticipation of Asif Aggi's 'free lunch', while Anna was just arriving home with her dad. Daniel Knight tried hard not to pry into his daughter's ordeal, and simply showered her with affection, but deep down he knew his daughter's innocence had been ruined. Nothing he could do or say could restore her lost virtue.

***

WPC Bev Gardener and PC David Cross from Dorset Constabulary had been given the dubious task of pushing Anna's case forward, and began their questioning at the Blue Lagoon camp site. When Daniel Knight found out his precious little girl had organised the caravan retreat all by herself, his views on her version of events began to change; after all, if she had concealed that, what else could she be hiding? Nevertheless, in the eyes of the Law Robin Bradford had instigated sex with a minor, statutory rape in fact. At first Anna's colleagues remained tight lipped about the things that went on, like key lending and shift covering, but when the gravity of the situation began to dawn on them, they soon started to loosen their tongues - mostly for fear of losing their jobs, or being implicated in some way. Constables Gardener and Cross worked out that Anna had played a massive part in her own downfall. It was clear that she was being somewhat economical with her account. Robin Bradford was still considered to have 'groomed' her, though, and all they needed to do now was work out who the hell he was and where he came from. Forensics was bogged down with other, more important cases, so Robin Bradford's semen sample would have to sit in the lab patiently waiting its turn to be processed. Anna couldn't place Robin in any of the trailers, as she had only seen him around the Park's Hospitality areas, so the police couldn't short cut to his details. Typically, he had booked the break in Lizzie's name, as she held the bank accounts, so nobody by the name of Robin cropped up on searches through the Camp's computer records. Cross and Gardener pressured the lab time and time again, always getting the same answer. "Wait your turn!"

***

Robin was home safe and sound, well away from the dramas in Weymouth, and spared little thought for his teenage victim. As far as he was concerned, she was a consenting eighteen year-old girl, even though he'd cottoned on that she was still at school. 'C'est la vie,' and all those other life mantras!" he thought.

***

In Weymouth the mood was quite a lot different. "Taking advantage of a schoolgirl! Grooming her... Preying on the vulnerable...Coaxing a minor into sex after having plied her with alcohol!" Everybody had an opinion of Robin Bradford, and none was pleasant. Though foolish and partly to blame, Anna received nothing but sympathy for her part.

If it wasn't bad enough that Robin Bradford had DI Vincent Ambrose stalking him, he now had WPC Gardener and PC Cross to contend with. Daniel Knight bore down heavy on Dorset Police, hell bent on getting justice for his girl. In reality of course he was venting his frustration in their direction for two altogether different reasons, the first being the natural knee-jerk aggression to mask what he considered was his own neglect. The second was more complex. With no mother for Anna, Daniel had assumed both roles. His own, prudish upbringing made it very difficult for him to guide and mentor Anna through puberty and the menstrual issues that all young women face. Now she had been deflowered he needed a focus, something to take his mind off the harsh realities of the situation. Vincent Ambrose's Achilles heel was Southend's Media, WPC Gardener and PC Cross's was the outraged and inconsolable Daniel Knight. Very soon both forces would unite in the hunt to bring Robin Bradford to justice.

CHAPTER 24

BIZZIE LIZZIE

Vincent Ambrose was resting on his laurels, safe in the knowledge that by the time the court date came around he would have enough evidence to see Robin Bradford banged up indefinitely. His love life had taken a turn for the better and young Vicky Ward was hell bent on showing him that there was more to life than work. She had even persuaded him to take a summer vacation, his first ever.

***

Robin's phone purred away enticingly in his shirt pocket as he left Asif Aggi's house in Thorpehall. Being extra vigilant in his new BMW, Robin eased towards the kerb to take the call. The car had been the first of many luxuries to creep back into their lives, as business was positively booming now. He opened the text that had landed seconds earlier.

Robin, I know things haven't been great between us lately. Planning a special night in with you. Will order a Chinese from Slow Boat for 8. Don't be late. LoL xxx
"Bingo! The ice maiden has finally melted!" Robin knew what 'special' meant. It meant he would need a shower, shave and probably flowers if he stood any chance of spending the night on the nest.

***

Lizzie smiled to herself as Maria handed her the package.
"Are you sure you know what this stuff does Liz?"
"Yes, Maria! Trust me! I just need to relax a little bit tonight, that's all."
"You'll do more than fucking relax with that shit, you'll be bloody comatose! You'll be too shattered to watch that DVD as well - not quite the sort of thing I would have put you and Robin down as wanting to watch, anyway."
"Oh well! I'm sure Robin will enjoy it, even if I don't. One thing's for sure, it'll certainly get him going. One last thing Maria, you tell no one you gave me this, no matter what happens. I've always looked out for you, and done things a girl should never even have to think of, just to keep you safe. This time I need you to keep my little secret safe too!"
"Of course I know what you did for me Lizzie, and I will always be grateful...and silent. Just be careful, Darling!"

***

Gardener and Cross came on duty about six in the

evening and were chatting idly in the locker room when one of their colleagues came in.

"Your forensic report on that Knight girl came in this afternoon. It's on your desk, Bev."

"The girl from the Blue Lagoon?"

"Yeah, that's the one."

Both of them went into the office and Bev scooped up the wedge of papers. PC Cross stood watching over her shoulder as she turned through page after page of scientific blurb. "Half of this crap doesn't make any sense to me anyway. I only want the bloke's details, for Christ's sake; this is like a bloody novel!"

"There you go, Bev! Look bottom right hand side."

"Oh! Well, looks like we'd better get the map out - we're off to Essex. Do I need to go and pack my white stilettos and peroxide so we blend in?"

"Dunno about that, but I'll be making sure we've got locking wheel nuts on the car or it'll be a long walk home!"

"I'll ring ahead to Southend while you get a car sorted. Hopefully, we can lift him and still be back in time for breakfast. He certainly has enough previous to warrant a few days down here."

"Jesus! I can't see Southend letting this one go quietly. Look! He's due in court for three murders in less than a month!"

"My God! That's the one off the News, remember?"

"They'll love us if we barge in and steal their thunder. We'd better be on our best behaviour Bev, or they'll be chasing us round the London Orbital for months!"

***

When the call was put through to Vincent Ambrose he nearly had a fit. "Are you fucking kidding me? You can't take him off our manor; you'll have to process him here. No way are you marching that bastard back down to the South Coast!"
PC David Cross wasn't going to argue with DI Vincent Ambrose: he needed Essex to help in picking up Bradford, so he bit his tongue and agreed to go straight to the station first. What he didn't tell Ambrose was that he was already holding papers from his own governor, securing Bradford's extradition to Weymouth. It was a done deal; Vincent Ambrose would have to roll over when he slapped those on his table. He would just be a little economical with his news until Bradford was safely in their grubby paws.

***

Cross and Gardiner grabbed all the relevant papers and started the long journey to Essex, knowing they were heading into a minefield of legal and moral dilemmas. They both knew how much a collar like Robin Bradford would mean to all those local Bobbies and suits who had spent hours poring over paperwork trying to detain him.

***

Meanwhile, Vincent Ambrose was gathering his troops and trying to get as much of the paperwork from Dorset as he could. If he played his cards right, he might be able to pull the wool over their eyes, but he was no fool. He'd been in the game long enough to know that, despite their reticence, PC Cross and WPC

Gardener would do their utmost to take Bradford back to Weymouth with them. If he could get the boss upstairs to agree, he could swipe Bradford right from under their noses.

"Right, Team! Listen, and listen good! We've got two officers heading up here as we speak. They've got Robin Bradford banged to rights on a Statutory Rape charge. I don't under any circumstances want those country shites walking off with my man. I've spent too many nights agonising over that tosspot to just lose him now! This is what we we'll be doing..."

***

Lizzie and Robin sat opposite each other making polite, yet meaningless conversation over their tepid Chinese takeaway. From time to time she gave him knowing looks in allusion to the forthcoming romp. He was on his best behaviour, being guarded with his remarks, to say the least; petrified he would do or say something that would scupper his chances of a sexual feast. "Slow down, Robin - we have all night!" Contrary to her own advice, Lizzie jousted with Robin's feet under the table, considerably raising the sexual tension. When the meal was over they indulged in preliminary kiss and cuddle on the sofa, Lizzie with one eye on her favourite Soap.

Suddenly she rose from the chair, telling Robin to sit tight downstairs for a while. "I have a few things to take care of!" Slipping quietly from the room, she headed first to the kitchen with their dirty dishes. Robin could hear her banging and crashing drawers and cupboards. He was intrigued, but held fast on her command. At last she bounded upstairs, leaving him pondering on the couch for a good ten minutes. Just as he was starting to give up hope his phone began to vibrate in his pocket. Fancy something a bit different? Call my phone and just play along with me x x Lizzie was inviting him into a little role play session, so he thumbed through his contacts and found 'Lizzie Mob'. He pressed the green button and waited with baited breath as the dial tone bleeped.

"Luscious Lizzie's Massage Parlour! How can I help?"

"Sorry? Liz! What are you doing?"

"Robin - indulge me, please!"

"It doesn't feel right!" he replied awkwardly.

"Please, Robin! Do it for me!

"Tonight we have Lizzie. She is slim, athletic and sexy. She also likes to play rough, Big Boy! Would you like an appointment with her?"

"Liz, this feels weird, Babe..."

"Yes, or bloody no!" She lost her cool momentarily and then apologised.

"Ok, if it's what you want - if you're sure. Yes, I would like to make an appointment!"

"Robin I need to know what it feels like, please? Get up here now, I'm ready for you."

***

Cross and Gardener had passed through the Dartford Tunnel and were now rocketing their way down the A13 at break neck speed. Their sat nav guided them through the maze of unknown roads, just as it had once led Bradford to Peldon. WPC Bev Gardener rang through to Vincent Ambrose's office, warning of their imminent arrival. "We're in a hurry, so can you get someone to whizz us through procedures. We still have a four hour slap to get home once we have him on board." Vincent didn't take kindly to Gardener and Cross trying to dictate events but was keen not to show his disdain, or hand just yet.

***

Robin cautiously entered the bedroom, to be greeted by Lizzie standing before him in a silk robe that only just hid her slender curves. Scented candles flickered around the perimeter of the room offering very little light, but alluring none the less. Lizzie had laid a towel across the bed, which Robin thought was ironic. It was just like Anja's bed.

"What service do you require Mr... Smith?"

Robin's worries had evaporated the second he saw her scantily clad body; he was hooked in now and more than willing to participate in her antics. "You said 'rough,' Madam?"

"Yes, rough!"

Lizzie switched on the bedroom's TV set. The screen crackled into life as she pressed play on the remote. An 'adult' movie flashed up on the screen, depicting a young couple in the throes of intercourse, the rampant man clawing and slapping at the busty, eager actress. "I want you to fuck me like that, Robin! I want to be bitten and scratched, hard and rough just like she's getting it." She handed him a glass of whiskey and took one for herself. "Here, drink this and loosen yourself up Babe!" She watched as he downed the glass in one swig, eager to carry on with their games. He stood beside the bed and loosened his clothing, one eye on Lizzie cavorting semi naked on the bed, the other on the titillating film.

Lizzie teased him to arousal and began giving him instruction on what she wanted. “Pull my hair! Harder!” she begged as he pulled her head to his penis.

“Suck me Lizzie.”

“No, don’t say it like that! Tell me I’m a bitch, a whore! I want to be your whore, Mr Smith.”

Robin was unsure but his urges took over and he pulled her to his hard cock and forced it in her mouth. He pulled at her hair as he rammed her mouth. His pace quickened dramatically, so she pulled away and presented him with her backside.

“Come on! Scratch me, you bastard - slap me! I want it fucking rough! I’m your slut aren’t I? Remember, you’re paying for this!” Lizzie pushed herself back on him. “Fuck my arse! I know that’s what you like. Fuck me hard, make me scream Mr Smith!”

Robin was now completely immersed in their role-playing and drew back his hand ready to strike her pale buttocks. Slapping the peach-like cheeks, he left an instant blotchy red handprint, and Lizzie screamed with pleasure. “Yes... that’s it! Harder, you bastard!” He struck again, harder and with much more aggression, then again and again till she screamed in a mixture of ecstasy and agony. She pushed him even further, despite her obvious discomfort. “Now scratch me, dig your nails in... make me fucking bleed! I deserve it - go on!” He duly obliged and dug his nails deep into the skin on her shoulders, dragging them furiously down her back.

"Oh... yes! You really know how to make me feel horny, don't you! God Lizzie, I never knew what a dirty tart you could be. I love the new Lizzie!" She gritted her teeth as the hot, stinging pain surged through her waif-like body. Robin built up to a utopian euphoria as he climaxed noisily, almost caveman-like, and Lizzie felt the warmth of his fantasies filling her insides. At last he slumped forward gasping for breath, panting like a dog, his lust subdued once more.

***

Vincent Ambrose went to the Front Desk to collect Constables Cross and Gardener, paying particular attention to his manners, despite his misgivings about their presence. The conversation was strained, to say the least, and Vincent was well aware that the duo was more than a bit keen to get the show on the road.

"My colleague WPC Vicky Ward and I will be escorting you to his house. We'll have a uniformed team on site with a custody vehicle to bring him back here. My boss is adamant that he is brought back here to be charged, and you can take it from there."

"Ok, let's be off then! Like I said earlier, it's a very long haul and there's a warm bed waiting for me!" WPC Bev Gardener was not unlike Ambrose in her ways - not one to waste time on pleasantries when there was work to be done.

"We need a few more minutes to assemble a crew. Please bear with us just a little longer!" Now Vincent was getting flustered by her impatience.

***

"My God, that was fantastic Liz!"
"Is that what it's like at your whore-houses?" she asked, grimacing at the wheals and scratches she could clearly see in the mirror.
"Oh, YES, Babe - that's exactly what it's like!"
"Good... now you have to pay!" Lizzie stood up from the bed smirking, and looking straight at Robin.
"How much, or what?" he laughed. "New dress? Weekend away? You name it..."
Lizzie cut him short as he lay there eyes rolling, grinning like an ape. "No Robin! You pay! I mean you fucking well PAY! You pay for all your bastard cheating and infidelity...you pay just like your whores paid!" Her spit was spraying over his face as she began to scream obscenities, with Robin understandably bemused by this unexpected verbal attack.
"Have you gone fucking mad? What did I say? You wanted to play the stupid game, not me!" Lizzie's response was to reach under her pillow and draw out a large carving knife. Aiming for his throat, she lashed out frantically.
"For fuck sake Lizzie, calm down! You've bloody cut my neck, you thick bitch!" Clutching his throat in bewilderment, Robin reeled back in fear and agony, scrambling off the bed in a desperate effort to escape. Lizzie let fly again with another volley of swipes aimed at his windpipe, and then just as Robin's backside lifted from the sheets, she lunged again. This time her aim was good, the blade slicing straight through the main artery in his neck. She retracted the knife and with a final lunge stuck it firmly between his shoulder-blades as he spun towards the floor, unconscious. She

looked on for what seemed like an eternity as his chest struggled to rise and his breathing became shallower. Finally his body fell silent, motionless, the last dregs of his mortality seeping from his veins.

"Fucking well paid in full now, ain't ya!"

Moving quickly from the bed, she grabbed her mobile phone from the dressing-table, along with her mirror and scotch. She opened the top drawer of the unit and uncorked the phial of liquid, carefully pouring it into her drink. Holding the mirror by the base, Lizzie struck herself violently across the temple several times till the glass broke leaving shards stuck in her forehead, momentarily losing her balance and causing her head to swim. She edged past Robin's limp, lifeless corpse and squeezed his hand round the knife handle, making sure his print was clear. Then she then went into the bathroom and wrapped the container in toilet paper, and flushed it down the toilet. The vessel surfaced again as the blue bubbling water cleared, and she panicked for a second as she waited for the cistern to refill. "Bollocks! Bloody thing - fucking well flush!" Pumping the handle furiously, she tried again and again but to no avail. Eventually she took a deep breath, put her hand into the cold toilet water and pushed the soggy package round the u-bend out of sight. The water flowed for a second time, with Lizzie apprehensively standing guard. The bowl was empty, the glass phial was gone! Now she could return to the bedroom and proceed with the rest of her plans.

Holding the glass of whiskey laced with Rohipnol in one hand and her mobile in the other, Lizzie dialled 999.

Reaching into the darkest depths of her soul, Lizzie had one final act to deliver. In a vague and semi incoherent voice, she pleaded with the operator for assistance. She told her tale with emotion and conviction, occasionally pausing for effect to portray a hysterical victim. Once Lizzie had imparted enough of her wholly plausible tale, she claimed to feel woefully dizzy. Moaning briefly, she slammed her hand down on the dresser as if falling, and dropped the phone to the floor. Silently saluting Robin's dead body, she downed her drink and lay quietly and patiently on the floor, waiting for it to engulf her in sleep. The overwhelming urge to shut her eyes could not be staved off any longer and she drifted into a semi-lucid slumber.

Throughout the early stages of her comatose state, Lizzie could hear sirens and voices, occasionally making out shapes moving slowly around her.

***

As soon as the emergency call filtered back through to Southend Station a wave of panic flooded through the floors and offices. WPC Ward and PC Semple were the closest unit, and dutifully took on the mantle, arriving within minutes of the first rumblings. PC Semple threw himself at the door with sense of purpose WPC Ward had never seen before.

"Hang on, Boy Blunder!" The more experienced and definitely more composed WPC Ward pushed him aside and tried the handle. No luck, so PC Semple hurled himself at the thick wooden door again.

"Wait, you prune!" Vicky Ward bent over and eased the small potted conifer to one side, exposing a shiny brass key. "Work smarter not harder, dipshit!" WPC Ward's assessment of Semple sounded a tad harsh, but sadly it was fairly accurate. The door creaked open as the key turned in the lock, leaving Semple rubbing his shoulder and nursing a bruised ego.

***

The ambulance blasted in from London Road, managing to block Vincent Ambrose's passage to the scene. He tried in vain to bully his way past, but they were having none of it, so he resigned himself to tuck in behind. Soon the road was jam-packed with police cars and paramedics, flashing blue lights around the houses like disco balls.

Each car came skidding to a halt, slewing and wayward, wherever they could find room. An army of plods, medics and suits beat a path to the door of Bradford's dreary abode, the pavement now swarming with onlookers hoping for a juicy glimpse of the macabre events soon to unfold.

When Vincent arrived at the scene, he made it very clear to PC Cross and WPC Gardener that things had changed and their interference wasn't welcome. "You stay in the car and keep your heads down! This is my investigation, so stay put!" They were livid at his blunt attitude, but powerless now to intervene.

Inside the house Vincent found a whole line of people queuing to mount the stairs. Like some latter-day Moses, he parted the wave of spectators and bounded up two treads at a time, his muscular legs working like pistons. As he entered the room his first thoughts were not for Lizzie or Robin but for Vicky Ward, who sat on the floor covered in blood, cradling Lizzie's numb frame. With total disregard for the Crime Scene, he shot across the room to check on his lover.

"Vicky, are you ok? Are you alright, are you hurt?"

"Of course I'm alright, you knob! It's her blood not mine!"

"Thank Christ for that, you nearly gave me a coronary!"

"She needs a paramedic and quick. Something isn't right!"

"And him?" Vincent gazed across at Robin Bradford.

"Bit late for him Vince, Semple couldn't find any sign of pulse, and his throat's been opened up like a bean can!"

Two medics entered the fray, parting to examine each of the victims. The first dealt with Robin, applying gentle pressure to his wrist, checking for a pulse. The room was hushed as they eagerly awaited confirmation that he was dead. "He's still with us. His pulse is very weak, but he's still alive. Get me a stretcher up here, now!"

"I want that bastard saved at all costs. Don't - please! - let him take the easy road out of his troubles!" Vincent Ambrose sought retribution, Robin Bradford had been his Achilles heel for months, and he wanted his due revenge in the Court Room. PC Semple helped the paramedic get Bradford down to the waiting ambulance as the others tended to Lizzie.

"The wounds are mostly superficial; nothing a couple of days in hospital won't cure. Looks like she's been drugged, though. Her pupils are dilated and she's swimming in and out of consciousness."

Semple stepped back into the room, catching the tail-end of the conversation and made a grab for Lizzie's glass, inadvertently wiping all traces of its user away. "This smells weird!" he said as he stuck his beak into the tumbler.

"Put it down for goodness sake, haven't you learnt anything yet?" If he hadn't intervened maybe, just maybe they would have realised that Bradford had never touched it.

"Vicky, do you smell that?" Not content with wrecking the scene, Semple now seemed bent on annoying Ambrose and Ward with his constant jabbering.

"Smell what?" they replied almost in unison.

"Bleach, or cleaning stuff. I smelt the same thing at Katya's - and Helena's as well!"

"So? Someone's been cleaning...what of it?" Vicky was well and truly rattled by his continual interruptions.

"But..."

"But, nothing!" Vincent could see Ward was ruffled, so he ushered Semple outside into the hall and demanded he wait downstairs. They managed to get Lizzie stable enough for a move, taking her down to the ambulance and then off to Southend Hospital.

***

The patient kept drifting in and out of consciousness, rambling veiled apologies and profanities. None of it made sense to the people looking on.

"What goes on in a delusional, drug-addled mind, hey Vince? She's been babbling on about all sorts of crap since we got here." Vicky was beside Lizzie Fenwick's bed as the nurses fussed around, checking this, prodding that and making the obligatory sighing noises whilst shaking their heads.

***

Robin Bradford was rushed into theatre with what was left of his pitiful existence ebbing steadily away. The surgeons and nurses virtually mobbed his trolley as they fought valiantly to save his wretched life. The slow but steady beeping in the background turned to a continuous long drone as the knife was caressed out of its wound. “He is going...quickly now!” One of the doctors placed the cold pads either side of his chest, letting a surge of electricity ripple through his body and into his soul. His large and bulky frame leapt momentarily from the sheets before landing again, silent and still, on the makeshift bed. All eyes were on the screen as the heart monitor flickered, then settled into monotone once more. “Again! ... Clear!” The second, equally violent charge was met with the same hush as before. Bradford lay motionless as the devil slipped quietly in and claimed his soul that night.

***

The following morning Lizzie Fenwick woke to find two Police Officers at her bedside. Naturally, she feared the worst, supposing arrest was imminent, as Vincent unfolded his notes.
“Miss Elizabeth Fenwick?” Although he knew the answer he felt the need to clarify this point, to try and make her aware that something bad was coming.
“Yes. Look, I’m sorry for everything I’ve done. I couldn’t help it! I just saw red and...”

Vincent interrupted her chattering, unaware that she was ready to confess everything. She thought they had worked it all out and the chase was finally at an end. "May I call you Lizzie?" His informal approach silenced her instantly as it dawned on her that he couldn't possibly know, or he would be reading her rights to her by now. "Look, I'm sorry to have to give you the bad news Lizzie, but Robin Bradford passed away at around two o'clock yesterday. We have decided not to press charges against you for the death of your partner, Robin. It has been accepted that you acted purely out of self-defence. It would appear he drugged you before forcing himself on you. I can only offer my apologies for not being able to detain him when we had the opportunity."

"But what about the women?" Still unsure of her fate, Lizzie probed Vincent for more information.

"He'll undoubtedly be credited, if that is the right term, with their deaths posthumously. As far as we are concerned it's case closed."

Lizzie took only seconds to realise her part in the fiasco had gone unnoticed. "So I'm free to go?" Still shocked, she sought confirmation again. Vincent smiled back, slightly puzzled by her questioning,

"Of course you are. Go home! - and look after yourself!" His head dipped respectfully as he turned to leave. "Oh, just one more thing Lizzie! I'll need you to come down to the Station on Saturday morning at eleven. One of my officers will help you make a brief statement. Once it's signed you will be able to get on with your life."

"Inspector Ambrose...Thank you! Thank you for everything!" She let out a huge sigh of relief as the two police officers shut the door behind them.

***

At ten fifty am sharp the following Saturday, Lizzie Fenwick was ushered into an interview room by WPC Vicky Ward and PC Paul Semple.

"Based on the events you have described at your home address on Friday of last week, we have produced this statement for your perusal. If you're happy with the content please sign at the bottom of every page, and by the last sentence on the last page. Sorry Lizzie, are you ok to continue?" WPC Ward was compassionately mindful of Lizzie's possible distress, allowing her time to compose herself before handing across the document to be signed.

About ten minutes later the biro was inking its way from page to page as Lizzie signed the papers.

"Thank you, Lizzie." Just one final signature...here. And that's you done." Vicky's sympathy in the face of another woman's distress allowed Lizzie time to wipe away her crocodile's tears. "Come on, chin up! It's nearly all behind you now!"

"I know it's a strange request, but could I have all of Robin's possessions. You know, from his car?"

"His phones and wallet - that kind of stuff you mean?"

"Phones!" For a minute Lizzie let her guard down and the cool exterior was replaced by a grim stare. "Sorry, it's just a bit distressing that's all. He had two or three I believe, but yes I would like all of his personal effects please."

"Lizzie, far be it from me to tell you what to do, but

some of his personal stuff holds some unpleasant 'surprises'. You'd be well advised to leave them alone; they'll only cause you more heartache."

"I want his stuff! If I go through it all bit by bit, it will help bring closure. Please!"

"If that's what you really want, I'll go and get them from the store for you."

"Yes it is, and thank you for being so understanding!"

Vicky Ward returned minutes later with a large black sack full of Robin's belongings: laptop, paperwork, porn stash, and most importantly his mobiles. Lizzie broke the seal from the top of the bag and delved in, watched by Semple and Ward. She retrieved both his phones from the sack and promptly replaced his work one back inside. Finally, she said her goodbyes and left for the automated doors. As she passed over the threshold she switched his 'personal' phone on and slipped it into her pocket, just as her friend and ally Maria approached.

Lizzie left Southend Police Station and headed for Maria's car. She gave the place one last cursory glance before heading off.

***

PC Paul Semple scooped up the papers before handing them to Ward, as they prepared themselves to leave the Interview Room.

"Vicky, I've been reading the case notes and forensic reports and they were adamant that the killer was left-handed."

"So! Your point would be what exactly?"

"Bradford was right-handed, agreed?"

"Well yes, on the face of it, but presumably he was ambidextrous!"
"Lizzie... she was left handed and always worked around bleach. She had motive and access to all of Bradford's computers, cars etc. Perhaps..."
"Semple, when you have mastered the basics, like walking and talking at the same time, then maybe you can do a bit more detective work! In the mean time I would suggest you leave it to the likes of Vincent and his team!" Frowning irritably, Ward marched off into the corridor, leaving her colleague to ponder, chewing his pen top. She walked straight into the arms of her lover and mentor, Vincent Ambrose.
"You'll never guess what that bird-brain Semple has come up with now! He reckons Lizzie Fenwick killed those toms, not Robin Bradford! What the fuck is that bloke on...how he got through training I'll never know!"
Vincent stopped dead in his tracks and pushed Vicky back to an arm's length. Still holding her shoulders he said. "What...! But why?"
"Well firstly he..." Vicky went on to repeat Semple's half-baked theories as Vincent listened intently.
"Where's Semple now?" a sense of urgency to his request.
"He is still in the Interview Room, why? Surely you aren't going to take him seriously?"

***

Meanwhile Maria was making small talk to Lizzie as they filtered through the busy traffic, but her friend was a million miles away. She was staring blankly at the

mobile phone that Robin had used so freely to tout his obsession, illicit affairs and prostitutes. Slowly, one by one, Lizzie worked her way through the call logs, messages and pictures. Some names and numbers seemed to come up time and time again, but Lizzie was inexplicably drawn to one number in particular. It began to eat away at her, so she pressed firmly on the green call button and waited as the dial tone followed. Just at that moment Maria's work phone sprang into life in the door pocket. Unaware of Lizzie's actions, Maria pulled the phone from its hiding place and looked at the screen to see who was ringing;
'Incoming call... Robin B'

***

Vincent Ambrose reached the corridor just as Semple, muttering loudly, left the Interview Suite. He ushered him back into the room and sat him down.

The End

More Fast Paced Novels by Percy Publishing:

The Honey Trap by DJ Priddle

Once a detective sergeant with the MET, Jonas Brock aims to rebuild his life. Having been investigated and arrested by his colleague, a bright young officer named Donovan Quinn; Jonas served five years in HMP Belmarsh for taking backhanders and protecting prostitutes. After his release, Jonas becomes a private detective in his hometown of Abbey Wood, and having investigated nothing more than cheating lovers for vulnerable clients, he finally lands the case that he has been waiting for; stolen evidence files for one of the largest fraud cases that the city has ever seen. With the help of Selena, the young prostitute that he has protected for over ten years, Jonas must put his mistakes behind him and focus his mind on solving crimes once again.

ISBN: 978-0-9929298-1-7

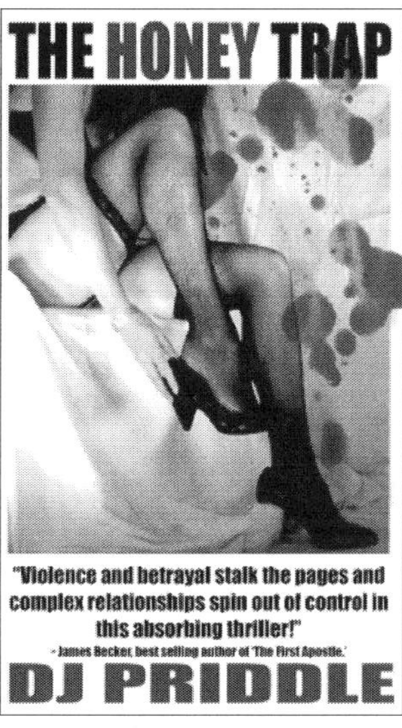

Hearts of Green by John Marsh

It's 1989 and Chris Carter has been seduced by the British Army. Seduced by the posters and the TV ads to live life to the max! Be the Best! Start a new life!

Leaving behind the traumas of a broken home, he looks forward to a warm welcome from his new family, and to giving his all in return.

It takes nearly one year of training to get there, but only one week to realise that what he's fall for is just the hype.

It has been one big mistake – a mistake that will push Carter right to the edge.

ISBN 978-0-9571568-3-8

Peoples Book Prize Finalist
Shortlisted for Costa Book Award 2014

Sabre Six : File 51 by Jamie Fineran

Michael Fox is on the way home to his wife and daughter after saving the life of a French Industrialists son.
On the way through Paris De Nord station about to catch the Eurostar he is propositioned by Stan an Ex-colleague from the SAS who now works for MI5.
Michael is to follow Ryan Killeen into London and report where he goes once he leaves the train.
Michael's life will never be the same after he accepts the simple task for £10,000.

"For Fans of Fast Paced Action Thrillers" Soldier Magazine.
"Fantastic Debut Novel" Phil Campion.
"A Must Read" Airsoft Magazine.

ISBN 978-0-9571568-3-8

Shortlisted Peoples Book Prize

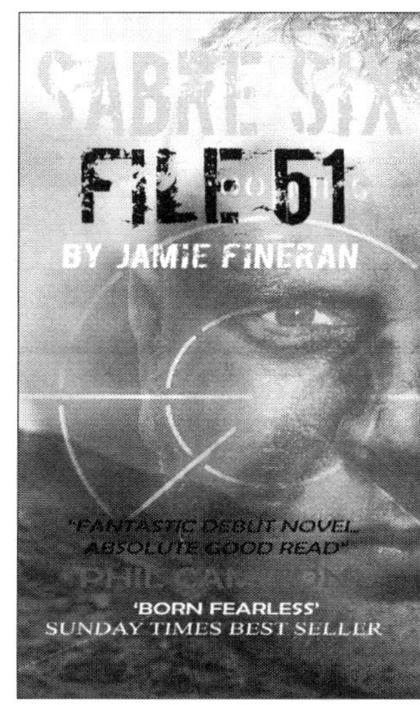

Ace of Spades : File 52 by Jamie Fineran

The year is 2015 and the Coalition Forces are pulling out of Afghanistan, leaving MI5 boss Stan to an embarrassing and delicate situation.
His perfect soldier with the impeccable 22 year Army record has gone rogue, taking Merlin Security with him - the very security assigned to safeguard the one thing the British Government needs.
Two mercenaries are deployed to restore Government control. It's a deceptively simple, but potentially deadly mission.
So who IS in control of the poppy fields?

ISBN : 978-0-9571568-6-9

Unsceptred Isle : Three of a Kind by Joseph V Sultana

Society has gone to hell.
And as the collapse spreads, Jon Maitland is building a wall.
A wall that costs him his family.
As the world implodes, Baker has become abandoned and lost in this new world.
Ridiculed and outcast in his youth, Latimer is now the lunatic in charge of this asylum known as Launceston.
Maitland needs out.
Baker Wants Out.
Does Latimer hold the Key to the Unsceptred Isle?

ISBN 978-0-9571568-0-7

To be released as a Film in 2015 under title of
'Reaper Shadow'
Directed by Phil Howard

Visit www.percy-publishing.com for more information.

Facebook: www.facebook.com/percypublishing

Twitter: @percypublishing

To Contact Colin Llewlyn Chapman.
Find him on FaceBook